PRAISE FOR
BEYOND HOPE'S VALLEY

From the last page of *Along Wooded Paths*, I couldn't wait to see how Marianna's story would resolve. I loved spending more time with the characters, watching them work through so many challenges as Marianna learned how to find true love as she learned to love her Father more deeply. This story will leave you sighing at a wonderful conclusion even as you long for just a few more pages!

—Cara Putman, award-winning author of *Stars in the Night* and *A Wedding Transpires on Mackinac Island*

The bond of obligation and the freedom of grace intersect *Beyond Hope's Valley*. Tricia Goyer writes with sensitivity to tough issues and passion for the truth in this compelling story full of love and loss . . . and love again. A definite must read!

—Nicole O'Dell, author of The Diamond Estates series and the Scenarios for Girls interactive series

PRAISE FOR
BESIDE STILL WATERS

This book is a keeper! When I opened *Beside Still Waters* I was transported into the world of the Amish. Tricia's expressive storytelling and vivid descriptions drew me into the heartache and joy of the characters as if they were real people. So compelling.

—Robin Jones Gunn, author of the Christy Miller series

Only a gifted writer like Tricia Goyer could present such a captivating story about a group of Amish forging a new community in Montana. Tricia writes in such a way that the reader can't wait to turn the page and learn more about main character Marianna's experience. Tricia's talent for connecting our heart to Marianna's plight also connects us to our need for one another. *Beside Still Waters* draws you in with its genuine characters, and it holds you there with its enduring bonds of love and family.

—Suzanne Woods Fisher, best-selling author of the
Lancaster County Series

PRAISE FOR
ALONG WOODED PATHS

A skillfully written blend of Amish and "Englisch" lives that will have you rooting for both sides. *Along Wooded Paths* draws the reader into Marianna's complex choices and swirling emotions, while exposing her deep-seated desire for a stronger faith. Tricia Goyer's beautifully woven tale captured me from beginning till end.

—Miralee Ferrell
author of *Love Finds You in Sundance*

A sweet, tender story about God's gentle workings in the hearts of His own. Tricia Goyer has a true talent for creating believable characters readers can identify with and empathize with. Anyone who enjoys Amish fiction will appreciate this moving tale.

—Sally Laity, author of *Remnant of Forgiveness* and coauthor of
The Daughters of Harwood House trilogy

BEYOND HOPE'S VALLEY

TRICIA GOYER

BEYOND HOPE'S VALLEY

B&H
PUBLISHING GROUP
NASHVILLE, TENNESSEE

ISBN: 978-1-4336-6870-8

Published by B&H Publishing Group
Nashville, Tennessee

Dewey Decimal Classification: F
Subject Heading: AMISH—FICTION \ LOVE STORIES \
COURTSHIP—FICTION

Published in association with the Books & Such Literary
Agency, Janet Kobobel Grant, 52 Mission Circle, Suite 122,
PMB 170, Santa Rosa, CA 95409-5370, www.booksandsuch.biz.

Scripture references marked NIV are taken from the
New International Version, copyright © 1973, 1978,
1984, 2011 by International Bible Society.
Scripture references marked KJV were taken from
the King James Version of the Bible.

Cover photo by Steve Gardner, PixelWorks

Publisher's Note: The characters and events in
this book are fictional, and any resemblance to actual
persons or events is coincidental.

1 2 3 4 5 6 7 8 9 • 17 16 15 14 13 12

"But blessed is the one who trusts in the LORD,
whose confidence is in him."
(Jeremiah 17:7 NIV)

DEDICATION

Dedicated to my friend Michelle Hill.

You are a treasure to me. I know God's story for you is going to knock your socks off. Remember, Michelle, there's hope beyond each valley!

ACKNOWLEDGMENTS

I am thankful for my friends who have continued to share the Amish lifestyle with me:

Ora Jay and Irene Esh
Dennis and Viola Bontrager
Martha Artyomenko
Elvie Miller
Lloyd Miller
Leona Mast

Also thank you to Amy Lathrop and the Litfuze Hens for supporting me and helping me stay connected with my readers. Amy, you're always coming up with creative ideas for how to promote my books. And whenever I need to talk you listen and encourage me. Thank you, friend!

I also appreciate the B&H team, especially Kim Stanford, Aaron Linne, and Julie Gwinn. I also send thanks to all the unsung heros: the managers, designers, copy editors, sales people, financial folks, and so on who make a book possible. And a special thanks to Karen Ball for your amazing editing! I waited a long time to work with you and it was worth the wait. My name may be on the cover, but I couldn't do what I do without all of you!

I'm also thankful for my agent, Janet Grant. It's amazing that we've been working together for fifteen years! You give me great advice, tell me "no" just the right amount of times, and are a great cheerleader. And yes, you're always right!

And I'm thankful for my family:

John, I'm so thankful to be married to you. You had no idea that an eighteen-year-old single mom would become a multi-published author did you? I am able to do what I do today because you believed in me. Even from the beginning when I told you that I wanted to write books, you didn't ask why. Instead you helped me to figure out how. Thank you for the sacrifice, for the encouragement, for late-night chats about my book ideas, and for loving me greatly. I hope you see that the love you show me is reflected through the characters of these novels in numerous ways.

Cory. Some days it's hard for me to believe that my little boy is all grown up and married with a son of his own. You know, son, that I'll keep bugging you until you write that novel that you have written in your mind and on your heart. Now all my readers will bug you, too! Yet even if it doesn't get written this year—or for a few more—know that I'm proud of you. I'm proud of the man you've become. You reflect your dad and your Father God in so many ways.

Katie. I've told you before that I've prayed for Cory's future wife since he was just a baby. I'm thankful that God heeded those prayers, cared for you, and brought you together like He did. I've never met someone with a smile that can brighten up a room like yours. I know how you caught my boy's eye! Thank you for your tender, loving heart.

And Clayton—my first grandbaby. No one can convince me there's a baby cuter than you! What a gift you are to us. I'm excited to see who God made you to be. We are just starting to get a glimpse of your personality, and I know there's a bunch more where that came from!

Leslie. Even though you are the most dramatic of all my children I love to see how God is using that "gift of exuberance" to impact peoples' lives. From the students you've taught English to on mission trips, to those you lead in college Bible Study and youth group, to the amazing people you connect with in the deaf community, it's hard not to want to be your best friend for life once someone meets you. I love your heart after Jesus and the decisions you make daily to keep your steps in line with His will. Your passion for reading and knowing His Word is an inspiration to me. Know I'm praying for you as you finish your last year of college. I'm eager to see what's next!

Nathan. God knew what He was doing when He gave me such a gentle-hearted and tender third child. You're so easy to love. I've been amazed to see you growing and maturing and becoming a man after God's heart. You're the one I turn to first when I need help with your little sister—mostly because you're always so willing and eager to offer a helping hand. You have many stories within you, and I want to encourage you to trust your heart as you write. Sometimes we can't see what holes we have until all the words are on the page. Keep going! There are many who will be amazed by the story lines you come up with. I know I am!

Alyssa. My sweet girl. A hundred times a day I thank God for bringing you into our lives. When I was most discouraged that God was taking years and years to allow us to adopt a baby from China God gave us a great gift in bringing us you! I'm forever thankful to your birth mom for choosing our family. Life around here would be boring without your smile, your giggles, and chasing you from one end of the house to another. One of my favorite times of the day is snuggling with you and reading stories. In the nearly two years since your birth I'm pretty sure I've been smiling more than ever in my life! You are a true gift little daughter.

Grandma Dolores. Some of my happiest memories growing up where those spent at your house with you and Papa. What an honor to have you here in our home. I know it's hard for you to depend on us for help. It's challenging when you can't do all that you used to be able to do, but I honestly say that the best thing that you can do is what you're already doing—holding our house up in prayer. Listening to you sing and praise God in the morning encourages me. A grandmother's prayers are a gift forever.

Nathan, Kayleigh, MaCayla, Audrie, and Donovan Stoltz. Kayleigh, I can still remember that day over ten years ago when you walked through the doors of Hope Pregnancy Center. I thought you were just another young, teen mom who needed a little support. I had no idea that God planned for you to join our family—you and your whole crew! You may not be a Goyer by name, but you are ours in heart! Even though having all of you in our home for a season is busy and noisy, I'm blessed by the joy all of you bring. Having eleven faces around the dinner table shows that God builds family in unique and wonderful ways.

Finally, to my best friend Jesus Christ. None of this would be possible without you. You remind me there's hope beyond every valley. Even during the hardest days I can lift my head and look forward to eternity with You. There's nothing better than that.

Dear Journal,

All my life I've lived plain, but emotions are far from plain even for us Amish . . . at least that's what the beating of my heart, the rush of heat to my cheeks, and the stirring deep in my gut—like the churning of butter—tell me as I feel Aaron Zook's breath against my neck. Aaron slumps in the seat next to me, his dreams taking him on some adventure as the train carries us back to Indiana. Or that's what the small smile on his lips is sayin'. I wonder if I'm included in that grand venture? If I were to guess, I am. Seems that's why Aaron came—to find me and to make me his own, like we'd both been dreamin' for so long. Seems like he'd carry that, carry me, into his dreams.

Please forgive the squiggly handwriting as I write these words. The sway of the train makes writing difficult, but I must get onto paper what I've been storing up in my heart. At this moment the mountains of Montana are only yet a memory. Farms, fields, and sky spread out as far as I can see. Of course, I can't see far. The first rays of dawn have just stretched out their brightening arms of welcome. A small ache pinches my heart as I consider leaving that wonderful wooded place and my family. Yet, I remind myself that what I found in Montana is something I carry with me—not packed within the two cardboard boxes under the train, but tucked away deep in my heart between layered memories, like colorful embroidered kerchiefs stored away.

God is what I've found—not Him exactly, but a deeper knowing of Him. Friendships, too, with the Amish and Englisch. Friendships to remind me that I'm more alike to those "outside" our community than different.

A smile fills my face as I write, not only as I turn over the memories I've collected, like small treasures in my mind, but also as I listen to Aaron's soft snores. I can't help pausing every few sentences to catch a glimpse of his handsome face. I can't help my chest warming at his closeness. To think in a few months' time we'll be married. Married!

The first order of business, of course, is to help Levi and Naomi—to walk through their challenges alongside them, holding their hands and maybe covering their ears from the comments certain to come. But when that task is done, I'm eager to step out in my life, with my husband. Just writing that word—husband—sends a thousand tingles, like pine needle pricks, movin' up my arms.

Indiana.

Aaron.

It's all I could think of when I left Indiana . . . and it's within the embrace of both that I'll finally discover home.

Chapter One

Marianna scanned the crowd and then she saw him. Levi the man—no longer the boy—strode to her. Tenderness for her brother, even with his close-cropped hair and Englisch clothes, tugged at her heart. But as Marianna approached, she was sure she saw something. A shadow of stubble on Levi's face, the beginnings of a beard. Evidence he'd soon be an Amish husband. Her heart leapt.

Marianna held back her questions. She wanted to know about his plans, about the wedding, yet she noticed other Amish milling around. This conversation was one to be shared in private, around family. Only after the engagement was published, a few weeks before the wedding, would they be able to talk about such things where others could hear.

Though it was far from ladylike, Marianna lifted her skirt and ran to him.

Levi opened his arms to her, and she stepped into them. His T-shirt was soft on her cheek.

"Thank you for coming, Mari. I can't tell you how much it means."

She swallowed hard and nodded. Her lips parted to answer, but the quiver of her chin stopped her words. She looked back. Aaron gathered their suitcases with one hand, as he leaned on his crutches tucked under the other arm. She should go help him, but first she needed a moment with Levi.

"Are you crying?" Levi's hands touched her shoulders and he nudged her back to see her face. "You don't have to cry. I'm all right and Naomi will be too. We're figuring things out." He wiped away a stray tear from her cheek with his thumb. Levi's touch was gentle. "Don't cry, Marianna."

"They're happy tears," she whispered. "Levi, you have to know that. The days to come, I can't even imagine, how full of happiness they'll be."

"Yes, Marianna." Levi hugged her again. "I suppose it's what we've always wanted. It's just that we didn't know."

"We do now, Levi." Laughter replaced her tears. "We do now."

Levi moved to help Aaron with their suitcases and boxes, but Marianna carried so much more deep inside. More than the clothes and her journal that she'd packed in Montana. She carried more sweet memories, more of God than she had when she'd headed out west.

She looked around the train station, letting it sink in that she was home. Other Amish families mulled around the station, bearing testimony that it was so. The lack of snow on the ground outside told her she was no longer in Montana. God had sent her there for a reason. Now, more than anything, she wanted to share what she learned with her friends and family in Indiana. She wanted them to know God as she did.

A child's pained cry split the air, and Marianna paused.

A small girl, who looked to be about five had tumbled off the bench and sat crumbled in a small heap on the white, tiled floor.

Without hesitation, Marianna turned and strode over to the girl. She knelt and reached out a hand. "Oh, sweetie."

The girl accepted the help and within seconds the little one crumbled into her grasp. The cries stopped, but the girl's shoulders trembled. Marianna looked around. A young woman with red hair pulled back into a ponytail hurried toward her with a baby on her hip.

"Ashley, oh no!" The mom rushed forward, offering an open arm to replace Marianna's. "I told you not too goof around like that!"

The woman met Marianna's gaze. Her eyes widened as if for the first time noticing it was an Amish woman who helped her daughter. "Thank you. I—I just left her for a moment to make a bottle for the baby in the restroom. I told her to sit still and watch our things."

Marianna patted the girl's soft, blonde hair. "I understand. I'm not a mom yet, but I have five younger siblings. Turn your back for one minute—"

The sound of a man clearing his throat sounded behind her, and Marianna turned to see Aaron and Levi waiting. Aaron shifted his weight from side-to-side and looked toward an Amish family who sat straight-backed—lined up on a bench from oldest to youngest—all eyes on her.

Disapproving.

Marianna swallowed as she rose. "Yes, well. She seems to be fine now. We must get going."

The stares of her fellow Amish resurrected the memory of how things were in Indiana. She'd been in Montana too long— had gotten too comfortable with Englisch ways, Englisch folks.

The girl's cries stopped, and the woman adjusted the baby on her hip. "Coming or going?"

"Coming. Just arrived home." Marianna took a step back, drawing closer to Aaron. "You have a lovely family. Have a *gut* trip . . ." She turned to the doorway—but not before she saw the woman's wrinkled brow. Was she more surprised that Marianna had helped or that she'd backed off so quickly?

Marianna hadn't meant to be rude. She'd forgotten that Amish and Englisch didn't talk much in these parts. She pressed her shoulders back and lifted her chin as she followed Levi toward the exit. It took every ounce of strength not to look back, not to wave and offer one last parting smile to the little one, who still whimpered at her mother's side.

So much I've forgotten . . .

Tightness formed around her chest, the same as when she tried on her childhood winter coat only to discover she'd outgrown it.

She looked to Levi and forced a smile. "It'll take some getting used to, being in these parts again."

He glanced over and nodded. "It does take adjusting going back, but it'll come to you, Mari. We can leave our home for a while, but our heart knows the way back." She read something in her brother's gaze. Thankfulness, in part. After all, at least they had a *gut* way of living to return to. Uneasiness too. She'd prayed for Levi to return to the Amish—yet questions, concerns muted her happiness.

Did he love Naomi? Did he feel returning to the Amish way of life is what God wanted him to do?

A silent knowing flashed between them. They were returning, but not the same. Never again the same.

Levi held the door open for them and pointed to a blue van waiting at the curb.

A biting wind nipped at her nose as Marianna, one hand on her kapp, hurried toward the waiting van. Seeing her approach, the driver opened the door and jumped out. Taking Marianna's satchel from her hand, he hurried around to the back of the van.

"I've got this. Get inside where it's warm. The front seat is the warmest. Don't want to fall ill on your return." The driver smiled, not only with his lips but with also his eyes, as he said those words.

Marianna narrowed her gaze. Did she know him? She didn't think so. Yet the Englisch driver, who appeared to be in his late forties, acted as if he knew her. Or more than that, as if he were excited to see her.

The wind picked up again, and she hurried to the van, climbing in the passenger's seat. He was right. It was warm. He'd kept the van running for them, which wasn't typical. In the cup holder was a paper cup of coffee from the Garden Gate Cafe, where her best friend Rebecca now worked. Marianna told herself to ask about this driver. She thought her family knew all the Englisch drivers in the community. Perhaps she'd been wrong.

She let out a low breath. A bit of tension released. Her feet again walked on the soil of Indiana—the place she knew best. She was to marry a good man who loved her. She had a home waiting for her. Her future waited too. *Montana is behind me . . .*

Marianna bit her lower lip. For some reason that thought didn't give her as much comfort as she imagined it would.

She turned in her seat and watched the driver load their luggage. As the rear door slammed, her brother Levi guided Aaron to the side door. Aaron's limp intensified with every step.

For most of the train trip Aaron's leg had bothered him. Even though the doctor had given Aaron clearance to travel, Marianna feared he was up and around too soon. Since Aaron hadn't been able to sleep for more than a few hours at a time, she'd stayed up with him as much as she could. They'd talked about her siblings, about their friends they'd gone to school with. They'd wondered if anything had changed in Shipshewana, the town closest to their farms. They'd guessed it hadn't. She and Aaron talked about new calves and spring planting. What they hadn't discussed was their future, their home, their someday family. As the miles passed, their dreams yet unspoken, filled the space between them and sat heavy upon their laps.

Aaron climbed in first and Levi followed, shutting the side door. Marianna was thankful her brother had picked up her and Aaron at the train station, and she wished she and Levi could get away to talk. But not today. She'd save their deeper conversation for another time. Today she needed to rest. Adjust.

Marianna turned back toward the front. The driver's eyes studied her.

She sat back in her seat. *Who is this man?*

He buckled his seat belt and checked his mirrors. "You look like your mother."

She glanced over, daring to look at him from the corner of her eyes. "You know our mother?"

In the backseat, Levi cleared his throat. The driver looked into the mirror, making eye contact with him. "A long time ago." The man sighed, then pulled out from the parking space. "Yes. I know her. My family's farm is near her parents' place."

Marianna studied the man. Had she met him before, when she was a child? No, she didn't think so.

"So, Levi, how's work yet? The community?" Aaron's weary voice broke the silence. He said nothing about Naomi.

"*Gut.* Things are busy at the factory, and I am moving into the *dawdi* haus on Naomi's parent's property. She's been busy as a beaver fixing it up. Soon as we wed she'll move in too."

At the mention of *beaver,* Marianna thought about the beaver lodge at the pond behind her parents' Montana home. She closed her eyes and tried to picture the still waters. She remembered the peace she found reading her father's Englisch Bible there. Before Marianna left Montana, her boss Annie had given her a Bible of her own, but as the van continued on, a sinking feeling puddled in Marianna's gut. Would she find the same peace in Indiana? Had God joined her on this journey?

How silly! Of course He had—but she needed to feel it, not just know it. Maybe . . . she would find a special place here where she could pray to God, where she could expect Him to meet her. If so, where? Someplace private, where she could pray about sharing with her family and friends the hope she found in God. Would they listen? They knew the Ordnung, but would they cling as fiercely to God? Would they tend their souls as diligently as they tended their farms?

She released a breath. She needn't worry about that now. She'd returned, but not alone.

Marianna looked back to Aaron. He offered a weary smile. A peace she hadn't seen in months radiated from his eyes. How brave of him to journey to Montana for her. Only a man who truly loved a woman would do such a thing.

The thrumming of her heart filled her ears. And she reached back her hand. Aaron's eyes widened, and he grasped it, entwining his fingers with hers. She turned her attention to the road ahead, but he didn't release his hold. They took separate journeys to Montana but returned together. This drive was the beginning of good things to come.

He squeezed her hand tighter, and joy rushed through her, prickling her skin and making her skull tingle under her kapp. They returned not only to a place, but a history. *Their* history.

As they traveled over familiar roads, and the Amish farms passed outside her window, the spoken rules of her childhood played in her mind. And the unspoken ones. From an early age their parents taught them about the plain dress code. They could use no electricity from the public grid, and travel was to be by horse and buggy. Additional "rules" were taught more by action than word.

Your dress and kapp must be pressed and neat.

Neighbors help neighbors.

The earlier you're up for chores the better, lest anyone think you to be lazy.

In Montana, the Amish way of life had been relaxed. Although most of the rules were enforced, folks didn't watch each other too closely. In Indiana, eyes had followed her all the time.

Would it be that way again?

She brushed a stray hair into her kapp, then adjusted the kapp, making sure it was just so.

They drove down the highway and passed the sign that read *Shipshewana City Limits.* Another rule swirled in her mind: *Amish must marry Amish.* That was an easy one.

She'd marry Aaron.

They drove through town. Shipshewana was ready for Christmas, with tree lights, wreaths, garlands, and other ornaments trimmed everywhere. Some Amish families decorated with greens and a few candles, but most focused on family gatherings and the religious meaning of the holiday. No decorations would grace Aunt Ida's home. One thing her aunt *would* celebrate with was special cookies and candies. Marianna guessed making plenty of both would fill her time next week.

This would be the first Christmas for her and Aaron in their new relationship. Last year she couldn't have dreamed they'd be this close. If his accident back in Montana had done anything, it had given them more time together. It also showed they could handle trials with grace and care.

If you had never tasted the bitter you wouldn't know what is sweet. The familiar, Amish proverb made her smile.

Thankfully they were on the sweet end of this journey—not only their journey back to Indiana, but also in their relationship.

They passed a small house tucked in a thicket of trees just outside city limits, and a new thought stirred. *The cabin.* Today it was too late to travel to the place Aaron had built for her, but tomorrow . . . tomorrow she'd see evidence of his love, displayed in wood, nails, and glass.

They spoke of simple things as they drove two miles past Shipshewana to her Aunt Ida's farm. As they approached, Marianna released the breath she'd been holding. Once inside her aunt's warm house she could forget about the Englisch driver and why he seemed to know her. She could take her mind off Naomi, and even off her own upcoming marriage. She could simply enjoy seeing her aunt again and partake of a good meal in front of the fire.

The van parked. The driver would take Aaron home next. They'd been together for so long, it seemed strange to be going separate ways.

Her eyes met his. She could see his weariness, but she also noted love.

"I can walk you to the door."

"No need . . . you've been on your leg too much as it is."

Aaron nodded. "Tomorrow then?"

She tilted her head. "*Ja*, I'll see if I can borrow my aunt's buggy." She sighed. "I just hope I can sleep. I'm eager to see our house."

Aaron's face brightened. Joy bubbled in Marianna's heart seeing how those two simple words—*our house*—brought so much happiness to the man she cared for.

She opened the van door and climbed from the front seat. Around back, their suitcases sat on the gravel driveway. Levi was paying the driver, but neither turned as she approached. Tension froze the air around them, and a shiver raced up Marianna's spine.

Levi slapped a tip in the man's uplifted palm then narrowed his gaze.

"So, just how well, sir, did you know my mother?"

Ruth Sommer eyed her husband and fingered the letter in her hands. Abe had brought a small stack of mail home with him, and she knew he had paid no attention to the letter from her sister, Betsy. Ruth hadn't paid much mind to it, either, until she started reading. Now her sister's words burned through the envelope, all but charring her fingers.

You'll never guess who I saw in town today. Who's moved back to care for his parents and set himself up as a driver for the Amish . . .

Ruth hadn't needed to read any more to know Betsy wrote of Mark. *Her* Mark. She and Betsy had shared the same room—the same bed—for eighteen years. Her sister alone knew the depth of

Ruth's feelings for Mark—and of Ruth's struggle to stay with the Amish and not go with him.

Outside the snow fell. The three boys built another snowman, complete with an Amish beard made of pine needles they'd dug up from under the snow. Ellie sat content, playing at Abe's feet with her doll. Like all Amish dolls it didn't have a painted-on face, but that didn't bother Ellie, who dressed and undressed it with the numerous dresses and kapps Marianna had made for it.

Ruth clutched the letter to her chest. "I'm going upstairs yet to check on Joy."

Abe nodded but didn't lift his eyes from the Bible. Ruth moved to the staircase and hurried upstairs. Joy would be sleeping for another thirty minutes at least. It would give Ruth time—time to read the letter and time to sort through her feelings before she finished up dinner.

Ruth reached the top of the landing and moved to her girls' room, sitting upon the bed that Marianna had shared with Ellie. She missed her oldest daughter, but the fiery nervousness moving through her limbs took all of Ruth's concentration. She opened the letter again, reading its message. Betsy had written the letter just for her, but had also not written names—or a specific name—in case Abe or one of the children picked it up.

Dear Ruth,

Christian greetings. Sending the love of your family as best I can in written word.

I wonder yet if another storm is raging in Montana. It seems every letter of late that I've received from you has started with these words, "It snowed again today in the West Kootenai." For as much as it snows you'd think the drifts would reach the rooftops by now.

Our whole family is eager to see Marianna on her return. That's good of her to come to assist Levi. We saw him in town wearing Amish dress once. I welcomed him back. Levi gave us an update of Aaron Zook's condition. How sad we all were to hear that Aaron was in a vehicle accident on his way to visit your family. Everyone here was thankful you did your good Christian duty and cared for him while he was on the mend.

You'll never guess who I saw in town today. Who's moved back to care for his parents and now set himself up as a driver for the Amish. It always seems strange when someone from our past returns and butts into our future. Seeing our neighbor made me think of our long conversations. I jest wanted you to know so that when you return you won't be surprised.

If you return for Levi's wedding will you go back to Montana or just stay at that time? Some are saying there is a reason Levi and Naomi are getting married. I'm not one to spread rumors so I do not agree with or deny their claims. I am glad for Levi's decision to return to the Amish. I know the world's offerings are a mighty draw for the young people today. I'm praying for my own children as they near the age they must decide. I am thankful that our family has chosen to follow the way of our ancestors— the way of peace. I know you are thankful, too, although the decision is not easy.

When Levi and Naomi come by for a visit after their wedding I will share a quote with them that you told me long ago. I've heard this proverb many times since, but I remember it meaning the most coming from your lips:

"Love, peace, and happiness in the home are infinitely more than honor, fame, and wealth."

I hope Levi realizes that all he is embracing will mean so much more than all he's left behind.

Well, I must go. The baby awoke and is crying. Know we are all sending our love and look forward to seeing you soon.

Love,
Betsy

Ruth's fingers trembled as she placed the letter on the bed. Without question she and Abe had decided to return for Levi's wedding. Even though only a few in the family knew about the baby coming, they would all celebrate Levi's marriage when it was publicly announced.

But could she still go? How would she handle seeing Mark again? She'd done well over the years, holding memories of him at bay—until he haunted her dreams with his smile and easy laugh. *Mark.*

Even his name made her feel young. Made her forget she was a woman old enough to have a son married, old enough to soon be a grandmother.

A soft cry told her Joy had awakened. Ruth went to care for her little girl, then returned downstairs and whipped up mashed potatoes to go with the roast in the oven. She avoided Abe's eyes as she set the table. The words of the letter refused to leave.

You'll never guess who I saw in town today.

Her shoulders slumped as she thought about serving the children, cleaning up, getting them ready for bed. Her head throbbed.

She put the food on the table. The boys gathered around, waiting for their supper. Joy sat in her highchair content. Ellie wasn't so patient. The young girl leaned closer to get a look of the potatoes and knocked over her glass of milk.

"Uh-oh." Ellie looked down at the milk.

"Sit down, now. Hands in your lap!" Ruth pressed her fingertips to her temples. "How many times have we told you to sit still, be good, obey?" She stomped her foot.

Abe stood and hurried to the kitchen for a towel. "Don't worry. I'll clean it up."

Ruth sat in her chair and scooted up. "You'll do something now, will you? All these kids, all these years, and now you help?" Angry words tornadoed. Trembling hands covered her face.

Why him? Why now?

CHAPTER TWO

he van driver's words wrapped around Marianna's mind even as Aunt Ida pulled her into an embrace. *"Your mother and I were friends for many years. She's a special woman."*

What did that mean? Marianna wished Levi had asked more questions, but before he had a chance, the driver had turned and hurried back to the driver's seat to take Aaron back to his parents' home.

Marianna forced a smile and melted into the older woman's arms. Most Amish weren't as affectionate, but Aunt Ida—her father's oldest sister—always had a soft place in her heart for her nieces and nephews.

"Look at you. More beautiful than I remember, and I see something special in your eyes. A lightness that wasna there before." Aunt Ida released her grasp without waiting for an answer and then patted her kapp, ensuring it was perfectly in place. "I have hot water on the stove. Let me pour you a cup of tea. Warm you up." She walked through the living area to the kitchen and busied herself with an old mug and tea bag.

Outside the window, a large cloud slipped across the dipping afternoon sun, sending a shadow of gray across her aunt's spotless living room. Marianna's eyes glanced from the worn sofa to the bookshelf to the quilt rack that held Aunt Ida's latest project. Aunt Ida said not a word to Levi. Marianna turned to him, and he shrugged. Walking to the mantel, he picked up the matchbox. After lighting the kerosene lantern, Levi slunk into the nearest chair with a forlorn look, reminding Marianna of their younger brother Josiah after he'd been reprimanded.

She raised her eyebrows. In all her days she'd never seen her aunt act in such a cool manner. Levi was returning to the Amish. Why did Aunt Ida treat him so?

The older woman's long dress swished against her legs as she busied herself around the kitchen. "I hope the trip wasn't too hard on you, Marianna. Was surprised that you were comin'. Told yer friend Rebecca I'd believe it when I saw it."

Marianna slipped off her coat and hung it on the coat rack by the door. "*Ja*, well, after I received Levi's letter I didn't want to stay away. There's nothing more exciting than a wedding."

"And how is Aaron's leg now? Did the train bring much trouble?"

She paused at her aunt's words, and the message became clear. Not only was Aunt Ida ignoring Levi's presence, she wasn't even going to let Marianna say her piece about his marriage to Naomi.

Marianna glanced to her brother. He occupied himself straightening the matches in the matchbox. An ache filled her chest. What other snubs had he gotten from the community?

She was sure Naomi and Levi had kept news of her pregnancy to those closest to them. A pregnancy outside of marriage wasn't something to rejoice over, yet it wasn't uncommon either. Most couples got married before too many months passed and one didn't know the truth until later, after they counted back. So if Aunt Ida didn't know about the baby, why was she acting this way? At least Levi had done the right thing—had returned to being Amish. An ache moved from her chest to her gut. Her brother *had* done the right thing, hadn't he? Returning was the only way . . . wasn't it?

She wished she had someone to talk to about it. Someone who could see things different than the Amish did with their narrow thinking. Someone like . . . Ben.

Aunt Ida neared with the tea, offering it. "I hear there is a singing this Sunday at the Yoders' place. When it's too cold out the youth have been gathering in that new barn. Might you go Sunday?"

Marianna took the cup into her hands, relishing its warmth. Instead of answering her aunt's question she turned to Levi. "Would you like some tea too? To warm yerself?"

"Nah." He rose. "I need to head back to Naomi's place. Gonna help with the chores." His eyes fixed on hers, and though she could tell her brother was pleased she was here, it was as though he was mere a shadow of the young man he'd been before. She thought of their last face-to-face conversation before she'd left for Montana. He'd been telling her the reasons he'd left the Amish. The reasons hadn't made sense to her, but at least he'd been passionate. At least there seemed to be light—a fire—in his eyes.

"I'll see you tomorrow then?" Marianna walked him to the door. "Perhaps I can meet you for chores—"

Levi waved a hand. "No need to get out in the cold. I'll come over in the mornin'. We'll get a chance to talk—I'll catch you up."

"*Ja, gut.*" She bit her lip and looked to her aunt. They'd have to find someplace to go lest Aunt Ida insert herself into their conversation. At this moment, her mind and body were too weary to worry about it. As if sensing they wanted a minute alone for a good-bye, Aunt Ida hurried to the kitchen, mumbling to no one in particular about pouring her own cup of tea.

Levi leaned close, lowering his voice. "Don't be so hard on her, Mari. She'll come around. She's an old woman, set in her ways. She's had no husband or children to smooth her rough edges. She'll come around."

Was the repetition to convince her . . . or himself?

Marianna nodded, then reached up and fastened the top button on Levi's jacket, just as she'd do with her younger siblings. For some reason he didn't mind.

Levi placed his hand on the doorknob. His eyes fixed on her and narrowed. "You going to be all right? The last few months haven't been easy for you—with the move, working, caring for so many folks, and now the long trip back."

She shrugged. "I've come from a line of hardy women. I'll be back to baking bread and tilling the field by sunset tomorrow."

They both laughed, glancing to the frozen ground. She offered another hug, hanging on a moment extra. Funny how she appreciated her brother more after their time apart.

Levi left, and no sooner had Marianna slipped off her shoes and set her stocking feet to warm by the fire then Aunt Ida filled her in on the comings and goings she'd missed. Marianna covered a yawn as her aunt went on about the new school teacher and the robbery of an Amish home close to Shipshewana.

"Then there is Bishop Troyer's daughter, Nancy. She married an Amish-Mennonite boy and broke her dat's heart. To consider one of the bishop's own daughters to be Beachy Amish now—that's what they call those Amish-Mennonites, you know. What a shame."

Marianna fidgeted and bit her lower lip. Her whole life her aunt's home had been a favorite place to visit. She'd come to cook and to can. She'd come to do crafts and borrow books from her aunt's library. She remembered her aunt had always been up-to-date with everything happening in their community, and she used to find that interesting, but now . . . Aunt Ida's words were like bags of feed pressing on her chest. Marianna's breaths were hard to take in. The words weighed heavy on her mind.

Marianna considered those who her aunt spread the "news" about. How was the young woman, just married, dealing with being shunned? Months ago, Marianna would have listened to her aunt and would have agreed in horror, but now? The Beachy Amish were still plain—just a bit more liberal. She'd heard the Beachy Amish read the Pennsylvania Dutch version of the Bible. This was unacceptable for those in their own community who only allowed scriptures in High German to be read in their church and their homes.

Marianna wiggled in her seat. She shifted from side to side as if sitting on tacks. How would her aunt feel knowing an English Bible sat in her suitcase? Would she be asked to stay somewhere else, or even worse, treated as if she weren't worthy of her aunt's attention?

Aunt Ida clamored on, and Marianna's mind drifted back to the events since she'd been in Indiana—first the Englisch driver who seemed to know her. Then the way her aunt treated her brother. Now this.

Please, let tomorrow hold no more unpleasant surprises.

"Did you hear me, child?" Aunt Ida leaned closer in her chair until her knees almost touched Marianna's.

Marianna refocused her thoughts. "*No*, I'm sorry. I think the lack of sleep on the train is getting to me."

"I said that if you hear any rumors about Aaron Zook you needn't let them worry you. Just people talking."

Marianna straightened in her seat. "Rumors?" What did Aunt Ida mean? He'd been with Marianna in Montana for the last six weeks. Whatever could have carried so far or lasted so long?

"Like what?"

"Do you think I'm gonna throw kindling on the fire of their words?" Her aunt clucked her tongue. "I'm not one to spread vicious talk like that. It's talk—that's all it is. Jest enjoy seeing that house Aaron's built for you. He's a good man he is . . . no matter what people are saying."

And just what *were* they saying?

A shaft of dread bore through her, and for a moment she considered walking out that door and catching the first train back to Montana. But she knew, all too well, that running away from her problems was never the answer.

If only she knew what, exactly, the problems were.

Ben sat on the leather sofa in Roy's media room and pressed his back deeper into the cushion. He'd been enjoying dinner at the West Kootenai Kraft and Grocery when he'd gotten a call from Roy on his cell. Roy had asked him to come over right away. Ben had finished off his roast beef and potatoes then denied a piece of peanut butter pie.

After driving the hour down to Kalispell, Ben wasn't disappointed. The news *was* big.

A smile lit Roy's face. "Your song hit the charts. You've got interview requests from *Entertainment Tonight* and *Country Music Magazine*. The record label wants you to go on tour. They're talking the biggest cities, L.A., New York, Chicago. Twenty-six venues to start. Then back to L.A. to cut another record. A million musicians would dream of such a thing."

Ben waited for the surge of excitement, but it didn't come. So why wasn't he happier? This, of all things, should defrost the numbness inside after Marianna's leaving.

Or Marianna's running. Away from him. From his feelings for her.

And hers for him.

Ben nodded and smiled. He tried to act happy for Roy's sake, but his excitement was dampened by the fact that the song's success wasn't appreciated by the one person who mattered. He'd written it for Marianna. Had she even heard the song? He doubted it. The Amish didn't listen to music, and she tried her best to follow the rules. Of course, she shouldn't need to hear the song to know his heart.

Roy rose from the sofa and strode to the bar to pour himself a drink. "So what do you think?"

Ben covered his face with his hands. His cheeks grew hot. His mind raced. The room seemed to spin. Like most musicians, he loved being in front of the crowd, feeling the pulse of a live event and the energy in the room. Yet . . .

He knew the temptations he would face while on the road. They'd gotten to him the last time, taken him to dark places, painful places. He lowered his hands and looked at Roy.

Roy laughed. "Speechless, I know. The money you'll make will set you up for years to come—minus my cut."

Ben pictured a cabin, a house. He could build his own place. Create a home, just like in his song. Yet he tried to picture the man he used to be on stage and shook his head.

That was then, this is now. I'll make different decisions. Better ones. I care about, and for, different things. I'm a different person.

God had allowed this to happen. Maybe there was a greater plan for Ben's life than he imagined. He sat a little straighter. "You know, this song hit it big for a reason. And that is what I want . . . to impact lives. If the venues are big, and if I can share what God has done—"

"Great. Yeah, there's always that." Roy rose and slapped his hands on the front of his thighs. "We have a lot to do. Don't start counting your converts before they kneel." He smirked. "We need to get to L.A. as soon as possible. Think you can pack tonight?"

Ben scratched the back of his head. "Sure. It shouldn't take too long." He wilted back into the sofa. Was this really happening?

Roy tossed an envelope onto Ben's lap. "Great."

Ben opened it. Two printed Internet confirmations slid out. One was a one-way ticket to L.A. for 7:30 a.m. the next day, leaving out of Glacier International Airport. The other a two-week reservation for the Sunset Tower, Hollywood.

"We'll be assembling a band, planning the tour, and rehearsing. Plan for long days and little sleep."

Ben swallowed and stood. "I've done this before."

Roy rose and extended his hand.

Ben took it, and Roy pumped it with a squeeze. "Congratulations. It's what we've been waiting for. I suppose you living like a hermit up in those mountains worked. Keep doing what you're doing. Keep those songs coming."

"Easier said than done." Ben's head felt like lead. "I'm afraid to say, Roy, I've lost my muse."

Dear Annie, Sarah, Edgar, and Jenny (and all the dozens of customers I'm sure you'll share my words with),

I've made it to Indiana. Seemed strange at first seeing so bare a horizon. The hills I used to love seem so small now. Nothing, I suppose, compares with Montana's grandeur. There's less snow here, so that's different too. It might take me some time to adjust. And I'll have to consider another means of exercise rather than stomping through tall snow drifts walking to work.

I know you all were concerned, but Aaron did well on the trip, considering. I had to convince him to take a pain pill once or twice. Stubborn men, they never like to let on a thing bothers them.

We've yet to set a date for our wedding. The typical month for Amish weddings is November, after the harvest is in. But I'd hate to wait a year. Whether we wait that long or choose a closer time I'll let you know. Unlike what I saw done in the West Kootenai with the Englisch, Amish do not plan weddings months in advance. When both parents agree the time is right we choose a day a few weeks prior. We also don't design formal invitations. Rather, we call on our friends and let them know of the event—we even call on those who we'll count on to help with the preparations and the food.

I know Annie mentioned hosting a reception in Montana after the fact. That is mighty kind. I'll have to confer with Aaron, but I have to say the minutes could not pass faster until I return. I miss the customers yet and all of you, and even though Aunt Ida prepared a hearty meal tonight, at the end I craved a piece of Sarah's peanut butter pie.

Heavens! You don't want to read a letter filled of my wishes and wants, but I'm afraid that's what I've done. I'll write again soon and tell you more exciting happenings. Tomorrow Aaron's taking me to see the house he's built. I'm anxious to see his home, or rather our home.

Say good night to the pines and stars for me.

Marianna

CHAPTER THREE

*M*arianna sank onto the double bed, her eyes moving to the bedroom window, which overlooked an idyllic farm scene. She'd finished the promised letter to her Montana friends and then slipped between the covers.

This was the bed Aunt Ida had slept in as a child with two of her sisters. Marianna pulled off her stockings and sighed. An unfamiliar uneasiness came over her again—she just hoped her friends couldn't tell from her letter.

She'd only been here a few hours and already her aunt had talked about nearly everyone in town—everyone but Aaron. Why of all things did her aunt have to consider that bit of news "a rumor"? How would she ever be able to sleep tonight not knowing what people were saying about him? Because the truth was if they were talking about Aaron, she no doubt was part of their conversation, too.

A small smile touched her lips. Levi had been so gracious— a stark contrast to the way Aunt Ida had treated him. He was right. She'd had no one to smooth the rough edges. Thank goodness her brother reminded her of that, for that kept anger and frustration from building. Growing up, Ida had no doubt dreamed of a husband, kids, and a home of her own, yet here she was living alone in her parents' place. Near enough to enjoy her family members—and to be reminded what she was missing. Though Ida got out often and was a part of more quilting circles than anyone else in their county, none of that changed the fact that she lived alone, spent most of her days alone.

Even this room seemed lonely.

Marianna took her English Bible from her suitcase and opened it on her lap. She closed her eyes, picturing the pond in Montana. So many warm days she'd spent reading there, imagining Jesus sitting beside her near the still waters. She opened her eyes and glanced around the room. *Yer with me here, too, aren't You?*

She glanced at the closet, where homemade dresses hung, and at her simple shoes on a simple rag rug near the foot of the bed. Not one decoration hung on the walls, and even the curtains were plain. She imagined Jesus finding comfort here. Not because of the manner of living . . . but because of her. He cared more about her heart than her plain ways. That thought pushed her lips into a smile and she prayed for Aunt Ida's lonely heart that tried to occupy itself with so many things. And she gave thanks that she didn't have to worry about being alone like that.

Thanks for Aaron.

Surely the rumors are nothing serious. What could he have done? He's been in our home for months . . .

She released a sigh. She offered those worries up to God, too, yet even as she prayed she didn't feel the same connection with God as she had near the pond. Marianna set her Bible to the side and moved to the window.

The fading sunset filtering through the bedroom window seemed brighter than the sunsets in Montana. Maybe because there were no majestic mountains for the rays of sunlight to stretch over, or tall pines to filter through. Marianna rose and moved to the window, placing her fingertips on the panes of cool glass. Her aunt's house sat on a small ridge, giving her a view of the farmland to the north.

The land her father used to tend.

In the distance, the roof of her childhood home peeked over a small cluster of trees. Not far beyond that was Naomi's house, right next to the house of one of her married aunts. Even though Marianna could not see the country road from here, her mind's eye continued down that road. All of her father's siblings lived along that road—all except Ike. That's the way things had always been, and she hadn't thought life would ever be any different until her father uprooted their family. Now their family home was occupied by another.

Marianna set her Bible to the side, recalling the verse she'd chosen to memorize after deciding to leave: "'For I know the plans I have for you,' declares the LORD," she whispered. "'Plans to prosper you and not to harm you, plans to give you hope and a future.'"

She readied herself for bed and slid into sheets that smelled of Aunt Ida's homemade soap. She closed her eyes, but her mind wouldn't settle. It was easy to memorize the verse, but for some reason it wasn't sinking into her heart like she hoped it would. How were Mem, Dat? Was Joy scooting around more? Did Ellie ask about her? What about the boys? Did they watch out for Charlie on their walk to and from schul?

Marianna yawned and closed her eyes, pretending she was back in Montana. Pretending that Joy slept in the crib across the room and the boys were snoring. Pretending she had to get up early to work at the store. Even though she was tired, that was the only thing that could make her peaceful enough to sleep—

Pretending she was back in the place she'd thought she wanted to leave for good.

Abe Sommer glanced at the clock one more time before blowing out the lantern and climbing in bed next to his wife. Ruth climbed into bed early. Said her head was aching. Abe should have gone to bed hours ago, but he couldn't get his mind to stop all its thinking. He worried about Marianna. Why he hadn't taken more time to talk to her about everything—about returning, about marrying Aaron, about the growing faith that he knew she shared. He'd seen the difference in her. Was hard to miss.

He could tell she'd been sneaking his Bible. The peace in her eyes was evident. He'd heard her whispered prayers through the wall in the next bedroom more than once. There'd been many times he'd felt ill-prepared as a father of grown children, but now more than ever. How could he lead his daughter when his own steps were unsure?

Ruth's body was warm under the covers, and he snuggled up next to her. He kissed the top of her head, his lips pressing against her sleeping kerchief.

"You awake?"

From the softness of her breath he knew she was. He most likely woke her when he entered. He should let her go back to sleep . . . but he had too much on his mind. He wouldn't be able to drift off until he found out Ruth's thoughts on returning to Indiana soon like.

She turned toward him. "Hmmm?"

"If you're sleeping we can talk tomorrow, but I've been thinking . . ."

"About Marianna?" Her whispered words carried through the dark room. "I keep wondering how it's going." Her tone was softer than it had been earlier tonight. He didn't know what had been bothering her, but he hoped his helping with the dishes and the children had put her in a better mood.

"*Ja*. Me too, but about something else. We'll be expected to return for our children's weddings . . ."

Ruth's body stiffened. "I know." She swallowed hard, and if he wasn't mistaken she scooted away from him, putting more space between their bodies and the warm breath of their words. "I'm not sure of Marianna's plans, but I imagine Levi and Naomi's wedding will happen quick like, before her pregnancy becomes evident."

Ruth reached a hand toward him, stroking his chin with cold fingers. If only he hadn't turned out the lantern. Then he could read the expression on her face. Something was wrong. Something other than Marianna.

"We can go, but we don't have to stay long. We'll see our family, of course, but . . ." She blew out a breath. "But we hadn't have the boys miss too much schul. Maybe a five-day trip, that should be sufficient."

Could this be the woman who argued about coming to Montana in the first place? Though Abe was thankful Ruth had adjusted to Montana, he knew it would take more than five days just to visit their brothers and sisters, aunts and uncles, not to mention travel time and wedding preparations.

"We'll be needed for the wedding for more days than that, and I was considering while we're there packing our things, bringing them back . . ." He whispered the words, and when silence met him Abe almost questioned if he'd said them aloud.

"*Ja*. We should pack up." She scooted closer, tucking her head under his chin. "There's nothing for us there now . . ."

He was surprised she didn't argue. *She's agreed too easily.* It caused him to pause. It was a big decision to make. Were they making it in haste?

"Yer right, there's nothing for us . . . except for our children. Levi will be married. Our first grandchild is coming. And soon Marianna will be marrying Aaron. I can't guess her to make to next Christmas without a wedding. Are you sure, Ruth? Can you live so far away from them?"

"I—I think we need to be here, uh, in Montana. It's the best for the boys and us. Haven't we been doing better here, Abe?"

Her voice sounded like she was about to cry, and he didn't understand. There was more going on inside his wife. Something she wasn't saying.

She sighed. "But our things . . . How will we ever get them here?"

"It's late, we don't need to figure all that out now."

"No. But tomorrow. Maybe you can talk to Ike. He did say he knew someone who moved the Amish, didn't he?"

Abe nodded. "Tomorrow I'll see what Ike says."

Ruth pressed tighter to him, but even then her soft body stiffened. Despite how close she was to him, her mind seemed far away, in another place.

What could be bothering her so? What would make moving to Montana for good so urgent in her mind?

If anything, Marianna returning and a grandchild coming should make her want to return to their Indiana home. Nothing mattered more to Ruth than her family.

Unless . . .

Something must have changed things. This morning she'd been cheerful and content. Tonight anything but.

The only thing he could think of was her sister's letter. Betsy hadn't written more than two or three times since their move. They'd been short notes, and Ruth had shared Betsy's words over dinner.

But today, after receiving the letter Ruth had been solemn. She hadn't said a word of the letter at dinner. Was there something in the letter that was bothering his wife?

Tomorrow. Abe allowed his body to sink deeper into the bed and his eyes to flutter closed. *I'll read the letter for myself tomorrow.*

Dear Marianna,

The long journey has me weary. The miles have taken their toll, but even in its heaviness my mind can't stop thinking of you. It's strange how I often find myself turning to letters to express myself. I suppose it's become my means of communicating. Strange how I now filter my thoughts through the written word. Pen to paper seems to calm me somehow.

There's an Amish proverb I've been thinking about. You know it, too, no doubt. The gem cannot be polished without friction, nor the man perfected without trials. *It's an easy one to quote when the warm spring breeze is upon you and the air smells of fields and trees, but the truth is I'd rather have the friction gone for now. The trials aren't from outside. If anything I should be happy that the dream I've held for so long is finally coming true. Tomorrow is a big day.*

Instead, the trials are within. In a perfect world I'd be able to share this letter with you. No, let me say that differently. In a perfect world I'd be able to share what's really going on with my words—by looking into your face and speaking my heart.

I picture you at this moment sleeping under a handmade quilt and dreaming of me. I hope that's the case. Tomorrow I'll put on a smile and no one will be the wiser, but tonight I'll still think about you—think about the truth of what I hold inside. A truth that, more than anything, I wish I could confess.

Written by the man who dreams of your smile.

CHAPTER FOUR

arianna entered the Stolls' barn. It was so like Dat's old barn. The scents of the hay and animals, the moist warmth inside despite the crisp air outside . . . it all reminded her of times spent with her father. A twinge traveled through her.

From the time she could sit balanced on a five-gallon bucket, she'd hung out with Dat. Gazing up at him and watching him work had been part of her earliest childhood memories. Even though her brother insisted she didn't need to help him with the chores—that she should stay in where it was warm—she hadn't been able to sleep. She'd woken up before dawn, missing the pines outside the window and Trapper whining to be let out. Unsuccessful at keeping her longing for her family at bay, she dressed, bundled up, and headed down the road to the Stolls' farm where Levi now worked. Even though her day would include going over with Aaron to see the cabin, she wanted to talk to her brother first.

She made her way to the *milich* room with soft steps. The twenty black-and-white spotted Holsteins all looked identical, but she guessed Levi knew them all by name—just like Aaron most likely had when he held this job. All of the cows wore hobbles—clamps that drew the cows' hind legs together just above the knee to keep them still during milking.

She studied her brother for a moment. Levi emptied a small hand tank of milk into a larger, refrigerated tank. He wore the Amish shirt Mem had made him years ago, and it was rolled up to his elbows. The muscles in his arms bulged as he worked. His shoulders were broader than she remembered. He seemed taller too. He'd lost some of the boyishness in his face and looked more like a man—more like Dat. It was strange to think he'd be a father soon too, and would be caring for a place and a family of his own.

"Naomi waited three months before she told me she was pregnant." Levi turned to her. He'd seen her come in after all.

"Why's that, Levi?" Aunt Ida knew so much about all her Amish neighbors, how was it she didn't know about Naomi's pregnancy. Or did she? Was that the true reason her aunt had acted as she had toward Levi?

"She was afraid of what I would say. What I'd do. She was hoping I'd have everything together for her to leave the Amish. When that didn't happen, she resigned to the fact we'd just have to make things work here." He glanced down at his feet, scuffing his shoe on the concrete. "Heck, maybe she didn't think I'd come back. That I'd return to the old grind."

Marianna nodded and realized that even though he wore the clothes of an Amishman, he'd picked up a lot of the Englisch talk during his time away.

Marianna picked up a piece of straw and twirled it between her fingers. "I have to admit I was surprised, ja. For when I left you'd told me you wouldn't be asking her to leave and that you'd be going yer separate ways . . ."

Levi finished emptying the small buckets of milich. His slow movements told her his mind was more on Naomi's pregnancy than his work. He finished up milking the last cow and walked over to Marianna. "I suppose the time apart made me realize I loved her. I dated a few Englisch girls, but their minds were busy with foolish things like clothes and makeup and movies. They knew nothing of caring for a home or family. They didn't give God a passing thought."

She sank down on a hay bale. "So it made you miss her?"

Levi nodded as he moved to retrieve more buckets. "I told a friend I wanted to find someone just like her, and my friend laughed. He told me the only way I'd get someone just like her was to go back. To tell Naomi how I felt."

"I'm glad you did. Did Naomi's parents say anything about you returning to the Amish?"

"They welcomed me and"—he shrugged—"I made mistakes, she made mistakes, but the more time I spent without her made me realize my friend was right. She is the one I want to spend my life with." Levi approached and crossed his arms, looking down at Marianna. Was that a glimmer of tears in his eyes? The questions, worries, fears she saw in her brother's face caused her own emotions to swell like a balloon being inflated.

"I just wonder if I'm going to be able to do this . . ." His hand covered his face.

"You can." She rose, touching his arm. For some reason she couldn't bear the thought of him crying—and feeling so weak. He'd written to her. He'd asked her to come. This was the main reason she was here. She'd have time later for her own happiness. Levi needed her.

"Maybe you should talk to Dat—see if he'll let you live in the house. You know, until they plan on moving back. You can start spring planting for him."

"You think I should ask?"

"*Ja*, of course. I'm sure the dawdi haus is nice, but how will you farm? Naomi's father makes just enough on his land to provide for his own family, I suppose. Didn't you think of it?"

"Of course I thought of moving back into our home. I didn't think it would be possible."

If only their parents were here. Marianna missed them so! Her heart had been aching since she'd awoken. More than anything she wanted to take a breath of fresh mountain air and look up to the jagged mountain peaks. She wanted to hear Mem's voice reading a story to the kids by the wood fire.

Maybe that's what she was really longing for, her family. In the last few months her parents had said little about their return to Indiana. Their plan had been to go to Montana for a year, but neither had said a word about returning, traveling back, farming their place. Maybe she should have brought that up before she left.

She exhaled a long, slow breath. Something deep in her gut told her that she knew the true answer—they wouldn't be moving back this year—but she didn't want to believe it. It had only been three days since she'd left, and her aching for them had already flared up something fierce.

"If you don't live in their house, how is Dat going to get seed in the ground this year?" She continued as if her words would make her parents' decision for them.

Levi paused and studied her. He cocked his head and his

mouth dropped open. Then his mouth closed and he turned back to his work.

Cold crept over her, as if the winter wind outside had snuck through the door and wrapped around her. She took a step closer to him. "You want to tell me something, don't you?" She placed a hand on his forearm. "Dat and Mem are coming back this spring, aren't they?"

He let out a sigh. "Your guess is as good as mine, Mari."

"But you will ask them about our place, won't you?"

"I suppose it wouldn't hurt to write a letter—now that I'm back on their good side. After working in the mill for a while, I am eager to get back to the farm . . . but it's more than that. It's . . . well . . ."

Marianna waited for him to continue, but part of her didn't want to hear. The hair on the back of her neck stood. Did he have something to tell her about Aaron? Aunt Ida knew something . . . did Levi too?

She stood up and brushed straw off her skirt. She should ask Levi—just get it over with—but she couldn't make herself do it. Instead, she smiled, pretending it wasn't evident that important words lay on the tip of his tongue.

"Remember what Grandpa used to say?" Marianna squared her shoulders and jutted out her chin. "'On a farm you can see God in all things alive and growing.' Seeing that, experiencing that, will be good for you. You're stuck between two worlds, Levi. You need to plunge your whole heart, whole mind in this community again. You can't live halfway between heaven and earth. Your feet need to be planted deep somewhere."

As Marianna spoke, she knew was talking to herself just as much as him.

You can't keep thinking about Montana and all you've left behind. This is a good place, with good people, and the man you love . . .

So why did her heart ring as empty as a milk bucket that her brother tipped over and drained? *How could I have everything I've ever wanted and suddenly it's not enough?* If anything, a good Amish woman needed to learn to be content—to be grateful. She needed to turn that over to God in prayer.

A barn cat hopped down from one of the rafters overhead and curled around Levi's feet, hoping for a drink. Levi ignored the cat and ignored her words too.

"I'm going to see the house Aaron made, today," she said, trying to brighten her spirits and get some type of response out of him. "And after that maybe I'll come by and see you and Naomi. I do have a question. In your letter a few weeks ago you said Naomi was moving into the dawdi haus, but yesterday you said she's fixing it up and you're living there. Why did things change?"

"They changed because Naomi's parents didn't want her staying out there by herself for so long."

"For so long? I'm not sure I know what you mean."

He paused his work and turned to her. "That's one of the things I've been wanting to tell you. We're not going to be getting married any time soon. Naomi's parents insist we wait to wed until the baby's born."

"They do?" Marianna's jaw dropped. Most couples married before the pregnancy was known, but this? "Do—do they have a reason?"

"They say they don't want us to marry because we have to. They wish for us to marry because we want to. I tried to explain . . . but . . ." He shrugged.

Marianna stared closer. His face softened and he released a sigh. A sigh of relief perhaps?

He reached down and stroked the top of the cat's head. "I've known since last week, but I didn't want to tell you. I was worried you wouldn't come." He looked like a small boy during a thunderstorm. Like six-year-old Josiah feigning bravery when he wished to hide under the covers.

She took her brother's hands between hers and squeezed. "What can I do?"

"Jest be there for us. You saw how Aunt Ida treated me. It's taking a while for me to gain the trust of the community. It's not gonna get easier when they discover Naomi's pregnancy."

"For you or for her."

Suddenly Marianna's own concerns melted from her mind like icicles under the sun's rays. Her brother had a long road ahead of him. Maybe over time he and Naomi would be accepted by the community again, but it wouldn't happen overnight.

At least she had Aaron by her side. She could be strong for her brother and Naomi as long as she could turn to him.

Abe had looked in the top drawer of Ruth's dresser where she kept the letters from home. He'd looked through the pile of papers on the kitchen counter. He'd even checked the pockets of Ruth's coat, but he didn't come across the letter from Betsy. Ruth had started acting like herself again, but she hadn't said much about their trip back to Indiana.

It made no sense. Ruth liked to plan and organize. With as large of a family as theirs it was a must. Still, she kept silent.

After breakfast, the boys practiced for their Christmas recital in the living room, and Ruth browsed through a seed catalog they'd gotten in the mail. Abe's coworker had stopped by to give him a ride to work at Kootenai Log Homes, but he told his friend he'd hitch up the buggy and drive himself in a few hours. His excuse was he wanted to enjoy the sunny day, and they were ahead of schedule on their project anyway, but the truth was he needed to talk to Ruth.

He poured himself another cup of coffee and sat down across from her. The noise of the children's laughter and voices filled the space. Trapper's barking added to the commotion. That usually brought a smile to his face, but not today.

"Ruth?" Abe fixed his eyes on her. Marianna looked so much like her mother, with her pretty face and thin form. Ruth's gray hair mixed in with the brown. She was just as beautiful as the day they met. Maybe he hadn't told her enough how much he loved her. How much he appreciated her. "Ruth, I was wondering if we could talk, I—"

"*Gut.*" She glanced up and stretched her hand forward, placing it over his. "I want to talk to you too."

He cocked an eyebrow. A bit of tension he'd been storing in his chest released. "Really?"

"*Ja*, I've been thinking about it fer some time. I've said some prayers. Last night I agreed we should pack up our things, but I believe we should do more than that. We need to sell the house in Indiana too."

"Sell the house?" Abe's fingers drummed the tabletop and his mind raced, thinking of all that meant. Yes, he'd been the one to want to come to Montana in the first place. He'd been the first to mention they should pack up their things, but in this own mind he'd thought of just renting the house. He felt secure knowing that if ever they needed it—if he lost his job or if one of them became ill—they would have that place, that community, to return to.

He ran a finger under the collar of his shirt. "You really want to make the move that final? I mean . . . things are different now. Levi's returned to the Amish. If we did have to go back someday I wouldna be so concerned about his influence over the young." His voice caught.

"Abe Sommer." Ruth rose and placed a hand on her hip. "Wasn't it you that talked me into coming? And now that I like it here, you're the one who wants to hold on to what we left? Montana's a good place. I can see that it's best."

"Really, you do?" He stood and faced her. She lowered her head and he studied the top of her kapp. "And what do you like about it, Ruth?"

"Like I told you before, not everyone's eyes are on me. I can breathe here, live. I don't have to be 'that woman' who lost her girls. I don't have to be 'that woman' who . . ." Tears touched the corners of her eyes, and two concrete bricks fell on Abe's shoulders.

The Amish woman who almost left her husband for an Englischman? Is that what she was going to say? From her down-turned lips and the way she refused to look at him, Abe guessed that's what it was. He tried to shrug, pushing the weight of the past off of him. The burden was heavy, even after all these years. He imagined she felt the same.

"Ruth, you know I don't see you as that woman. Most people don't remember, much lest care, about that anymore. But I understand, and I want to support you." His hand stroked her chin and tilted it up until her eyes met his. He hoped she could see the love in his gaze, but worried it was distorted through her own pain.

"If you believe selling the farm is our best decision, then I do too. My home is where you are, Ruth. I want you to always remember that."

Jest tell Abe about the letter.

Ruth argued with herself as she peeled a bag of apples that Annie from the store had dropped by. She turned over the green apple in her hand and worked the sharp knife to extract the peel in one long strand. The love she'd seen in Abe's eyes as they'd talked this morning brought tears to her own.

"Don't go getting all misty. You're gonna cut yerself," she mumbled under her breath.

"Owie?" Ellie asked from her place on the chair next to Ruth. Ellie washed the peeled apples in a bowl of cool water—not because Ruth needed help, but because young Amish girls need to learn how to work. How to be useful.

"No owie yet . . . and I have to remember you're a smart one. I've got to watch that. You most likely know more English words than I realize."

Ellie lifted her head, nodded, and wrinkled her nose. Laughter spilled from Ruth's lips, and Ellie joined in. How much the young girl reminded her of Marianna—always watching, always so willing to help and give and serve. If Ellie grew to be as industrious and kind-hearted as her old sister, Ruth would have no complaints.

She glanced at the clock, counting the hours until Abe

returned. She hoped he'd have a letter from Marianna with him. She wondered what Marianna thought about being back in Indiana. Unlike Ruth, Marianna had always been highly respected there.

Ruth handed the peeled apple to Ellie, who dunked it into the water, and then Ruth picked up another. She'd been jest a newly married woman when Mark had caught her attention. When Abe was out in the fields it was Mark who came by to check on her parents. One cup of coffee would turn into two, and they'd get lost talking about the people he'd met and places he'd visited. He opened a world to her she hadn't known much about. More than that, he'd asked her about her dreams.

Where would you like to travel to some day, Ruth? What's your favorite book? What do you do for yourself? Shouldn't you think about what makes you happy instead of just caring for everyone else?

Looking back now, Mark's words had a certain hiss to them. Like the sweet, tempting words the serpent had spoken in the garden to Eve, they had stirred dissatisfaction. She and Abe had read that Bible story just last week in their English Bible, and the story caused her to look at her past in a new light. Made her see Mark in a new light. Maybe it was God preparing her—preparing them—for what was to come when they returned to Indiana.

Still, she had to admit the way he'd wooed her caused heat to fill her chest even now. Although she'd made the right choice in focusing her heart on Abe, and living life as his wife, her sister's letter—and even her memories—stirred emotions in Ruth she hadn't felt in a while. Like a campfire she'd thought had grown cold, the letter had been a stick stirring the ash. And she was surprised that sparks had kindled underneath.

She finished peeling the last apple and handed it to Ellie.

Ellie washed the apple and then set it on the clean kitchen towel. "All done?"

Ruth set down the knife. "All done." She smiled and wished she could speak so confidently about what was inside. She wished her feelings for Mark were all done. Then again it didn't surprise her that she'd been drawn to him in the first place. She'd always been drawn to fancy words, fancy things.

"Ellie, can you go and see if Joy's still sleeping for me, *ja*? Be a big girl and hold the handrail as you go upstairs."

"Yes, sir!" Ellie turned and stomped off.

Laughter spilled from Ruth's lips. Now that was something Ellie never would have heard in their Amish community in Indiana. She no doubt picked up that phrase from the Carash boys down the road.

Ruth turned to the cupboard and pulled out the oatmeal, deciding to make an apple crisp for dessert. A memory stirred of when she was Ellie's age. She reached for the sugar and smiled, thinking about the day at the flea market and her purchase.

She'd gone with her grandparents to Shipshewana. It was one of the few times she remembered being with them without her other siblings. Her grandmother had given her some dollar bills— how many she couldn't remember now—and told her to pick out anything she'd like.

Heat rose in her face even now to realize she'd picked out the fanciest thing possible—a delicate china cup with intricately painted flowers! She'd been used to drinking from tin cups, and for the rest of the week she drank from that cup with her mother looking on with a disapproving gaze.

Her younger sisters, of course, thought it was beautiful too and tried to sneak it when they could. It was then Ruth had real-ized what she had to do—she packed it away in her hope chest. Even as a young girl she knew that's what Amish women did to prepare for their future.

After getting married she considered pulling it out, just to look at it, but her first baby came nearly nine months later and more children after that. Not wanting it broken, she left the china cup where it was. Where it was still packed away.

"Baby wake!" Ellie called from upstairs.

"Coming!" Ruth started for the stairs. When she was in Indiana she'd have to go through her things and get that china tea cup out. Maybe she'd even get rid of it. Heaven knew she needed to start purging old things.

Most especially old feelings and thoughts.

CHAPTER FIVE

*M*arianna had just finished her last bit of toast with blackberry jam when she heard the clomping of a horse's hoofs coming down the gravel roadway. Looking out the window her heart leapt to see Aaron. She'd missed him.

Though the air was cold outside, the sun shone brightly. How many days had she imagined this—Aaron arriving to take her on a date? She'd bathed and dressed after returning to Aunt Ida's house from talking with Levi, and she'd also determined not to let her brother's challenges disrupt her day. She'd do what she could to help her brother tomorrow. Today was Aaron's day.

Marianna stood and walked to the door, smiling.

Aunt Ida hurried into the room with quilting needle in hand. "Is that Aar—"

"It's Aaron, *ja*, we're going to see the cabin." Marianna moved back to the table where her plate sat.

Aunt Ida waved a hand. "Leave it . . . I'll wash that up yet. You git now, you hear. You've waited a long time for this."

Marianna didn't argue. She hurried to the coat rack and put on her coat. Pulling her mittens from her pocket, she slipped them on as she hurried out the front door. She reminded herself again not to worry about Levi or Naomi today.

Aaron parked and looked as if he were preparing to climb down when she rushed up to him.

"No need to get down, I'll just climb in. I don't want to dawdle. We have our house to look at."

Aaron settled back down, holding the reins with one hand and rubbing his leg with the other. "I like the sound of that. I've been waiting"—he turned to her and she saw sadness in his smile—"I've been waiting a long time for this."

She nodded, not wanting to get their conversation bogged down with what could have happened or what should have been if she never would have moved to Montana. Instead, she climbed up and scooted next to him, tucking a lap blanket over her.

She placed a hand on Aaron's shoulder. "Do you know this is our first official date?" Laughter slipped through her lips.

Aaron removed his hat from his head and scratched his blond hair. "I guess that would be right. Had to find out if you'd be willing to marry me before I spent any time courting you . . ."

"Aaron Zook!" She punched his shoulder with a soft fist.

He returned his hat and then turned toward her, running a finger down her cheek. His hand was cold, but she didn't mind. The gaze in his eyes warmed her even as the wind picked up.

"You're worth it, Marianna. Worth everything. Now, let's get going so you can see what I got for you." He winked and then turned his attention back to the horse. "I've been waiting for this day fer quite a while," he said with a flick of the reins.

They rode to the Zooks' place in near silence. As the buggy passed the small Amish schul where she'd first met Aaron, a verse they'd memorized filtered through her mind.

I must be a Christian child,
Gentle, patient, meek and mild,
Must be honest, simple, true.
I must cheerfully obey,
Giving up my will and way.

Uffgevva. The word played through her mind. It was a Pennsylvania German word that had been as natural to her as the farm, fields, and community. *Giving up* was its literal meaning, and she'd done it in daily tasks, putting down her quilting to tend to her siblings. Putting down her book to make dinner. Anything she desired mattered little when it came to submitting to parents, teachers, church leaders. And soon to her husband.

She thought even about the sermons she heard while growing up. Every minister started his sermon with a confession of his unworthiness and ended it by asking the other ordained men to correct any of his mistakes. It was giving up your day to raise a barn or your time to help finish another's quilt. She hadn't thought much of it until her father's step of boldness. He'd traveled to Montana to protect his family. He'd stepped out on his own, going against the good of the community to consider the good of his children. Her father's "adventure" was tolerated, as long as he had plans to return, but what if he stayed?

Leaving for good wasn't an option. Those in the community would make it clear he wasn't yielding. To yield would be to stay and continue life as he always had, no matter what Dat's heart desired.

She glanced over at Aaron, and her own heart was conflicted. He'd always followed the way of the community, that she knew— but what if protecting their family called for something different?

She had a feeling the community would still win. And up until the last year she was fine with that. But now?

She'd returned to Indiana with Aaron . . . but there was so much more that she hadn't expected in Montana. She'd learned to appreciate a new place and a different type of lifestyle. She'd worked in an Englisch store and had made new friends. She'd grown closer to God too, thanks to Ben.

Even as his name filtered in her mind, her stomach twisted into a knot. *Is this how Mem feels, even after all these years?*

Mem's tears had been real as she'd confessed her love for an Englisch man. Marianna had never actually confessed she loved Ben, but she did care for him more than she should. A cloud passed over the sun, dimming the light around them, and she wished with one breath she could blow away her dark thoughts as well as the clouds.

Twenty minutes later they pulled into the Zooks' property and parked. The last time she'd been there was the night of the youth sing. That night she'd just started getting used to the idea that they might be leaving Indiana. Now she'd left and returned. And they'd survived the parting. Aaron had come to her to win her heart, and it had worked. Here she was. Here *they* were. Their future presented itself in wood and glass, and Marianna sucked in a breath.

It was a small cabin with wood siding and a green metal roof. It sat in a peaceful alcove between the pasture and the woods. Marianna glanced around. The woods blocked the view of the Zooks' main house and the road. They had their own slice of earth where no one would bother them.

Aaron cleared his throat. She turned to him. Pride gave his face a warm glow.

"What do you think?"

"It's beautiful . . . I . . . I don't know what to say." She turned back, taking in the porch that ran the length of the front and the tall windows that flooded the house with light.

She placed her small hand in his larger one, squeezing. "I can imagine a swing hung on the porch, and curtains in those windows. I'm sure around back there's the perfect place for a garden, and is that an apple tree over there?" She pointed, and laughter bubbled from Aaron's chest.

"*Ja*, it's an apple tree, and I can see the house does suit you."

"Can we go inside?" Marianna curled her lips in a smile. She wouldn't let thoughts of Ben ruin this moment.

She climbed down from the buggy and extended her hand. "Do you need help down?"

He smiled sheepishly and then placed his hands on her shoulders, lowering himself, stepping down onto his good leg first.

Honest, simple, true. She couldn't think of three better words to describe Aaron.

Even as he stood, Aaron's hands stayed on her shoulders—a lingering excuse to touch. Heat rose to her cheeks, and she lifted her chin. A deep longing for his kiss surprised her.

He studied her eyes, smiled, and then leaned forward, offering the kiss she waited for. His lips were warm and the kiss was gentle, but the tightening of his fingers around her shoulders told her he desired more.

A rustling sounded behind them, and Marianna pulled back, looking over her shoulder.

"It's only the wind in the brush." His voice was husky.

He leaned forward again for another kiss, but she pulled back. She knew better than to let the desires of their flesh lead them where it ought not. "I'm ready to see the house now."

"Don't you want to kiss me, Mari?" His Adam's apple lifted and fell. His blue eyes widened and her heartbeat quickened, doubling its beat. Something inside urged her to step forward, to wrap her arms around him, to absorb his warmth and allow him to kiss her—to hold her. To discover each other in ways they never had. But even as her body longed for that, warning bells chimed in her head.

She released the breath she'd been holding and stepped back. "Of course I want to kiss you, but we can't let ourselves get carried away . . . it'll only make the months until our wedding more difficult."

He opened his mouth to say something, then closed it again.

"Someday there will be no waiting." Her voice escaped as a whisper.

"*Ja.*" He stepped back and cleared this throat. "That's something to look forward to."

She approached the front door, and anticipation pushed against her throat. A sluice of joy struck her. She was really here. This place would soon enough be her home.

"You better step inside now, Miss Sommers, before I pick you up and carry you in myself."

She stepped through the door behind Aaron. He hurried to the center of the living room and lit a lantern, although that wasn't necessary. Bright mid-morning light shone through the windows.

She stood in the living room archway and glanced into the kitchen. Though simple, the rich wood that Aaron used for the cabinets and the stone countertops made the house look far from plain. She walked through the large, empty living room into the kitchen with slow steps, taking it all in. Her fingertips trailed over the countertops, and she considered all the wonderful meals she could make here. Food to sustain them, cooked with love.

"Granite," he said. "The man at the lumber yard recommended it. You can put a hot cookie sheet right on top of it without hurting it."

"Already thinking of cookies, are you?"

Aaron patted his stomach. "Of course." He winked. "It keeps my mind off other things."

She noticed small squares of fabric on the kitchen counter. Picking them up, they were some of her favorite colors—blue, red, pink. "What's this?"

"I know the curtains must be white, plain, but this place needs some color, *ja*? If you pick out your favorites I'll get the fabric for a quilt on my next trip into town."

She returned the fabric to the counter and then clapped her hands together. "Really?"

He chuckled as he removed his hat and then hung it on a hook by the door. "Didna think you'd get that excited. I cannot wait to show you the rest of the house and the bed the quilt will cover."

She followed him to a large bedroom just off the living room. A simple bed frame had been set up with a new box spring and mattress.

"I figured you had sheets and things in your hope chest at home."

"*Ja*. I've been preparing for some time now." After a pause she added, "It's what all young Amish women do, you know, plan for their future. Although I never imagined anything like this." She walked to the window and placed her fingertips on the cool glass. "Has your ma been here?"

"No, not yet. I wanted you to see it before her."

"Just think." She released a sigh and sat on the mattress. "I'm the first woman to sit on this bed—in my home." Her eyes scanned the frozen ground and the trees that stretched naked limbs into the air.

She turned back to him and noticed the color had drained from his face. "Are you all right? Is it your leg? I told you you've been on it too much."

"*Ja*, maybe I have." He lowered his head and then sat on the mattress next to her, running a hand down his smooth-shaven face. He circled a finger around his shirt collar and then nodded his chin toward the doorway. "There's another room you have to see."

Marianna rose and followed him back into the living room and toward a closed door. With his eyes fixed on hers, Aaron opened it. With a sweep of his hand he motioned for her to enter. A smile tugged at the corners of his mouth.

She walked into the small bedroom and the first thing that caught her eye was the large window and window bench. She placed a hand to her chest and rushed forward, taking in the view of the pasture and trees. Tears came to her eyes, and she didn't understand why.

Aaron approached and placed a hand on her shoulder. "I hope those are happy tears."

She nodded, hoping they were too. The tears rolled down her cheeks, but weariness overwhelmed her. Her limp hand refused to swipe them away. "This will be a perfect room for our child."

She pictured a small girl with dark hair like hers and bright blue eyes like Aaron's. She imagined sewing her dresses and kapps. She thought about welcoming Aaron home every night and their family around the dinner table. She thought about their child growing and more children coming. A family, a real family, gathered around the dinner table and reading stories by lantern light. Butterflies danced in her stomach and more fluttered around her heart.

The impact of what she was about to do by marrying Aaron hit her like never before.

Marianna placed a hand to her forehead. An overwhelming feeling came over her like it had that dark Montana night when the spooked horse carried her and Sarah away in the buggy through the trees and brush. She tried to contain herself. Tried to calm the swift surge of bittersweet joy.

She sat on the window bench. "Can you imagine a baby here, Aaron?" She brushed away her tears. "Can you picture yourself as a father?"

He didn't answer, and she turned to face him. His skin was red above his shirt collar. His hair rumpled, as if he'd run his hand through it. A hint of sweat glistened upon his brow.

"Are you all right?"

"Just my leg." He sat down beside her. "I think you were right when you told me I've been doing too much."

Was it really the pain in his leg that caused this reaction? A nagging feeling inside Marianna told her there was more. There was a moment's hesitation where each assessed the other. She opened her mouth to ask what she knew she ought, but no words came.

Aaron turned his attention back to the meadow. "*Ja*, that's why I built this, with the thought of a child in mind." Even as he said the words Marianna could tell his mind was on something else. *Someone else?*

How can I marry him when he won't even share his heart? His thoughts?

She sighed and turned her eyes to the small winter finch that hopped from bare tree branch to bare tree branch. The day seemed colder than it had a few minutes ago, and she crossed her arms and pulled them tight, feeling a shiver carry up her spine.

Dear Dat and Mem,

Hello from Indiana! I suppose it's cold in Montana, but I imagine you reading this letter in front of the warm fire. Knowing Dat he would have wanted to open this letter as soon as he saw it in the mail, but knowing you, Mem, you would have bawled him out if he did . . . so I assume that you're reading this letter together. I'm glad you are, because there so much I'm wanting to tell.

Today was the day. The one I've been thinking about for a while. I visited the house with Aaron. It was more beautiful than I expected and it's hard to believe one day yet it will be mine . . . ours.

Levi looks well. He has news for you, but I'll allow him to share it in his own time. News that might mean my wedding won't be as soon as I imagined, but I'm adjusting to that idea.

As I pray, I feel deep inside that I should give to and care for Levi and Naomi first. My own marriage will come in good time. I told Aaron such, and he stated

he understood, yet his eyes were full of questions—
worry even. Maybe he wonders if I am having doubts?
If I cannot convince him with my words maybe the
commitment I'll show him in the months to come will
speak otherwise. Love, as you've always told me, Mem,
is more than jest a warm feeling deep inside. It's the
standing by someone in the good days and bad.

   Tell all the children hello for me. I miss them with a
deep ache. I tell myself I'll see them sometimes soon.
I hope that indeed will be the case.

   Love,
   Marianna

CHAPTER SIX

*I*n Hollywood, everyone wanted to be a star. So why did Ben wish he could just catch the next flight back to Montana?

He rose early and drove his rental car down to Sunset Boulevard. He'd paid twenty dollars for all-day parking, even though he knew the studio had a spot for him. He could have had a limo pick him up if he wanted, but for some reason he didn't want to be "that star" yet. He wanted to feel normal, ordinary, broke.

Years ago, when he first came to Hollywood, all he could think about was his name in lights. He'd tried to picture his CDs being sold in the music stores—his songs playing on the radio.

A smile tilted up his lips, and Ben lifted his face slightly, letting the sun warm his face. The cold of the Montana winter was behind him. So was his desire for fame.

Continue to work in me, God. Your glory, not mine.

A gentle peace descended with the rays of the sun. God was with him here. Not only his head told him that, his heart too. That's the reason why Ben's footsteps carried on. He wouldn't go back to Montana, not until he completed the work God had for him here, whatever that was.

God had saved his soul—saved him from self-destruction. He shared that in the letters he wrote every week to teens who'd been caught with alcohol. He learned the hard way, and he hoped the letters he sent would somehow make a difference. It didn't mattered if the kid crumpled up the letter after reading it and tossed it in the trash, if something Ben said about God stuck, well, that would be worth it. Just one more seed to take root when the time was right.

The streets were nearly empty. Hollywood was more alive at night, he supposed. Christmas lights framing many store windows had yet to be plugged in. Trash littered the gutters and neon signs blinked from tall store windows. At least two stores every block sold cheap Hollywood souvenirs: shot glasses, miniature statues of Marilyn Monroe holding down her white skirt, and T-shirts in various colors made from thin material that looked as if it would unravel after one wash. Bars and restaurants sat empty. A few dedicated fashionistas strolled into shops that sold trendy clothes, shoes, and items that only people in Hollywood could get away with.

He shook his head as he strode by one window that displayed high-heeled shoes in a rainbow of colors. He couldn't imagine anyone back home wearing nine-inch, red leather stilettos with metal buckles at the ankle and fringe in the back.

A woman walked by in a skimpy outfit, her hair rumpled and her makeup smeared as if she'd just woken up. His heart went out to her. How different could she be if she were taken out of this place and surrounded by people who cared about *her*, not what she had to offer? People who would become her friends and welcome her into their community.

As he said a quick prayer for the woman, two teenagers strode by in coffee shop uniforms, chatting about seeing Kate Hudson ordering a chai tea the previous evening.

So different from Montana.

In Montana the stars that came out at night were the ones God created in the broad heaven—not the people who made too much money and partied too hard, all in the name of entertainment.

He walked the street, looking at the Hollywood Walk of Fame stars that led toward the Chinese Theater, amazed by how many names he didn't know.

Jean Hersholt, Julia Faye, Ann Margret, Vincent Price . . . who were those people?

Today most entertainers no doubt strode through these streets, picturing their names on the walk, yet fame was fleeting. The biggest names now would hardly be a blip on the radar screen in fifty years. What was he doing here?

God must have a purpose for this all . . . I just can't wait to find out what it is.

He didn't know how far he walked, but as it neared noon he strode toward the studio. The guard at the gate seemed wary as Ben strode up to the security point. The tall man's eyes widened in surprise when he noticed Ben's name was indeed on the admittance list.

After being led through the gate, Ben found the correct set of double glass doors to Studio A. Inside, the left wall was lined with bronze, silver, gold, and platinum records as far as his eye could see. Roy was already there in the front area, chatting with the receptionist. He didn't even glance down at his watch when Ben entered, or reprimand him for being ten minutes late. Roy was already treating him like a star.

Amazing what a difference having a hit on the radio could make.

"Ready to get started?" Roy nodded a good-bye to the receptionist and turned toward the hall.

"As ready as I'll ever be."

"Did you bring some new songs?"

Ben nodded. He'd been writing off and on over the last month, which was a good thing. He just wished he'd had a better topic. Then again, heartbreak always made for best-selling records. "Wrote some new stuff, revamped some of the old stuff too. But it all needs work."

"No worries. That's what we're here for. By the end of these three weeks you're going to be the star everyone knows you are." Roy placed a firm hand on Ben's shoulder.

Ben forced a smile. "Sounds good to me."

Roy released his hand and then motioned down the hall. Ben followed him.

"You're going to ride this wave all the way to the top, my boy," Roy called back over his shoulder, his voice lifting with the excitement and charisma of a minister in a radical church, rising and falling with each step. "All the way to the top. Just go easy on the booze and the girls." Roy pointed a finger into the air. "Both are the ticket to spending too much money and time. Both will claim your soul."

Why was Roy telling him this? He'd walked that path before—and had lost big time. No way he'd make those mistakes again.

God, You know.

I'm a different person. He closed his eyes. *This time . . . This time I'll use my influence to make a difference.*

Aaron slowed his horse as the buggy approached Aunt Ida's house. "Here you are. Whoa, Jessie."

Marianna smiled at him. Aaron was handsome, there was no doubt. And what other Amishman had built such a place for his bride? None she knew. To add to that, what man would be so patient with meddling family members? Aaron had proven himself there too.

After looking at the house, Aaron had taken her to visit her aunt Betsy and all her cousins. It was meant to be a short visit, but her aunt had chattered all afternoon. It was only Aaron's pain in his leg, which he tried to hide, caused Marianna to stand up to Aunt Betsy and insist they had to go.

"Hurry back to see us," Betsy had said with a wave. "If you have time, stop by on Christmas too. The more the merrier yet."

Marianna found it hard to believe the holiday was in only three days, but the short days and cold, frosty air told her it was true.

He parked, and she leaned over and kissed his cheek. She climbed down from the buggy. "I thank you kindly, sir. Would you like to come in?"

Aaron turned his gaze to the row of windows behind Marianna. Marianna followed his eyes and she noticed Aunt Ida standing by the kitchen window. The lantern hanging over the sink had been dimmed to give her aunt a better view of outside.

"I think I'll pass. My mem has been prodding me with enough questions about Montana, 'What were the mountains like? How did the Amish there act?' If I hafta go another round, answering yer aunt's questions I'll get an aching head for sure."

A giggle slipped through Marianna's lips. "I understand." She took two steps back to allow the buggy to pass. "Although it's worse with Aunt Ida because she often forgets the answers and asks more than once."

Aaron chuckled, and then he loosened the reins and clicked his tongue, urging his horse forward. "Tomorrow then?"

"Yes, tomorrow. I'm looking forward to it."

Aunt Ida's words spilled from her as soon as Marianna walked inside. "That leg isn't bothering Aaron Zook, is it now? He did run home awful quick."

Marianna nodded. "*Ja.* Sadly it is. He's been on it more than he ought."

Aaron hadn't said he was hurting much, but she could see it. He tightened his jaw when he was in pain. His gaze had narrowed as the pain increased.

She smiled as she removed her coat and hung it on the hook, not because Aaron was hurting, but she realized their time together had made a difference. She knew Aaron. Knew how to read him. But more than that she knew he would be a good husband who rarely complained.

"Is it cold out?" Aunt Ida tucked her quilt around her lap, even though the woodstove poured out warmth.

"Not bad. Not compared to Montan—"

She caught herself. Mem had told her before leaving that the folks back in Indiana wouldn't want to hear about Montana in every other sentence.

"Not bad," she said again, "but before I get too warm and cozy I best get to choring."

"I can get Ezekiel next door if need be." Aunt Ida said in a way that told Marianna she didn't want to pay the young man if she didn't have to.

"*Nein*, no problem."

Ten minutes later, Marianna entered the barn and grabbed up a milich stool and bucket. With quivering hands she plopped herself beside the nearest cow. She took the warm teats in her hands and milked as quickly as she could, but her efforts told her she was long out of practice. Being in Indiana again—working around Aunt Ida's barn—was like being in a familiar dream, but one that no longer seemed to fit.

Looking into the bucket at the warm, frothy milk reminded her of Sarah whipping up cream for the peanut butter pie. As her hands did the familiar work, her mind took her back to the kitchen at the West Kootenai Kraft and Grocery. Were Millie and Jebadiah chatting in the restaurant or had the snow kept Millie home? Was Edgar feeling better? Was Mrs. Shelter still helping to care for Jenny's little girl Kenzie?

The sound of scampering caught her attention, and she turned to see two kittens chasing each other through the hay bales. Racing by, the second kitten gave up the chase and approached the bucket, gazing up at Marianna.

"So you think you need a drink, *ja?*" She turned the teat toward the kitten and gave a firm tug. A stream of milk shot out, spraying the kitten's face. It meowed and darted, then paused to lick the warm goodness.

"I sort of feel the same way," Marianna whispered to the small creature. "I thought Montana to be an assault, only to find it a gift." She bit her lip and then swallowed down emotion.

When chores were finished, Marianna washed up, letting her hands warm up in the basin of water Aunt Ida heated on the woodstove.

With a wagging of her head, Aunt Ida walked to the kitchen with her hands perched on her narrow hips. "Nearly forgot," Aunt Ida called. "Got a letter from yer mem today."

The image of her mom's brave wave as Annie had driven them away filled her mind. Marianna lowered her head, blinking fast.

"I am sure Mem's jest asking about the trip." Marianna tried to keep her tone light. "Either that or reminding me to change my stockings every day." Marianna forced a laugh. "Once a mother, always a mother."

Marianna waited until after dinner to escape into her bedroom with the letter. She opened it with eager fingers.

Dear Marianna,

My words cannot tell you how thankful I am that you've returned to Indiana and have agreed to marry Aaron Zook. Although I am not thankful you are far away, you've made the best choice. You haven't been gone but a few days, and I miss you already. What I am thankful for is that you have returned to the way of our ancestors, that you did not fall to the temptation of the outside world as I did for a time. You are stronger than I, dear daughter.

There are those our hearts turn to, who will lead us the wrong path. Even as I know it is right for you to

*return to Indiana, I also know that it may be right for me
to stay away. My heart demands a fresh start . . .*

Marianna paused, and she thought again of the van driver
who'd picked her and Aaron up at the train station. Could he be
the man Mem had cared about so long ago? A chill traveled down
her spine. He had mentioned her mother, had he not? He stated
Marianna looked like her. She hadn't seen him before, but he
seemed to know her. Seemed to be a part of her mother's past. She
thought about what the driver had told Levi, *"Your mother and
I were friends for many years. She's a special woman."*

If it was the same man, what would Mem think to know he
was back in town? If so, she might *never* wish to return—even for
a visit. Marianna's lips compressed. She placed the letter on her
lap and wiped a hand across her forehead. Even though she hadn't
pursued her relationship with Ben, as Mem had with Mark, she
understood the depths of where one's feeling could plunge.

Marianna wilted against the pillows on her bed. Her eyes fluttered closed, and she let the memories carry her back for just a
moment. Talking to Ben at the auction. The tight hug he'd given
her at her father's birthday party. The way he'd tried to save Ellie's
color-book from the puddle within five minutes of their meeting.

She had other memories of Aaron, more memories. Aaron
walking barefoot in the creek and the smile of a freckled-nosed
boy of thirteen. Yet, how come the thoughts of him did not stir
her in the same way?

"Love is a choice," she told herself. She would love Aaron. She
did love Aaron. The love she had for him was something that
would last—not the swelling emotions brought on by a man who
had no right to her heart.

The scent of his loafing shed welcomed Aaron as he entered. With winter set, the cows and young cattle nestled inside. Taking a look around, he saw a fresh calf was in the stall box along with hogs and chickens tucked in their spots. It was good to be here—to have his own space. Although he appreciated the extra time to get to know Marianna in Montana, nothing about that place appealed to him. The mountains were beautiful, but he missed the wide open plains and rolling hills. He did not like the friendships between the Amish and Englisch. Did not like Ben Stone being anywhere near Marianna.

He wasn't blind. He'd seen the way Ben and Marianna's eyes found each other across crowded rooms. Aaron considered giving Marianna the rest of the letters he'd written when she first left Indiana for Montana. He'd given her two already and he'd seen her response. After she read them all, she'd be even more committed to their marriage and all thoughts of Ben would vanish. Yet part of him held back. They shared more inside than he'd ever shared with another person.

After we're married, he convinced himself.

The door to the loafing shed opened, and Aaron's eyes widened as his mother walked in. He could count on one hand the number of times he saw her in the "menner's territory." He studied her face, hoping nothing was the matter.

"Mem?" He raised his eyebrows.

"Do ya want to tell me what's on your mind? What's going on with you and Marianna? You were so happy when you left to show her the house and you returned not so happy."

He cast her a glance and then filled the feeding bins with ground ear corn and silage.

"Aaron?"

"Nothing. It may be my leg, the pain, that's the problem." He rubbed it for emphasis.

"*Ja*, well if there is a problem . . . I offer a listening ear. I wouldn't blame ye if you need to talk. Everyone speaks of a difference in Marianna already."

"Everyone? Who's had a chance to see her? She's hardly left the house yet. Has her aunt been saying things?"

"Well now, I'm not one to be speaking what I have no business to say."

Not in front of me, that is.

Aaron knew his mother had no qualms about sharing her "concerns" with friends.

When Mem left, Aaron braced an arm on the wall and hung his head. The truth was he didn't know what bothered him. He'd waited to show Marianna the house for so long and finally had the chance. Maybe that was the problem. Maybe he'd dreamt about it for too many nights. Maybe he'd put too many expectations about how Marianna should react. Maybe it was what he hid that bothered him even more than what he'd revealed.

Should he have told her the truth about Naomi?

Marianna had assumed she'd been the only woman who'd sat on that bed and enjoyed the view. He didn't have the heart to tell her that Naomi had done so . . . more than once. It would lead to too many questions.

Questions about things he didn't want to think about . . . let alone confess.

Dear Marianna,

I wonder when I'm going to give you this letter. Part of me wants to put it in today's mail. Another part tells me to wait. Wait until I know your heart. Lately, I've been thinking a lot about the Amish way: gentle, simple, peaceful, forgiving.

Although the Amish are sometimes called simple people, we both know that is not the case. The Amish love, laugh, celebrate, mourn like any other human. There is nothing simple about their emotions. There is nothing simple about my emotions.

When you left I thought a lot about the Amish response to life. There is so much that must be "given up": modern conveniences, normal society, one's right to himself or herself. Only equal to that is the determination not to give in. Not to give in to the trappings of wealth, give in to pride, give in to temptations of what they ought not have.

I'm sad to say I've given in to many temptations. I'm not the man that I see in your eyes when you look at me. I wish I were.

Yet since I've known you, one thing that has not failed is my love for you. It's hard to explain, hard to deny.

Do you love me as much as I love you? I wish you were here with me now. One glimpse in your eyes and I think I would know.

Why do you have to be so far away, my sweet Marianna? Why couldn't you be tucked next to my side? Dream of me tonight if you would.

Written with the pen of the man who loves you more than you know.

Naomi entered the dawdi haus without knocking and then moved to the back bedroom. She'd seen Levi leaving thirty minutes ago and she'd waited near the back porch for fifteen minutes, making sure he wasn't going to come back.

She entered the bedroom and paused in the doorway. At first she'd planned to stay in this house, but her parents didn't like the idea of her being in her grandparents' cabin alone. She ended up staying in her room, and her older sister Judith moved in with their younger sisters. It worked better that way since Levi didn't have a home to return to once he became Amish again.

She'd cleared out her things weeks ago, until she remembered something she'd tucked away on a high closet shelf. Naomi just hoped Levi hadn't stumbled upon the drawing.

She entered the bedroom that smelled of Levi—of his manly presence and the Englisch cologne he still wore. Her heart hammered.

Turning to the closet, she hurried over and stood on her toes. Her fingers brushed the edge of a piece of paper and she let out a sigh. *It's still here.*

Naomi pinched her fingers on the edge of the paper and pulled. She didn't know why she kept the drawing. She'd be horrified if anyone saw it.

Aaron had drawn her with her kapp off, hair down, and apron sitting beside her. He'd used colored pencils to capture the red of her hair. She bit her lip and ran her finger over her captured image. She'd never considered herself beautiful until Aaron drew her like this, but she couldn't risk the chance of Levi finding it and asking questions. With one smooth motion she ripped it in half. Taking those two pieces she ripped them again, and continued ripping, until only small pieces remained in her hands.

Only then her breathing slowed.

She carried the small pieces in her hand and placed them in the trash, hiding them under potato peels. Relief lessened the tension in her chest. Still, she didn't feel whole. The evidence was destroyed but the deeds would never be undone. Her heart felt like the paper—torn and in pieces. Naomi placed a hand over her growing stomach.

When had everything gone so wrong?

CHAPTER SEVEN

He finished the concert, his mind and heart heavy for the words he had shared, the song he had sung.

He stood at a back table and noticed the line growing for autographs. His head ached and his eyelids weighed a hundred pounds.

A woman approached wearing bright blue eye shadow. She looked to be his mother's age but gushed like a teenager. "Can I take a photo for my Facebook page?"

Ben nodded. "Uh, sure." He smiled, but felt the life getting sucked out of him as he did.

More people joined the line, and he knew he should stay there for them, but tonight . . .

He just couldn't.

He turned to the assistant at the table. "Sorry. I need to scoot tonight. I'm not doing too well." He turned to face the line of people, raising his voice so they would hear him. "You know what folks, it's been a long day. I need to hit the hay."

A moan carried through the crowd as Ben offered a wave and strode away.

Backstage, the rest of the band members were loading up their instruments, but instead of helping he excused himself and headed to the tour bus. The night air was chilly, but a warm breeze seemed to blow over him when he noticed a woman standing by the door of their bus. Tall, blonde, beautiful . . .

He slowed his steps as he approached and said a silent prayer for strength. "Hey. You looking for someone?" Ben glanced over his shoulder. Were the band members setting him up? They'd teased him on the flight to Chicago about taking one of his groupies up on their offers to "keep him company." It would be just like them to place a temptation before him, then hide someplace with a video camera. Well, as temptation went, this woman was top notch.

"Lookin' for you."

Yeah. It was a setup. "That's kind of you, but I don't—"

She held up a hand, stopping him, then tucked her thumbs in the back of her jeans. She wore a low-cut shirt and it took all Ben's reserve to stay focused on her eyes.

She smiled, and oddly enough, her smile seemed . . . friendly. Nothing more. "I know it can get lonely and boring on the road. And I bet you get tired of fast food. I thought you'd like a home-cooked meal."

Ben's eyes widened. He'd been on the road before and he'd gotten a lot of offers—but none like this. "You're offering me food?"

"Yeah, what did you think?"

"Well . . ." He shifted from side to side trying to figure out how to tell her he wasn't interested. Well, he was interested, but knew he shouldn't be.

"Actually, I make it a policy never to go home with a stranger, even one as pretty as you."

Laughter bubbled from the woman's lips like suds in a sink of warm water. "Oh man, I must seem pretty desperate. Look, I'm serious about the meal. My dad owns a restaurant down the street. Home cooking at its finest." She lowered her gaze and looked up at him under long eyelashes. "After hearing the story of the girl you like I wouldn't want to get in the middle of that. You just looked like . . . you could use a friend."

No doubting the sincerity in her words. Clearly, he'd misread the situation. And the woman. "Sure." Ben slid on his jean jacket and buttoned it half way up. "I could always use a friend and home cooking does sound good." He patted his stomach. "Especially tonight. I forgot how empty I get pouring everything out on stage."

Something inside told him to get on the bus, to walk away. But the woman's smile drew him in.

He motioned to the bus driver and when the man approached, Ben told him he'd be back in an hour. It would take the rest of the band that long to pack up.

With slow steps he followed her to a waiting sports car.

"I'm sad to hear you're empty. My dad's cooking is sure to fill you up."

"Thanks. Appreciate that." If only he were just talking about his stomach. But his chest felt just as hollow. With late nights and long days on the road, he'd hadn't spent time with God like he had before going on tour. He needed quiet time, time to think, time to pray . . . but for right now he'd settle for a good meal, followed by a slice of pie. Coconut cream, if they had it.

She clicked the key fob to unlock the car door, and he placed his hand on the door handle. The stirring came again, stronger this time, urging him to go back to the bus. The woman was beautiful. He could use the company . . .

But he knew he had no right getting into the car with her.

A battle waged inside him between what he longed for and what God was asking him to do. He couldn't believe how quickly those old desires popped up. He'd gone with many women like this in the past—and for a whole lot more than pie.

Ben released the handle and stepped back. "I've changed my mind. I told my fans back there I was heading to bed. I do need the sleep, and I need some time with God. As much as I appreciate your offer—"

"Are you sure?" The woman hurried around to the side of the car. "I can get something to go." She stepped closer to him, peering into his face. "I can be back in twenty minutes. It's no problem."

The skin on her face, her neck, was so smooth. He imagined the feel of it under his fingertips.

Ben swallowed hard. "Sorry." He raised his hands and turned away. "I'm sure you're a nice girl, but I have to set limits. More than that, I need people to trust my word." He didn't look back, didn't wait for her response. Instead he hurried back to the bus.

God, keep me strong.

It was a simple prayer, but so true. He needed to be strong against those who had the power to draw him away. And against himself—

And against the desire to run to those he truly longed to be with.

Abe swung the axe high over his head and let it fall onto the wood. A crack split the air and the log broke into two pieces, each side tumbling into small piles stacking up on the dirty snow.

He squatted and loaded his arm with wood. Biting edges snagged on his jacket, and he piled wood up to his shoulder and then turned and strode toward the front porch of his house. The woodpile was already tall and neatly stacked, but he was one to be prepared. If things worked out as it seemed, they'd most likely be around next winter too. He could use the extra wood then.

Stepping onto the first porch step, Abe saw Ike standing with a coffee mug in one hand and patting Trapper with the other. His brother was just a few years younger, and they'd grown closer over the last year than they'd ever been. Ike had always been the wanderer, the adventurer, and this time—as the word had spread back home—he'd talked Abe into wandering along with him.

"Jest got here a minute ago." Ike lifted his mug. "Walked over from the store. Ruth was kind enough to let me warm up by the fire for a minute and pour me a cup of coffee."

Abe stacked the wood against the log siding. "She does make the best coffee. Glad you could make it."

Ike chuckled. "Well now, it's not every day I get a message on my answering machine in the shed from my brother. In fact, I think it's a first."

"I jest wanted to talk to you about packing up our things in Indiana. You said you knew of a driver who could help us." Abe wasted no time letting his brother in on the whole truth of the matter. "Ruth wants to sell the house, too, which means packing up and moving everything."

Abe finished stacking the wood and brushed off wood chips from his jacket. "The more I think about it, the more it seems the right thing to do. I won't need any of the farm equipment. I'll try to sell it to the Moser lad or take it to auction. Most of the things we bring will be from the house."

"That's good, the less you have to move the better. The problem is the driver I was thinking of was Ben Stone. That's not possible now that he's gone to California to make his music."

Abe nodded. He didn't like that they'd have to come up with another driver, and yet . . .

Just as well his daughter was far away from that Englischman.

Ike rose, and Trapper jumped up on his leg, wanting more attention.

Abe patted his leg, and the dog lunged toward him, tail wagging. The poor pup hadn't been the same since Marianna left. He stroked the top of the dog's head.

"Too bad you couldn't pack up those trees you planted behind the barn." Ike added a log to the stack. "I know they were planted in memory of Marilyn and Joanna, and even though those were the darkest times . . . well, seeing the trees helps me remember."

"That was a hard time, all right." Abe lowered his head. And that was the strange thing about moving. Leaving Indiana felt like he was turning his back to the pain and the loss, and in a way it saddened him to walk away from all that. It was a part of what made him who he was—what made *them* who they were.

"There were other dark days too." The words escaped before Abe understood why he was saying them, but as soon as they were out a chill dripped down his spine. Even though losing his daughters in the accident had been devastating, he knew his children rested in the arms of God. The *darkest* day was different.

That was the day Ruth told him she loved another.

He'd come in from laying seed, not having a care in the world, and there sat his wife, holding their infant daughter and looking at him as if he were a stranger in their own home. Her parents had both been ill, and she'd been spending time helping in their home. She'd been distant, but he believed it was because she'd been trying to do too much. But the words escaping from her downturned lips told Abe a different tale.

"My parents' neighbor has been over every day. Mark was my friend as a child—before I understood his friendship wasn't to be. We've been talking . . . he says he still loves me, Abe. Has always loved me." She lowered her gaze. "I believe I love him too."

She'd spoken as simply as if she'd been sharing her favorite recipe rather than shredding his heart.

Over the following months, although Ruth still lived at home and went through the motions of being his wife, her heart wasn't in it. Abe thought he'd lost her for good.

Then one day she returned. She'd never left physically, it only seemed that way. One day, though, she laughed as she did the dishes. She smiled again and cared for him as she had when they'd first married. He hadn't asked the reason for the change— he was just happy it had come.

Ruth's childhood friend moved away soon after that, and they never again brought up the subject of her struggle. It had been enough for Abe that the man was gone. It had been even better when their next daughter Joanna was conceived just a few months later—a second representation of their union. Another proof of their life, their family.

But now? Deep down he had a feeling what Betsy had said in her letter stirred his wife's buried emotions. No, he hadn't read the letter, but his wife's distance and tension these last few days told him what her words couldn't.

Mark Olsen had returned.

Abe shook his head.

Was he making a mistake in taking Ruth back to Indiana for Levi's wedding? Maybe he shouldn't return. Or just go without her. But no. He couldn't leave Ruth in Montana alone. There was nothing else to do. They would return.

He just hoped Ruth would be stronger this time around.

Ike cleared his throat, bringing Abe back to the present. "There is a phrase that Edgar at the store uses . . . penny fer your thoughts." Ike cocked one eyebrow.

Abe released a sound that reminded him of escaping steam. He considered telling Ike his struggle, but he didn't want to damage Ruth's good name. Back when it happened, word had gotten out that Ruth's eyes and heart had been turned to an Englischman, but like any "news," it had dissipated into nothingness as soon as the next community member did what they ought not.

"A penny is about all my thoughts are worth." Abe sighed. "I was jest trying to consider who would be a good person to drive us instead," he lied.

"I can ask around." Ike tucked his hands into his pockets. "In the meantime can we head inside?" He patted his stomach. Looked to me as if Ruth is almost done making up breakfast."

Marianna opened her eyes, stretched her arms, and expected to hear her younger brothers and sisters running through the house and playing. Instead, she heard the chiming of Aunt Ida's clock, stirring her to full wakefulness. Oh, yes. She wasn't in Montana.

She closed her eyes again, picturing Aaron's smile. Then she recalled Mem's letter. Montana . . . her friends and family . . . they all seemed so far away. Especially Ben . . .

How come it was that last thought that pierced her heart so?

She pushed all thoughts of Ben from her mind. That was a different time and a different place. She didn't need to think about that now—think about him. Instead, she needed to focus on what really mattered. She was back in Indiana for a reason. She was here to help Levi and Naomi prepare for their baby. She was here to think about her and Aaron's wedding and their future together. She wished they had talked about that more. Thought and talked about their future as they rode the train. Maybe they didn't need to. Maybe it was enough to accept each day as it came.

Marianna pushed the covers back and rose. She swung her feet over the edge of her bed and slid them into the slippers that she'd laid out the night before. At least there were some familiar things—the slippers she'd brought and her journal that sat on the dresser, waiting to be filled with today's adventures.

Before she'd moved to Montana, life in Indiana had a certain rhythm to it. Frozen ground warmed with spring. Broken ground opened for seed. Tended ground produced crops. And once the crops were in, there came a season of rest and partaking of the bounty.

Marianna stood at the window, pressing her fingertips to the cold glass. Outside, the ground lay at rest, but nothing inside her could claim the same. In the days to come, she'd sit by the fire. She'd quilt. She'd look through her grandmother's cookbook in search of something nice to make for Aaron, but she couldn't imagine not wondering what everyone was doing in Montana. Would anxiety stir even quiet days?

Enough of that.

She walked over to the dresser and looked in the mirror. Her hair had slipped out of her sleeping kerchief and a few strands fell around her face in soft waves. She brushed a long strand of hair behind her ear. What it would be like to wake up and look not only at her own reflection but also to look into Aaron's loving gaze? It felt gut to be desired. To know that she would soon be his. It made her smile to think she'd have her own home, cooking her own meals, creating her own menu, washing their clothes. She needed to start thinking about a garden too. Even if she and Aaron weren't married before planting time, maybe she could design a plot and Aaron could break up the ground and till it. If so, she'd be able to plant the seeds as a single gal and then cook up the harvest as a married woman.

She tried to picture that—pictured going out to her garden and picking the best produce and then bringing it inside for her husband's meal.

A soft humming outside the door interrupted her thoughts. Aunt Ida hummed one of the hymns they sang at church. But the way Aunt Ida hummed the song seemed more heartfelt than it did in Sunday service.

To be like Christ we love one another,
through everything, here on this earth.
We love one another, not just with words but in deeds. . .
If we have of this world's goods (no matter how much or
    how little)
and see that our brother has a need,
but do not share with him what we have freely received—

how can we say that we would be ready to give our lives
    for him if necessary?
The one who is not faithful in the smallest thing, and who
    still seeks his own good
which his heart desires—how can he be trusted with a
    charge over heavenly things?
Let us keep our eyes on love!

That last line resonated. She had to keep her eyes on love—
the love she had for Aaron. She needed to be faithful in the smallest things to him, and this included her thoughts.

"It's a new day," she told herself as she rose and dressed.
Today, she would see old friends. Today, she would think more
of the community she was a part of rather than the one she left
behind. Today, she'd think of her future with Aaron, and not let
her mind take her back to her feelings for Ben.

No matter how her heart longed to go there.

Marianna walked toward the Garden Gate Cafe. It was a small,
yellow building with a white railed porch. In the summer, small
clusters of comfortable chairs were placed outside, offering
customers a chance to sit and take in the warming sun. But today
the chairs were put away, and no one was sitting and relaxing.
The Christmas rush had hit the Englischers, and they moved
from building to building like ants around their anthill.

As she entered the cafe, Rebecca sat at a round table with
two of her coworkers decorating Christmas cupcakes. Marianna's
eyes widened. Rebecca wore her Amish dress. Last time she'd
seen Rebecca she'd been withdrawn, somber, ready to leave the

community. Had her friend decided to remain Amish and get baptized into the church? Had she chosen the better way?

"Mari!" Rebecca stood and hurried over to her, arms wide. "You are really here. I saw yer aunt Ida at church last week and she told me you were on your way."

Marianna stepped into her friend's hug, then smiled as she stepped out of the warm embrace. "I see yer wearing Amish dress, I—"

Rebecca's lifted hands halted Marianna's words. "Wait, you don't understand." Her mouth neared Marianna's ear and she lowered her voice to a whisper. "I wear this because I get better tips. I haven't decided to go back. Doubt I will."

Marianna's heart deflated as if had been pricked by a dozen sewing needles, but she tried not to let her disappointment show. Emotion stirred within her and she took Rebecca's hand. "You don't feel called to the Amish, but that doesn't mean you're leaving God, does it?"

Rebecca's eyes widened. "I-I am not sure what you mean." She led Marianna to a back table, to avoid her curious coworkers overhearing.

They sat and faced each other. Marianna took a moment to enjoy the closeness of her friend before continuing.

"I've changed since being in Montana. I see things in different ways." The image of the still pond came into mind. "If you stay Amish it would make many people happy, but if you decide not to . . . well, I know many Englisch who love God."

Rebecca's mouth fell open, and she stared at Marianna as if she'd just confessed that she'd been living on the moon for the past six months.

"Were you friends with the Englisch?" Rebecca leaned in

close. "You of all people . . . the one who always did everything right. Do yer mem and dat know?"

How could Marianna explain that Mem and Dat had Englisch friends too? She was sure she mentioned she'd worked at a store . . . did Rebecca think the store served the Amish only?

"Things were different there. I enjoyed getting to know my neighbors, Amish and Englisch."

Rebecca nodded and a slow smile curled on her lips.

Marianna placed a hand to her chest. "What? What are you smiling about?"

"Well, it may be selfish, but I think you'll give our neighbors something to talk about." Rebecca shrugged. "I'm afraid they may be bored of talking about me—with my Englisch boyfriend, my driver's license, and . . ."

Marianna didn't know what should shock her most. The driver's license she supposed. "I'm afraid to ask what else."

"I've signed up for college. I don't want to care for a home and children my whole life. I want to do something with myself. I want more."

Rebecca's eyes brightened as she talked about her plan to go to nursing school. Marianna never seen so much excited chatter spout from Rebecca's mouth, yet even as her friend talked an uneasiness came over Marianna. She had the strangest feeling that eyes were on them, or more accurately were on her.

She turned to the front bakery counter where a man was buying bread. The man glanced to the clerk as he paid for the bread and then turned and focused his eyes on her.

It's him. The driver . . . Mark.

Marianna tried to focus on what Rebecca was saying, but she could see the man's intent gaze from the corner of her eyes.

A shiver traveled up her spine. Should she say something to Rebecca? No, to say something would mean she'd have to explain who this man was.

Thankfully he paid for his items and left.

Rebecca's eyebrows narrowed. It was clear from her gaze that Marianna hadn't fooled her. Rebecca could tell Marianna was no longer paying attention and she let her story about her first math test trail off.

Rebecca straightened her shoulders. "Listen, can we get together sometime next week?" Her voice hinted of disappointment. "I've already taken my break and this cupcake order has to go out tonight."

"*Ja*, of course. How silly of me to keep you from your work."

Marianna bid Rebecca a farewell and headed back down the road to the grocery. She folded her arms across her chest and tucked her hands under her armpits to warm them. Her thoughts were on Rebecca driving an automobile as she turned onto the sidewalk outside of the cafe. Just then, a man stepped out of the shadows, moving toward her.

A squeal erupted from Marianna's lips and she jumped toward the street.

"Whoa now!" Mark reached out a hand, snagging her arm.

Her eyes widened, and she tugged against him. "What . . . what are you doing. Let me go!"

"I mean you no harm, Marianna." With his free hand he pointed to the street. "There's just a car coming, and I didn't want you to get hurt."

The car drove by slowly, but the driver's eyes were fixed ahead. *Should I call to him? Call for help?* She opened her mouth but the words didn't come. Instead she pulled against the man's grasp, attempting to free her arm.

"I won't jump in front of a car, sir, you can let me go."

The Englisch man released her, and she pulled back, crossing her arms over her chest. Glancing around she noticed the street was filled with people doing their last-minute Christmas shopping. Surely he wouldn't try to harm her with so many people around.

"I didn't mean to scare you. I just wanted to tell you that if you ever need a ride . . ." He pulled a business card out of his coat pocket and handed it to her. The warmth of his breath fogged up the air.

"Thank you, but I don't think that'll be needed." She raised her hands, shielding off his extended hand.

"There's no charge. You know, as a favor to your mother."

"Yes, sir, I understand, but I'm staying with my aunt, and I have transportation, and soon I'll be married. Aaron watches out for me." She hoped he'd get the hint, despite her quivering voice.

The lines on the man's face softened.

"I'm sorry." He put the business card back into his pocket. "Forgive me. I didn't mean to scare you. It's just the shock, that's all . . . looking at you takes me back twenty-five years. Are you thinking I want to hurt you? Never. I just . . . well, I want to be here to help you as a way to honor your mother. She's a good woman, you know."

"*Ja*, she's *gut*. Both she and *my father* are."

Marianna said a silent prayer for wisdom, and before it had played through her mind she already knew the words she needed to speak.

"You seem like a nice enough man, but the best thing you could do for my mother—for me—is to leave us alone. We have a family, our own family . . . and even though Mem has favorable memories—"

He ran a hand through his graying hair. "Does Ruth still think of me?"

A cold wind came up, biting at Marianna's cheeks. She considered lying, but she couldn't bring herself to being dishonest. Instead, she cocked up her chin and stared into his eyes.

"It really doesn't matter what place you had in Mem's life. She has a good family now. She's committed her life to another. I suggest you leave her alone. And me as well."

The man's eyes widened and then he lowered his head, looking like her dog Trapper after he'd just been scolded.

"You're right. I'm sorry. I don't know what's gotten into me." With a sweep of his arm he motioned down the street. "I won't bother you again, Marianna. And when your Mem comes into town . . . well, I'll do my best to steer clear of her too."

Marianna nodded and strode away, watching her footing on the icy sidewalk. Aunt Ida would be wondering where she was, but that didn't matter. She'd finally voiced what was on her mind. All her life she'd given the kind answer. Even when kids treated her poorly at schul, Mem and Dat had always taught her to return their scorn with kindness.

She noticed Aunt Ida ahead and waved, hurrying toward the buggy.

But sometimes being right had to overcome being kind . . . didn't it?

"*Kindness, when given away, comes back.*"

Marianna pursed her lips at the Amish proverb, because the

fact was she didn't want that man to keep coming back. What he offered wasn't kindness.

It was destruction. For Mem. For their family.

Marianna forced a smile as she approached her aunt. She just hoped that when Mem returned, she would stand strong.

Dear Marianna,

I don't know why I'm writing you another letter. They're stacking up and I still don't know when, or if, you'll ever read them. I smiled when I read that line I just wrote because I realize that maybe this time is to develop patience in me. Uncommon patience, it is the Amish way, isn't it?

The world around us, it seems, is quick to skip from one thing to the next. Yet don't you find it hard to wait and pray rather than to seek a quick fix? I do. If I had my choice this moment I'd walk out my door and find my way to you. That would be a quick fix, yet I doubt it would really fix things. Maybe our time apart is for us to know who we are separate, so that we will be better together. My heart hopes that is the case.

As I wait, I am also reminded that demanding an immediate solution signals a lack of trust. Do I trust we'll find our way to each other again? No. Do I trust God will make everything right even if things don't turn out as I want? I wish I could say a firm yes. It's my lack of faith that makes my confidence weak. As the days pass maybe my yes will be more firm.

If I could change your being far away, I would. If I could change the problems that keep us apart I'd do that too. Yet instead of resisting the path of things, I'm trying to resist despair and fear. This is also the way of the Amish, is it not?

While despair and fear are hard opponents, they are battled best in places beyond the noise and haste. I've been seeking those places more often than I used to. If it were possible, I'd seek them more often.

Finally, I will end with yet another note of my love. If I've learned one thing, love grows even if it isn't offered, yet the burden of its weight grows too. I console myself by believing that God hasn't brought you into my life only for pain and longing. If the love I carry for you is only for myself and my understanding of what's important in life, then it's a burden worth carrying.

Written with the pen of the man who dreams of you more than you realize.

CHAPTER EIGHT

*A*fter shopping in town, Aunt Ida suggested they stop by Naomi's parents' house to pay a visit. This surprised Marianna, until she remembered her aunt didn't know about Naomi's pregnancy. Surely Aunt Ida wouldn't want to visit a young woman in such a "condition." Either that or Aunt Ida knew, and she wanted more information.

A smile curled on her aunt's face—like a cat that had just caught a mouse—when Marianna parked Aunt Ida's buggy in front of the barn.

Levi was walking into the barn with a harness in hand. Seeing them, he spun in his tracks and approached Marianna's side of the buggy. "What a surprise."

"We've come to visit." Aunt Ida smiled.

"*Ja, gut.* I am certain Mrs. Studer will be eager to see you yet." Levi walked around the buggy and helped his aunt down. "While you visit with the Studers, I'll take Mari back to see Naomi." He pointed to the smaller place in back. "She's been telling me she can't wait to see you, Mari."

A pout rose on Aunt Ida's face, and Marianna could tell she was hoping they'd all visit together. *"Ja,* well, I suppose I can visit with Naomi another time."

"I'm sure she'd like that." Marianna slid from the buggy. "And I'll at least walk you to the door."

Thankfully, Levi took care of the horse. Perhaps that was easier for him than helping with their aunt. With careful steps she led her aunt up the steps of the porch.

Naomi's parents' big white clapboard house was newer than others in the community. Marianna remembered when the house went up. The smaller, older farmhouse where Naomi's grand-parents had lived was in back. As soon as she said a proper greeting to Mrs. Studer, she hurried to the dawdi haus.

From the dawdi haus, Marianna could see the trees her parents planted after her sisters' deaths. And beyond that she could see her parents' property and house.

Yet, it didn't feel like home any more. Home was where her parents were, where her siblings were. And Montana seemed very far away.

She'd get over to visit her parents' old place soon enough. She still had a hope chest upstairs in her old room filled with her things, including the many journals she'd written. It would be interesting now to go back and see what she'd said. Did her words come across as sad as she'd always felt? Could she read the weight of trying to live her life for two sisters lost? It would be interesting to find out.

The front door swung open, and Naomi stepped out. Even though her dress and apron hung loose, her pregnancy was already evident.

Wasn't it too soon for that?

"Marianna, welcome!"

Just inside the front door of the dawdi haus was a trunk. Naomi took Marianna's coat and placed it on top. Then Naomi led her to the worn sofa where they both sat.

"We're moving all our things to the dawdi haus," Naomi said. "I'll be setting everything up for after the wedding, of course. There should be plenty of time to get everything in order, especially since we'll have more time than we thought."

Marianna nodded. Naomi's parents had asked them to wait, but why? Because Naomi's pregnancy was so evident? Or were there other reasons? An icy sensation traveled up Marianna's arms. Oh, why didn't she allow Levi to share more of the burdens on his heart?

"Are you excited that you'll be living on your own—on your own together, I mean?" Marianna tried to keep her eyes off the one thing she wanted to talk about most—the baby growing in Naomi's womb. "It seems like a big commitment."

"With the house and Levi's income I s'pose we'll have enough to make it. And after the wedding, as we go around visiting, we should get enough for me to keep a home." Naomi rubbed her belly. That surprised Marianna. It also surprised her that Naomi talked like things were happening no different than with every other Amish young couple. The truth was, though, it wasn't uncommon for Amish girls to get pregnant out of wedlock. What *was* uncommon was for their boyfriends to come back from the world.

"Would you like some hot tea? I have water on the stov—"

The door opened and Levi stepped in. Instead of the look of admiration Marianna had seen a hundred times, Naomi dropped her hand from her stomach and looked away. Then she sniffed the air. "I think my pie is done. I'll be back in a minute."

Marianna smiled at Levi, and Levi smiled back, sitting on the sofa next to her. As soon as Naomi was out of earshot she turned to her brother.

"Are you certain, Levi?"

"Certain?"

"With this decision?"

Levi looked deep into Marianna's eyes. She could see he knew what he ought to say—that he was happy about the marriage. She could see he was going to do the right thing—the honorable thing—but that didn't mean it would be easy.

She swallowed hard and folded and unfolded her hands on her lap. The conflict was clear in his eyes, but so was the commitment. Something struck her deep within. She had a feeling gazing into Levi's eyes was like looking into her own soul. Did others see the questions, worries, in her gaze too?

Levi sighed. "Love is a choice, not a feeling. Didn't you write that in one of your letters to me?"

"*Ja*, it is a choice, and you're not making an easy one." Marianna forced herself to speak the question she'd been wanting to ask. "It isn't your baby, Levi, is it?"

Levi stiffened. "Why would you say that?"

"There is something different about you and Naomi. Distance. She . . . it's as if she's worried you're going to walk out at any moment. And you—you have the same look in your eye as when you were ten. Dat had given up on that newborn calf, but you stayed with it day and night for a week, feeding it at all hours until it was strong enough to nurse. You were proud. You were weary, too, but that didn't compare. It was as if the sacrifice was worth it."

He looked away. "You're seeing things where they ought not be."

"Am I? It's me you're talking to, Levi. I've come all this way to help. Shouldn't I know the truth?"

"And you'll not speak it to anyone."

"Of course not. You know me better."

He turned back to her, leaning forward and resting his elbows on his knees. "I have not slept with her, Mari. After all these years. I may not have followed the Amish ways, but I believed Dat when he told me that physical union ought to be saved for marriage."

Marianna's trembling fingers touched her lips.

"Whose? Whose baby is it, then?"

Levi shrugged and lowered his head. "Would you believe me when I tell you I won't ask. I don't want to know?"

"But why? How could you not want to know?" Marianna's stomach churned. She touched her forehead, suddenly light-headed.

This couldn't be happening.

"I want to love this child like my own, think of it as mine. As far as everyone else is concerned it is." He covered his mouth with his hand and then wiped it, as if wiping poison off his lips. "I don't want to think of her with another. Don't want to think what I'd say to a man who would do such a thing. Who would do that, Mari?"

He looked away, but the anger in his words was evident. "Who would leave a young woman pregnant and alone?"

Who, indeed?

The cold air nipped at Marianna's nose as she walked from Naomi's house to Aunt Ida's place. She hadn't wanted to be rude, but nearly as soon as Levi confessed the truth she had to get out of there. She needed fresh air. Needed space to think.

The steady *clop-clop* of a slow horse met Marianna's ears, along with the rasp of buggy wheels in the gravel. In Montana they'd driven on dirt roads and later snow. Both made different sounds. The loud rolling of wheels over gravel caused a longing for the quiet, snowy mornings. The longing started as an ache in her gut and moved upward to her heart.

As she turned, she expected to see one of Aunt Ida's neighbors. Instead, her eyes widened to see Aaron's buggy. Aaron's bright-eyed gaze. Aaron's smile.

She paused, and then hurried his direction. The horse picked up its pace, approaching. "What are you doing here?"

"Mem had me drive her over to visit Naomi's mom. She mentioned you'd just left. I wanted to make sure you were all right. Thought it too far for you to walk home in the cold."

Aaron smiled at her, his bright blue eyes sparkling. "Do you mind, Mari, that I've come to offer you a ride?" He leaned toward her. "Problem is, you walk faster than I'd imagined. You're nearly halfway home."

"Well, not having to walk the other half is much appreciated." She tried to keep her tone light yet the knowledge of what her brother was facing—what he chose to do—was still sinking in.

Aaron reached a hand to her and she took it, allowing him to guide her into the buggy.

"And the thought means as much as the action. I appreciate you coming fer me. Checking on me."

Aaron chuckled, then winced as she scooted closer.

"I'm not hurting you, am I?"

Aaron shook his head. "I'd take ten times the pain to have you near."

"Glad you think so because otherwise the last month or so wouldn't have worked." She chuckled, letting her gaze drift over the frozen ground and the gray clouds that filled the sky. Her emotions felt as barren as her surroundings and she told herself to cheer up. Aaron was here. Everything would be better now.

They rode along for a while in peaceful silence, both scanning the barren trees, the patches of snow and quiet farms as they passed.

"Feels good to be home."

She nodded, but mostly because she was afraid to express her thoughts. She couldn't describe it any other way than an emptiness—an ache she'd been nursing since the last glimpse of the Rocky Mountains had disappeared from the train's window.

Marianna rested her head on Aaron's shoulder. She thought about Levi's love and dedication to Naomi. Would Aaron make such a sacrifice? Aaron was a good Amish man. He always did what was right, but how far would he go to show her his love? What if she'd come to him in the same situation?

"My parents asked me to invite you over for Christmas dinner."

"Really?" She took his hand and squeezed it. "Of course. It'll be *gut* to get to know your family better."

"I told Mem you'd say yes. You'll enjoy everyone."

"Everyone?"

"*Ja*, many siblings from both my parents' sides and all their kids. The house will be full. Good thing you like children. I've already had some of them ask if they can call you cousin too. I've spoke of you often. They tell me you sound too good to be true."

"I do not know whether to take that as a compliment or not."

"Of course, it is the truth. There is no one as good as you—as pure."

As he spoke, tension froze up her limbs and tightened her stomach. "That's kind of you, Aaron, but I'm far from perfect. I've already disappointed you so many times, and in our married life I'm sure I'll do so again . . . often."

He nodded but didn't answer, and the longer they rode in silence the more she found it hard to breathe. All her life, all she'd wanted was to be the perfect Amish daughter to make up for the loss of her sisters. The amazing thing was the closer she grew to God the more she realized she was far from perfect. In fact, relief had flooded over her when she realized she wouldn't have to carry that burden any longer. Or at least she thought she wouldn't be carrying it. Did Aaron realize she'd have bad days now and then? Would he allow her to be herself—her true self?

And what if she wanted to read the Bible, to sing aloud to God, to pray out loud? None of those were what a *gut* Amish woman would do . . . but all of them had transformed her life as she grew to know God in new and different ways. Would Aaron accept that? She considered the gift she'd brought him for Christmas too. Would giving it to him ruin everything?

The horse's hooves clomped on the gravel with the same tempo that worry knocked against her heart.

"You are bein' mighty quiet."

She shrugged and lifted her head, looking at him. "I was

thinking about yer Christmas present. It—it's something . . . special. If possible, I'd like you to open it when we're alone and not at the family gathering."

"I don't think that'll be a problem. Will you give me a hint?"

"Hmmm . . . The hint is it's something you keep opening every day and find new treasure inside."

"In that case, I already have it." He released one of the reins and brushed her face with his fingers. "Your heart is that to me, Mari. The more I touch it, the more treasure I find . . ."

His words melted the tension that had been building, and she told herself not to let her own worries ruin all she had that was good. She closed her eyes, relishing in his touch, and letting her concerns drift away.

"Yer sure a romantic talker for a simple Amish man . . . a girl can get used to this."

"You're not a girl, Mari, you're a woman. One who's captured my heart . . . and I can't wait to spend the rest of my life not taking that for granted." He sighed. "If you only knew, Marianna. If you only knew."

Dear June-Sevenies,

You may have heard by now that I am back in Indiana. The trip went well, and I enjoyed the train ride, especially with Aaron by my side. I haven't told many people, but I cannot keep the news from you—my cherished friends—for much longer. As soon as we are able Aaron and I will be marrying! The last few months spent with him has reminded me of all I loved about him. For so long I'd watched him from afar, dreaming of getting to know him better. The days spent caring for him as he healed from his broken leg confirmed what a gut man he is. I cannot think of another Amish man I know who lives as honorably as Aaron. And what Amish man would be so diligent at preparing for his wife even before he started courting her? Aaron has made it simply impossible for me not to allow his dreams to become my own.

The wedding will not be soon, but I wish for each of you to attend. You're as close to me as sisters and I cannot think of a better day to have us all together. It's something we've dreamed of—have we not?

I know most of you made it to Clara's wedding. My thoughts were with you from Montana. And speaking of Clara, congratulations are in order, a baby! Or perhaps babies? I do remember you telling me that both your mother and grandmother carried twins the first pregnancy. Double the blessings!

Wish you sunny thoughts to cheer up the dreary winter days.

Marianna

CHAPTER NINE

*O*n Christmas Eve, Marianna sat down at the table with Aunt Ida to follow one of their favorite traditions—designing and creating their own greeting cards. From the time she was a child the tradition was to come to Aunt Ida's house on Christmas Eve to work with rubber stamps, colored inks, decorative cutouts, and scalloped-edged scissors.

The scent of gingerbread cookies filled the air. The heat from the woodstove filled the room with warmth, and a gentle snow fell outside the windows. Colorful scraps of paper were spread across the table, and the plain room brightened with their presence. Like the quilts Aunt Ida made, creating Christmas cards was another acceptable way to display color and beauty. And Marianna could lose herself in the making of them, even forgetting for a time about being plain. She couldn't help but smile.

Marianna wrote down a list of those she wanted to give cards to, and the majority of the list was made up of her friends from Montana: Annie, Edgar, Jenny, Kenzie, the Carash family, Eve and Hope Peachy, and of course Ben. Since Christmas was tomorrow her greetings would be late, but she had a feeling her friends wouldn't mind.

She pulled out a piece of cardstock and nibbled on her lower lip. What special events were happening at the West Kootenai Kraft and Grocery? Did Annie host a small Christmas party for the employees? Marianna guessed she did.

Aunt Ida worked beside her, cutting and gluing as she created three cards in the time it took Marianna to create one. Marianna enjoyed writing a personal message in each, but when she got to Ben's card she didn't know what to say. She decided on an Amish proverb that her grandma used to tell her. "Courage is fear that has said its prayers," she wrote inside then added:

> *Thank you for giving me the courage to seek God in new ways. My fear has always been that knowing God better would give me more rules and lists to follow. Instead, I've discovered a Shepherd who leads me beside still waters, a Guide to whisper His love to me along wooded paths, and a Protector who will be there no matter what valley lies ahead. Thank you for being an example to me. I wouldn't have known Him better without seeing God in you.*

She read the message again and her heart warmed. Then, instead of addressing each envelope individually, Marianna put them all inside one manila envelope and sealed it up, addressing it to Edgar at the store's address. She laughed out loud as she imagined his face when he realized she expected him to play Santa.

After the cards were finished, Marianna took the decorated paper upstairs to wrap the items she'd gotten for Levi, Naomi, Aunt Ida, and Aaron. For Levi she'd brought with her deer jerky from the West Kootenai Kraft and Grocery. She'd quilted two small potholders for Aunt Ida and the same for her soon-to-be sister-in-law. And for Aaron . . .

She pulled the Bible from the box it had come in and held it to her chest. *Please, let him understand. Let him be open to reading Your Word for himself.* Aaron had attended church his whole life . . . wouldn't reading the words of the One they worshiped be a joy? It was a joy to her now, but she also knew how shocked she'd been when she first discovered Dat with an Englisch Bible . . .

Yet, all she could do was try.

It wasn't until Marianna had finished wrapping Aaron's gift that she realized she hadn't created a card for Aaron. She set the package to the side. Was it too late to ask Aunt Ida where she'd put away the card-making supplies? She started downstairs, but noticed all the lanterns had been put out. There was no soft glow coming from under Aunt Ida's door either, which told Marianna her aunt was already in bed.

At least I can write out a message to put into the card, she thought as she returned to her room. Yet when she sat down she couldn't think of what to say.

Marianna put down the pen and paper. Tomorrow. She'd think of something tomorrow.

She'd arrived at Aaron's parents' house early on Christmas morning just as Aaron had requested. As she approached the front door of the Zook house the door opened and Aaron emerged.

He shut the door behind him, keeping his hand on the doorknob. His eyes watched her as if transfixed. Heat pulsated through her limbs as she looked into his eyes. So bright. So blue. So filled with affection, love.

She touched her kapp and paused before him. What was it about Aaron that made her feel like a schoolgirl with a crush? He raised an eyebrow but didn't move. Her gaze moved from his eyes to his lips, and she wondered if he waited for a kiss. From his soft smile she knew he did. She also guessed that at least a dozen eyes watched from the window. She didn't need to turn to know his siblings watched their interaction—most likely his mem too. She took a step back and held his gift tighter to her chest.

"What are you doing? It's cold and you have no coat," she teased.

"Is it? As soon as I saw you I didn't realize." He winked. "For some reason my whole body seems warm now. Seeing you warmed me from head to toe as if I'd swallowed the sun."

"Really now." Her cheeks warmed. "You aren't gonna keep me out here—on the porch—all day, are you?"

He took her hand and led her off the porch, leaning heavy on the railing as they descended. "No, but I won't let you inside. Not yet. I wish for you to come to the cabin first. "I'd want a few minutes alone with you while I still have the chance. Once everyone arrives you can be certain we won't have a moment together."

They walked side by side to the cabin. As they strode up to it, she imagined decorating it next year with simple candles and maybe greenery in the window—not too much to be prideful, but enough to beautify their home in a simple, lovely way.

"Can I give you your present first?" Aaron led her through the front door, shutting it behind him.

"*Ja*, if you insist." She smiled as she looked around. The woodstove was lit and a plate of his mother's Christmas cookies sat on the counter.

"Mem accused my younger siblings for sneaking those." He chuckled. "No one guessed that I was the thief."

She pulled a sugar cookie from the top.

Aaron smiled and held up a hand. "Wait here." He strode to the second room and soon emerged with a wooden crate, setting it down before her.

"This is for me? A whole crate? What could be inside?" Marianna sunk to her knees and opened the top. Lifting the lid her eyes widened.

Inside were books—hardback, old, dusty—exactly the type she liked to read.

"Aaron . . . there are so many!" She picked up a copy with a burgundy copy and turned it over in her hand. *"My Antonia.* It looks good." She continued looking through them. Some were titles she knew, others she'd never seen before.

"Can you imagine?" She looked around the room. "Us sitting here, enjoying the fire and reading."

"That's what I was thinking." He walked into the room and carried out a small bookcase, placing it by the woodstove. "I want this to feel like your home, Mari. I want you to enjoy our life."

Marianna smiled and then pulled the decorated package from the satchel she'd been carrying. Her gift seemed too simple compared to his thoughtfulness. Then again, the words in this one book were even greater than all those he'd offered her.

Aaron opened the package. He set the wrapping on top of the bookshelf and then his blond eyebrows folded into a scowl. "It's . . ."

"A Bible."

"I know." He glanced up at her. A hint of anger in his eyes caused her breath to catch in her throat. He tucked it under his arm. "I have a Bible already."

"Yes, but yours is in German and . . . well, you've told me before that you don't read it often."

"*Ja*, well, if I were to read any Bible it wouldn't be this one. It's English, Marianna." He lifted it into the air. "What am I supposed to do with this?"

A creak sounded, followed by a breeze of cool air. Marianna turned with a start, and Aaron tucked the Bible back under his arm, but not before Mr. Zook spotted it.

"Sorry to interrupt. I shoulda knocked." He stroked his beard as he entered, closing the door behind him. "You mother jest asked that I come for ya. Everyone arrived early and the children are eager to open their gifts." He spoke to Aaron, but his eyes stayed on Marianna. She saw no light in his eyes. No smile on his lips.

"I see that some presents have already been opened."

Marianna nodded and swallowed hard. Would Mr. Zook confront her, or would he wait to talk to Aaron after she left? He turned and exited the way he'd come. She lifted trembling fingers to her lips, uncertain of what to say. What to do. What had she been thinking? This is not the type of entrance she wanted to make into a family. What did Mr. Zook think of her now? What type of good, Amish girl would give such a gift? They had their rules. They had their Bible . . . she could imagine Mr. Zook's thoughts even as he stalked back toward the house.

"Well, you heard him, we best get back." Aaron tossed the Bible on the top of the stack of books.

Marianna followed, her eyes on her feet, ignoring the way

Aaron's shoulders slumped. "I'm sorry if I've disappointed you. I thought—"

"You thought—!" Aaron spun and pointed a finger toward her chest. She glanced up to his eyes. His angry eyes.

"You thought you can change me? That you could persuade me to follow the Englisch ways?"

"It's not the Englisch ways, it's God's way." Her voice was no more than a squeak. "God tells us—"

"God tells us to obey our elders. That's what He tells us. And here you are thinking you know better?" He removed his hat and ran a hand through his hair.

Marianna kept her gaze fixed on his, not knowing how to explain. If he would read God's Word for himself he'd understand . . .

The tears came without her expecting them. She paused and covered her face with her hands. Her lip quivered despite her best efforts to keep it still. This was supposed to be a special day— their first Christmas together and here she'd gone and ruined everything.

"Oh, Mari." Aaron rushed back to her. His arms wrapped around her, holding her tight. "I am so sorry. I didna mean . . ." His large hand stroked up and down her back. "I know you heard about new things concerning God . . . and I don't want to say they're all wrong, but can you give me time? I want to be a good husband to you, and someday I'd like to talk more about this. But not right now. I'm still trying to figure it all out."

She nodded but she didn't speak. More tears came, but not from Aaron's outburst. Rather because of her own foolishness. She should be more patient. She should be more understanding.

Dat did not push anything on her. Ben or Annie or Sarah didn't try to make her change all her beliefs at once.

"I'm sorry." Her voice emerged as a simple whisper. "I . . . I don't know what I was thinking. Today is a special day. Your whole family is waiting."

Aaron used a finger to lift the tip of her chin. She took a deep, shuddering breath and dared to look into his gaze. Surprise struck her heart when instead of anger or frustration she was met with his smile. "I'm sorry, too, I didn't mean to raise my voice. I appreciate the gift." He kissed the top of her nose. "I appreciate it because it came from you, understand?"

Marianna nodded, and then Aaron's lips met hers. She grasped the fabric of his shirt and didn't want to let go. She clung to him, attempting to draw from his strength. She clung to him, reminding herself she was loved—deeply loved.

It wasn't until their lips parted that she realized that she needed this—someone who would help her remember that being married wasn't always about agreeing.

It was about coming together as two people and finding middle ground as one.

No fewer than seventy people gathered in the Zooks' living room and dining room area. Lucky for them, church service was going to be at their house Sunday next, and Mrs. Zook had the foresight to ask for the bench wagon to be brought early. The benches had been set up around the edges of the room and a pile of brown paper-wrapped gifts sat in the middle of them all. There was no tree, no blinking lights, and no Santa decorations as seen in

Shipshewana. Instead the prettiest decorations were the bright eyes of the children—Aaron's siblings and cousins—eager to open their gifts.

But before they could open presents, Marianna knew Mr. Zook would read the Christmas story. He opened up the large Bible, written in High German, and read from the Book of Luke. Growing up in church, Marianna understood most of the words, but as she looked at the faces of the children she notice their eyes glazing over. More than anything she wished she could hurry back to Aaron's cabin for the English Bible and ask Mr. Zook to read from that instead. It was not tradition—that was for certain—but at least the children would understand the story and revel in the joy of their Savior's birth.

After the story was read, the children of Mrs. Zook's sister rose and sang a familiar Amish hymn. Marianna smiled at their bright-cheeked faces and was inspired by their voices that surely were as beautiful as the angels' highly heavenly songs around God's throne. She couldn't help but consider how many others in the community would love to hear such singing—of course that would never be. To perform in such a way would be prideful. It didn't matter that God imparted their talent, to display it wasn't the Amish way.

Ben's face filled her mind. Oh how his music had moved her. She said a silent prayer, thanking God for not only giving them life and families, but special gifts like these children singing that pointed to a Creator who didn't just create what was necessary, but what was extraordinary too.

When the song finished, Aaron handed out the presents, calling each child by name and playfully teasing them before relinquishing the brown packages. As the children opened their gifts of handmade dolls, wooden tops, books, and colored pencils, Marianna couldn't help consider what a good a father Aaron would be some day. Again she told herself to look at the goodness of Aaron and not focus on his weaknesses. No one was perfect, after all.

Marianna glanced around. *This will soon be my family.* The thought had barely finished its journey through her mind when she noticed Mr. Zook's eyes studying her. Her back straightened, and she pretended not to notice both his stare and the displeasure that was clear on his face.

Suddenly, she knew she had to set to work doing something; otherwise, she'd burst at the seams with anxiety. Standing, she hurried to the kitchen where some of the women busily prepared Christmas lunch. The wonderful aroma of pot roast, potatoes, rolls, and creamed corn made her stomach growl.

Without waiting to be asked, she started folding a pile of napkins into a bell design. It was something simple her mother did every Christmas, and Marianna noticed the women's curious eyes on her as she worked.

"You wouldn't believe what happened at schul just last week," Aaron's twelve-year-old sister, Glenda, said as she whipped the potatoes. "Our teacher had to ask Eleanor three times to pay attention to the math lesson. Her mind was on another place . . . or on some*one* else." She sniffed as she tattled on her best friend. "You should have seen her stare at Barney Yoder. I was sorely embarrassed for her."

"I believe I've heard their mothers talk about how *gut* it would be to have them marry someday. I'm sure they've heard plenty about it too," Mrs. Zook added.

Marianna heard footsteps behind her and noticed Aaron

approach. "I remember days like that." Aaron looked at Marianna out of the corner of his eye. "There were times I was concentrating on my math facts and I'd feel eyes bearing down on me. I'd glance over, and sure enough, Marianna Sommer would be staring as if I had a mouse sitting on the end of my nose."

A gasp escaped Marianna's lips as all the women turned her direction. "I did not! Aaron, how could you say such a thing?"

Aaron's laughter filled the air. "*Ja*, you're right. She was much more sly about her looks. I'd turn her direction just in time to see her look away."

"You've had an eye on each other for a time. I couldn't imagine it any other way." Mrs. Zook smiled as she said those words, but her voice held little hint of happiness.

Breathing in, Marianna released her breath. The Zooks seemed pleasant enough, but there was something strange about the way they interacted with her. It was as if they knew something she didn't . . .

And she wasn't at all sure she wanted to find out what it was.

Dear Marianna,

The cold of Montana is just a memory, but I cannot help but think of you when I consider that place. The cold here reminds me of the moments we walked alongside each other on well-worn paths, more aware of each other's presence than the world around us.

Today as I thought of you I considered what it would be like for you to get to know my family—really know them. Though there is much the same, I think you would

*find the differences appealing. There is a quiet humor
that most outside our family don't understand. You'd pick
up on it in time. My father might scare you. I'll have to
remind you often he's not as intense as he seems. Since
I was a child I could read a story in his every gaze. Some
stories I did not like, but if you learn to ask he's quick to
tell you what he really thinks.*

*I've written more letters to you. I have a small pile.
I've been thinking more realistically about giving these
to you. Maybe in the spring. Spring is a time of new life.
Maybe it can be a time of a fresh start for us. I'm tired of
hiding the truth.*

*I hope you are enjoying time being back in Indiana.
I imagine your laughter as you share in the dailiness
of life in you aunt's home. In my dreams the "dailiness
of life" includes us laughing together. I can't imagine
anything better.*

*Written with the pen of the man who dreams of a
future by your side.*

CHAPTER TEN

arianna smiled at the first sprigs of green grass as she strode from the barn to Aunt Ida's house after choring. She paused, bent down, and plucked it up. Was it possible? Had three months already passed since Christmas? Her life had settled into an easy routine, doing Aunt Ida's morning chores, heading over to spend the day with Naomi—cleaning the house, sewing baby items, or reading the books Aaron gave her for Christmas. Her friend seemed thankful for her company, and they chatted and laughed about silly things while they always made a nice lunch for Levi. Her brother's relationship with his wife-to-be hinted of a deeper closeness as Naomi's stomach grew. From the way he tended to her, Marianna would have never guessed the baby Naomi carried wasn't Levi's child.

Her eyes wandered to the orchard west of Aunt Ida's house, with windbreaks on the north and west side of it. She could picture Levi's and Naomi's child climbing those trees just as she and Levi had done. This was a wonderful place to nurture a child.

Her steps slowed, and Marianna turned toward the orchard. The ground was soft from spring melt, and water pooled in low spots. Marianna stepped around the puddles. Her shoes squished deeper into the ground as she moved toward the nearest apple tree. Gray branches stretched into the sky like gnarled fingers. The tree wasn't much to look at. Yet somehow that only drew her to it even more. It was easy to love a tree full of green leaves and apple blossoms. It was delightful to approach such a tree, with branches weighed down with fresh fruit. The offering and the display might change but the tree was still the same.

She neared the trunk and leaned her back against it, looking through the branches to the sky dotted with clouds.

"Is that how You've seen me at times?" She lifted her face to God. "I useta be so dead, with nothing to offer. I thought I was doing fine in my life. I followed the teachings I'd been taught, but it was the truth that changed everything . . ."

The truth of God's Word *had* brought new life, like fresh green leaves. And the more she soaked in the Word, the more the living water fed her. And with the presence of the Son, Jesus, she'd begun to bear fruit. Begun to help and serve others in ways that truly mattered.

She considered her time with Naomi. Her friend had never minded Marianna reading her Bible in the dawdi haus, and recently she'd begun asking questions. Marianna couldn't live with Naomi—help her—for the rest of her days, but perhaps Naomi would fall in love with God as she had. A closer relationship with Jesus would change her life. Make what she had to face in the community easier.

Marianna leaned her head back . . . so much to think about. So many prayers to offer for friends and family. It wasn't the same as the pond behind their home in Montana—there was only one place on earth as special as that—but then God He met her here too. Maybe she could bring the baby out here some day, to hold him and tell him about God.

As she headed back to Aunt Ida's house, Marianna couldn't help wonder again about the baby's real father. Was he Englisch? Amish? Would he ever try to butt into their lives? Would the child know? Would he or she be told?

Those weren't things for her to worry about now, she supposed. Or any time in the near future. Since Naomi had a doctor's appointment, today meant going to a sewing circle with her aunt, followed by a stop by the Farm and Garden store to pick up baby chicks. Every spring they always put baby chicks in the brooder house, with kerosene brooder stoves to keep them warm. Since she was a child, it was always a day to look forward to, and with the quilt circle it was two good things in one day.

"You have to make an effort to make new friends," she mumbled to herself as she climbed the porch steps. Since returning she and Rebecca had only seen each other a few times—her friend often found more joy in spending time with her Englisch friends. And other than Naomi and Aunt Ida, Marianna spent little time with other women in the community. And yet, they were no longer just Mem's friends. She was soon to be married, so she needed to make them her friends too.

It was just a short buggy ride to Lynn Over's place. The older woman with almond-shaped brown eyes welcomed them in.

"Marianna, it is *gut* you joined us. Please have a seat while I beg of yer aunt to help me with the last of the snacks." Lynn hurried to the kitchen, Aunt Ida on her heels.

Marianna moved that direction too. "I'd be glad to help."

"Oh no, dear. No need. Jest have a seat in there. Guests do not need to lift a finger in my home." Lynn pointed to the living room where a large quilt was already set up in a frame.

Marianna nodded and did as she asked, sitting gently on the pristine sofa, not wanting to rumple the throw pillows Lynn had set up there.

The house looked like a museum, everything neat and in place. She could hear the two women in the kitchen, but the living area was silent, lifeless. Why did Aunt Ida have to be the one that was always early?

Marianna thought back to Lynn's welcome. She was used to being welcomed into the sewing circle in Montana with open arms and hugs. With smiles. She'd never been called a guest before—especially not in this community.

The women arrived one by one. As more filled up the living room, Marianna moved to the wooden chair to the side, taking in the sight of the other women at the sewing circle. Two of Rebecca's sisters were there, wearing identical dark blue dresses, white aprons, and pressed white kapps. Last year about this time Marianna had invited them to Mem's sewing circle, but both had confessed they'd rather spend their day in the fields than inside.

Marianna smiled. As young women grew, the young men in the community often caught their attention . . . and unlike the Englisch who often though of romance first, Amish young women knew their ability to care for a home and family would make them attractive to a suitor. Even the toughest tomboys often settled down to work on their sewing and cooking as they neared marrying age.

Each woman brought over a dish for lunch and set it in the kitchen. They all knew their places around the quilt frame, and after they set up, Rebecca's sister, Christy, motioned to Marianna. "There's a spot here next to me if you'd like."

"Denke, that's kind." She pulled her needle and thimble from the small satchel of her things. "I have not quilted for months and I'm jest a bit out of practice. The one thing that is good though, whether in Montana or here, quilting varies little."

The women didn't respond, and Mrs. Troyer pushed her glasses up on her nose, a slight frown evident. "I hear things are different in Montana. Liberal."

Amazing the woman could speak through such pursed lips. Marianna threaded her needle. "They're not much different. Maybe a bit more relaxed in their dress—many work at Englisch businesses too, which means they sometimes have Englisch friends."

"Englisch friends?" Lynn Over clucked her tongue and scanned the faces of the dozen other women, who seemed equally shocked.

Marianna looked to Aunt Ida. She, too, sported lowered eyebrows and squinty eyes. The other women glanced at her aunt, as if gauging her response. Aunt Ida closed her eyes, opened them, and let out a longsuffering sigh. "No comment."

The quilting continued in silence, the women puncturing the quilt, reversing their needles and raising to the ceiling in unison.

The conversation picked up again, as each woman shared her garden plans. Excitement for spring planting was evident.

"I found some seed for baby eggplant and they were wonderful gut," one of the ladies mentioned.

"Do you have any extra seeds? I can do a trade," another commented.

Marianna kept her head bowed over the quilt, making her stitches as perfect as possible. Maybe they'd forget she was here. When the woman next to her cleared her throat and leaned closer, she knew it didn't work.

"So Marianna, do they do much gardening in Montana?"

Heat rose to her cheeks. "*Ja*, of course. Would an Amish woman be an Amish woman without a garden?" She laughed, but noticed that no one joined her. "Of course, the growing season is much shorter. They don't start planting until the snow melts off the Rockies, and that can be as late as June. Mem had a small garden, and the neighbors down the street had a greenhouse. They gave Mem some starter plants—"

"Were they Englisch friends?" Mrs. Troyer's question resonated with disapproval.

Marianna patted her kapp. "*Ja*, but I don't see how that makes a difference."

Her words stilled the motion of the women's hands. Marianna glanced up and noticed needles hung in the air, as if frozen in time.

Marianna's fingers picked at a stray thread on the quilt.

Mrs. Troyer eyed Marianna. "It doesna matter?"

"They're good people, Christian people. I learned a lot from them. I've learned about God in new ways."

The room was so silent she could hear Mrs. Over's dog lapping up water in the next room.

"Learned about God from the *Englisch*?" Mrs. Troyer's voice rose in pitch. "I have never heard of such a thing."

"Maybe you should spend time with some Englisch. I learned more about what a personal relationship with Jesus means. I learned it's more important to accept Him into your heart and life than it is dressing a certain way." She thought of Ben. "In fact, the faith of some of my new friends inspired me. One of the greatest things I learned was the importance of reading the Bible for myself."

Mrs. Schmucker's, the bishop's wife's, voice fell to a disdainful purr. "Don't you think it's prideful to say you know a better way?"

"I understand the importance of not being prideful, really I do, but being a Christian woman, don't you think you should read the Bible for yourself? If God took the time to have His message to us written down, do not you believe we should read it? That's all I'm saying, really."

Mrs. Schmucker's eyes widened. "You're judging me, and more than that, disrespecting a bishop's wife!" She rose, moving away from the quilt and turning her back on Marianna. "I don't know how you think there's a place for yourself in this community. And if you do stay, your confession will be long."

Marianna looked at her hands. "I believe that would be true of all of us if the impurities of our hearts were known."

Gasps erupted around the room.

What had she done?

A hollow sensation filled her. She grew hot, unable to breathe. Surely it wasn't her they were talking about. And certainly she didn't answer as she had.

Fear coursed through Marianna's chest. She covered her lips with a trembling hand, and then stood, straightening her shoulders muscle by muscle, her eyes never leaving Mrs. Schmucker's face. "I'm sorry, please forgive me. I do not wish for you to believe those words were directed to you." She swallowed back tears. "I know in my own heart there are struggles I need to bring before God. Each of us has struggles."

"Speak for yourself." Mrs. Troyer crossed her arms over her waist. "Some of us know how to be more self-controlled in our word and deed."

"*Ja*, I am sorry. I best be going." She turned to Mrs. Over. "Denke for inviting me. I'm sorry to ruin your afternoon."

Lynn Over nodded, but didn't speak.

"If you take the buggy, I'll ride home with one of my friends." Aunt Ida's voice was no stronger than a squeak of a mouse. Marianna looked to her aunt's face and then scanned the room. The women in the room had pity for her aunt.

Pity that poor Ida Sommer should have such a misguided and rebellious niece.

"Thank you, Aunt Ida. I'm sorry for the trouble." Marianna stood and hurried out of the room, out of the house. Tears blurred her eyes as she rushed to the buggy.

Nothing would ever be right again.

The beautiful spring day had mocked her on her buggy ride home. Now Marianna sat heavy on the couch. Why had Aunt Ida's friends treated her so? They'd always taken so kindly to her. They'd been Mem's friends too. She'd known them since she was a child. When had things changed?

Maybe they hadn't changed. Perhaps it was her changes they despised so.

"God, I want to know You more. I want others to know You— know Your Word as I'm jest starting to."

A hint of peace calmed the emotions whirlpooling in her heart, and she tucked her stockinged feet under her. Marianna crossed her arms over her chest, pulling them tight, and then leaned forward, elbows on knees, staring at the untilled field out the window. Would things continue this way even after she married Aaron? She supposed if she tried to share the importance of the Bible and reading God's Word for oneself that they would. She supposed if she returned to the young woman with no interests other than her home and no convictions beyond the Ordnung that over time they'd once again welcome her back into their fold.

"The more like them I am, the more I'll be accepted," she muttered to herself. "If I model myself in their image rather than the image of Jesus Christ . . ." she let her voice trail off.

Not able to sit in the quiet house any longer, Marianna adjusted her kapp and headed outside for a walk. As she got to the door she nearly turned around, looking for Trapper to follow. Her chin quivered thinking about how far away her dog was—how far aware those were who really cared.

She hurried down the steps and then headed toward the orchard once again. She'd spent simple days there, playing with her brothers and friends without a care in the world. She walked past the orchard and found the small valley that separated Aunt Ida's place from the neighboring farm. Marianna walked down the sloping hill and into what some would consider a gulch. The ground was soft and in shady spots patches of snow still clung. At that moment she wished it were May, not March, and that wildflowers were scattered across the fields. Their spots of colors would have given her hope. Even after hard winters, the most delicate wildflowers reemerged.

Marianna continued on, knowing that no one could see her in this place from the gravel road. And isn't that what valleys in one's life were—a time when one felt unnoticed, unloved?

She lifted her eyes to the sky, hoping for warm sun. Instead, she noticed gray clouds drifting across the plains.

Maybe she should hitch up the buggy again, go to see Aaron. They saw each other three days a week at least. Usually he came to Aunt Ida's house for dinner and they'd talk until his yawns overwhelmed their conversations. Yet what would he tell her? Would he be upset that she'd caused such a stir?

She lowered her head and kicked at a clump of dirt, then allowed a sad smile. She wouldn't be surprised if he showed up at her house instead. It wouldn't take long for word to get around on what she'd done. Who knows, Mrs. Zook could already have alerted him.

The first drop of rain hit her on her cheek, but Marianna barely noticed. When had everything gone so wrong? For a moment she considered what things would be like if Levi hadn't written her. Would Aaron have stayed in Montana? Would they still have plans for getting married?

She thought about going back, but she knew that wasn't the answer. Naomi had another few months of pregnancy yet, and she'd already committed to staying until the baby was born.

Wait.

The word came as a gentle whisper. It's wasn't an audible voice, but more like a stirring in her heart. She didn't know what she was supposed to wait for, but she did know she wasn't supposed to run.

More raindrops fell, and Marianna turned back to Aunt Ida's house. She needed to apologize to her aunt—really apologize. She also needed to figure out how to live this life she'd chosen. She couldn't spend the rest of her life knowing she should live one way but conforming to another. She needed to find her way out of the gulch—the valley—she found herself in.

Marianna hurried up the front porch steps and peered

through the screen door. She hoped Aunt Ida was still at the quilt circle, but she was not in luck. The older woman was seated at the long wooden table writing a letter. Her aunt paused as Marianna opened the door and entered. Aunt Ida glanced up under lowered eyebrows, and Marianna guessed the letter was about her. When Aunt Ida slid it between the pages of the dictionary, she knew it was.

Aunt Ida stared at the rain outside. "I see it started putten down."

Marianna nodded and crossed her arms over her chest. *"Ja,* just a sprinkling of rain."

Aunt Ida continued looking at the water falling from the sky as if it was the most fascinating thing in the world.

"I'm sorry, Aunt Ida." Marianna approached and sat across from her.

"I know. It's your father's fault. For making you go."

Marianna opened her mouth to explain that moving to Montana wasn't a bad thing, but she knew it would fall on deaf ears.

"I'll make dinner tonight if you'd like." Marianna rose and moved to the kitchen. "I can use the rest of that ham and—"

"No need. I ate plenty at the sewing circle."

Marianna headed to her room. *Where should I go? What should I do?* There were evening chores—she would do that. But tomorrow? What did she have to look forward to then?

It's not about what I want. It's about my commitments, she reminded herself. To Naomi and Levi, to Aaron, to God.

For somehow in the valley she knew what He was asking her to do. To look to Him. To wait. She didn't know why, but did that matter? In the Amish community she'd grown up learning her life wasn't her own. There was no time she understood better than at the present.

She just wished she had even the smallest sense of hope that everything would work out in the end.

Dear Journal,

I'm sorry I've been neglecting writing within your pages. It's not that there hasn't been a lot on my mind. It's more that I'm afraid to commit my words to paper. If I tell the truth of what's going on inside me—what I'm thinking about, dreaming about, wishing for—then my words could be found by someone I love and hurt him deeply.

It's not that I'm meaning to hurt no one. It's more that my mind's having a hard time forgetting what I left behind. Who I left behind.

My focus needs to be on what I have in this place. I found a special spot today by a leafless tree and I felt God speaking to my heart. If God can speak to me in that spot, He can speak to me anywhere. I learned that in a new way. And if anything . . . that's worth jotting down.

CHAPTER ELEVEN

aron looked up at Marianna's window as he strode up to Ida's house. Work had taken him longer than he'd expected, but as soon as he heard Mem and Dat talking about what had happened at the sewing circle, he knew he had no choice but to head over.

He needed to talk to Marianna.

Having been in Montana himself, he understood where she was coming from, but Marianna had to know that if she continued with her words—with her attitude—that she wasn't just going to make things hard for herself, but for him. With Naomi's pregnancy now evident, folks were already talking about Marianna's family. He just hated to see it go any farther than it already had.

Aaron took a deep breath. Should he tell her he'd read the Bible she'd given him a couple of times? He had to admit he was surprised by how much he enjoyed it, but as he lifted a hand to knock on the door, Aaron knew he wouldn't say a word about that. They needed to handle one issue at a time.

Aunt Ida opened the door and welcomed him in. Did he see relief on her face?

"Come, Marianna's just made some cherry cobbler. I told her I wasn't hungry, but I'm glad now that she didn't listen."

"Aaron." Marianna said his name as a whispered breath. She hurried over to him and took his hands in her. "I'm so glad you came."

She clung to him as a lifeline, and Aaron noticed a deep longing in her gaze. For him to hold her? Maybe. For her to be held? Yes.

He placed a hand on her shoulder and winked. She smiled, understood. Later, out of Aunt Ida's view.

They sat around the living room with their bowls of cobbler. Marianna's leg pressed against his, and he couldn't help but smile.

"I'm so glad to see you two together," Aunt Ida said after taking a big bite. "There were so many of my friends who believed you would stay in Montana and marry an Englischman. My friend, Bertha, told me that since Levi left the Amish maybe you would too. I tried to argue, but she said that history proved her point. Not only now but during your mother's time."

Aaron watched as Marianna's throat contracted, and her cheeks brightened with color. "What do you mean?"

"Surely you know, don't you?" Aunt Ida leaned closer. "She almost left the Amish too. Thank goodness your mem came to her senses. Thank goodness Levi did too."

Marianna set down her fork on her plate. She leaned back against the couch. Aaron eyed her. Was she going to cry? Mrs. Sommer loving an Englischman? It didn't seem possible, but from the look on Marianna's face, it had to be true.

Aunt Ida stared at Marianna's plate. "You're not coming down with a fever, are you?" She reached a hand and touched Marianna's cheek. "You didn't eat much."

"It's been a long day."

Aaron was going to wait until they were alone to discuss the situation, but from the hopelessness in her eyes he knew he had to speak.

"Mari . . . At his whispered word, she glanced up at him with those gray eyes he loved so much. "Don't pay them no mind, Mari." Aaron reached for her hand. "They are just busybodies and they don't know what they are talking about."

"The problem isn't with their facts. It's how they use them," she said, trying to act as if tears weren't going to overwhelm her.

He reached over and took the plate from her hand, placing it on the side table. "You're going to take their side?"

Marianna lowered her head. "Neither my mother nor I are innocent. There have been friendships—" She looked away. "Mem and I haven't protected our hearts as we should have." She rose and turned her back to him and pressed her palms against the windowsill.

He approached her and placed two hands on her shoulders. *Why won't she turn around?*

"Don't go there . . ." He wasn't sure if he was saying the words for her or for himself.

"I did have feelings for an Englischman, Aaron. My Mem did too."

"And now?"

"Mem's been married for twenty-five years. I believe her commitment speaks for her heart."

"And you?" The words came out on a whisper.

She turned to him and looked into his eyes. "I know you're the right one for me. I care for you, Aaron. Just be patient with me as I try to figure out how my changed heart fits into this old life."

Dear Ruth,

The purpose of this letter is to call your attention to some questionable things that have been taking place with Marianna. I am not sure what teachings she received in Montana, but to speak with her one would believe they're talking to an Englisch woman.

Of course I must start by saying that I do not write this letter to point a finger. As a child of God I cannot boast of anything except His grace. I write not of my personal observations, but write from the heritage of faith from our Anabaptist forefathers that is over four hundred years old.

Marianna seems the same pleasant young woman as the one who left, yet after she visits homes I've heard people talking, and today she boldly disagreed with the bishop's wife! Marianna shares about reading the Bible and praying and listening to God. She talks as if she knows more than the bishops—knows more than our ancestors who taught us our ways. We follow a heritage of faithfulness. Should we turn our back on the way we've been taught? Who are we to say our personal ways are better?

Rumor has it that you will be coming to Indiana soon. Perhaps you are moving back? I am thankful for that. I think everyone needs adventure in her life and I'm sure you enjoyed your time in the mountains, but it will be good for you to return. After seeing the changes in

Marianna more than one person has noted their concern for the rest of your children—and for you. There is a reason why our ancestors have chosen to live together in community. Outsiders have greater influence than we think and sometimes their thinking becomes our own when we do not guard our hearts and minds.

Aaron Zook has been understanding, but I am worried he won't stand by her for long. What young man will want a young woman as set in her harmful ways as that?

Thankful for all God's mercies,
Ida

Ruth folded the letter and placed it back into the envelope. Then she tucked it into her jacket pocket and glanced around the general store. Where was Abe? The store was full today. The gray clouds had cleared and the sun filled the sky. It was enough to get folks out and about. She nodded and smiled at the Peachys and the Vontragers, who strolled by and filled shopping baskets.

Ruth blew out a heavy sigh. If only the news from Shipshewana were brighter. The changes in Marianna worried her. Not that Marianna had grown to love God more—not that at all. But how folks back home treated her. If their Indiana Amish friends and family resented one thing, it was change. Folks built their lives on tradition. They centered their heart on things staying the same.

Ruth bit her lip. What was Marianna saying . . . and to a bishop's wife no less!

She spotted Abe in the dining room. His shopping basket was at his feet and he was enjoying a cup of coffee with one of the Amish bachelors and an Englischman who ranched down the road. Last year when she and Abe arrived, she'd never imagined such a thing. Now, it seemed normal—

Right even.

How would they be seen when they returned? Would folks consider them changed too? She picked out some apples from the bin and placed them in her basket and nodded to herself. Of course people would notice. They *had* changed. Difference was they'd be packing up and returning to Montana. And Marianna? Ruth would jest have to pray harder for her daughter. But it would not be easy for Marianna . . .

To fit into an old world that her expanding heart and convictions had outgrown.

Ben slicked his hand through his hair. Why did he let Roy talk him into letting it grow?

"You look more artsy," Roy had said. "Like you fit in with the other musicians." The thing was, longer hair and the right clothes didn't make things even easier. He didn't fit in. He didn't feel comfortable sitting at the table with the concert planning team. They were all nice enough, but they didn't talk to him . . . they talked about him. About his songs, his schedule, his merchandise. They didn't know him. Could care less how he liked his coffee and had no idea that when he locked up his cabin, leaving inside the photo of he and Marianna, he'd cried. He was an image to them, a voice, a paycheck.

As if reading his thoughts, Roy slid a paper across the table. "Did you read this? Four hundred and thirteen stations have had your song as their top request in the last week! It's spreading. People can picture you there, Ben, in that cabin, hoping for what you don't have."

Bernice Nutzhorn, Roy's assistant, piped up. "More than that, they feel like they're there themselves. Even if they're in a relationship, the song makes them long for what they're missing out on. That's the mark of a true hit, one the listener can identify with. One that brings tears and a wistful smile." She tapped her red painted fingernails to her lips as if giving herself kudos for coming up with something so profound.

Yet her words were like a pinprick to Ben's heart. Since he'd grown closer to God, he'd wanted to point folks to a life of peace. Happiness was as fleeting as dandelion puffs carried on the wind, or icicles on a warming winter's day. Happiness couldn't be contained, protected. There was nothing peaceful about his song—or about the longing within him.

Roy steepled his fingers and rested his elbows on the table. "The concerts are going well. You've been on the road three months?"

Ben nodded. "Yes, with three more to go."

The room went silent and everyone looked to Roy.

"Actually, Ben, we wanted to talk to you about extending that. We were thinking sixteen more weeks. The venues are falling into place—in fact we're getting calls left and right."

Five sets of eyes looked at him. He'd done well with the traveling, the guys on the bus, the concerts. He enjoyed the fans, but . . . he missed Montana, the mountains and the people. Then again, could he handle being there with Marianna so far away, planning her wedding, starting a new life?

"The concerts are being set up in the Midwest—Illinois, Iowa, Indiana . . .

"Indiana?" Ben ran a hand through his hair.

Bernice flipped through some pages on her clipboard, stopping on one that was highlighted. "Yes, that's right."

Ben shrugged. He was a man drowning in a massive ocean, alone and desperate, and so he reached for the hand that was offered him, no matter how thin and weak it was. "Sure. Why not."

Roy rose, tossed his car keys in the air, caught them, and pointed to Bernice. "Set it up." Then with a parting wave to Ben he hurried out of the room. "You won't regret this, Ben. I have a good feeling about this one."

Ben walked out of the studio and made a beeline to the rental car, then paused. Great. Which car did he have this week? Oh, right. The black Bentley GTC convertible. He walked over to the car and got in, then pulled out of the studio parking lot and drove toward his favorite destination in these parts: the Santa Monica Pier. Roy had taken Ben car shopping a few times, but it seemed foolish to spend money on something like that. His old truck in Montana did just fine. After a while he'd convinced Roy of that. Now if he could just convince Roy to stop renting these fancy cars. Roy, of course, said that one never knew who'd be snapping a photo and when, and Ben needed to *look* like a success to *be* successful. He'd tried to tell Roy his greatest success was who he was inside because of God, but his manager only nodded and smiled, like he always did when Ben tried to share his faith.

He turned the car west onto Sunset Boulevard, heading to Palm Avenue. Thankfully, he'd escaped the studio before rush hour. He could feel the tension slipping away as he drove. Maybe he should go sit on the sand to watch the sunset, pen and paper in hand.

Roy got Ben a smart phone, but most of the time Ben forgot the thing back in the hotel room. There was something about writing his thoughts in one of the cheap, lined notebooks he picked up. He wrote letters to folks back up in Montana, and a few more letters that would never be mailed. He also made sure to write his weekly letter to a young man or woman who was getting in trouble with alcohol. That was his mission today.

Twenty-five minutes later, Ben parked at the pier. It being a weekday, the parking lot was almost empty. Only a few people walked their dogs on the sand. One young couple sat in jeans and sweatshirts and shared a picnic lunch. There was a slight breeze, but he wouldn't call it cold. The sun hung in the sky over the horizon and streams of light rippled in from the distant waters. He strode toward the water and picked a random place to sit.

In the front cover of his notebook he'd written the name of the kid he needed to write this week.

"Jordan Marie Dyson," he mumbled under his breath. Above Jordan's name ten others were listed. Since Ben had been released from prison five years ago he had a dozen notebooks like these. He always made sure to pray for the names listed in the front covers. Maybe in eternity he'd find out how his prayers made a difference.

But right now, his thoughts were on Jordan, whoever she was.

Dear Jordan,

You may be wondering why you're getting this letter from someone you don't know. I'm writing you because I got your name from my parole officer. You see, about six years ago I did something very stupid. A good friend and I had been drinking a lot. He passed out and instead of realizing the trouble he was in, I laughed at him and went to bed. Unfortunately the next morning I woke up and he was dead.

Ben paused, and kicked off his shoes. He pushed his toes deep into the cool sand. He closed his eyes and pictured that awful moment. A heaviness settled on his chest and a tremor moved through his gut. He'd never forget the feeling of picking up Jason's cold hand, searching for a pulse in his wrist. When he didn't find one, horror jabbed a knife into his heart.

Ben picked up his pen again.

For a long time after Jason's death I thought I deserved bad things. I felt as if experiencing any happiness would be like throwing rocks at Jason's grave, but over the years God has shown me the best thing I can do for my friend is to share the memories about his life. And try to reach out to young people like yourself so they don't have to learn the hard way like I did.

In the Bible, Psalm 147 talks about God healing the brokenhearted and bandaging up their wounds. What I didn't realize until about a year after Jason's death is that I was brokenhearted long before he died. I'd pretty much decided that life wasn't fair and I was hurt God didn't do more to give me a fair shake. I buried my disappointment and anger with booze, but once I turned my life over to God, and realized that He'd be with me in good times and in bad, well things started looking brighter.

It's not that everything changed and became perfect overnight. In fact, I'm going through a tough time right now because a woman I hoped to marry some day is in love with another person. Yet, even when life doesn't turn out how I wish it would, God is with me. I can feel Him, just as I can feel the sun on my face. And I want you to know that I'm not telling you this because I'm court-ordered to do so (even though I am).

Instead, I'm sharing my heart because even though I don't know you, I believe in you. I also know that it is not just by chance that your name was sent to me. God has been trying to speak to you. Maybe you should just pause for a while and think about all the different ways He has. Also, pause and think about what He wants to say. My guess is that it's something like: "I love you, Jordan. I have good plans for you."

Ben ended the letter as he always did, sharing how it was possible to have a personal relationship with Christ and writing out a simple prayer she could pray. When he finished, he tore the letter out and placed it in an envelope, addressed it, and sealed it. Then, holding it with two hands, he lifted it up, with the setting sun and the rippling waves as a backdrop, and prayed over it. He prayed that God would prepare Jordan's heart for the words to come. He prayed for the other names in his notebook. Prayed that the words he'd sent to them in the past weeks would resurrect when they needed them most.

A new thought stirred as he prayed. For so long his name hadn't meant anything. He'd just been some guy from Montana writing these letters. But now—with his songs on the radio and his face in tabloid magazines—maybe getting a letter from him would matter more.

He smiled. Wouldn't that be just like God to make him a star so one kid would pay closer attention to the words he had to share?

Ben tucked the letter into his back jean pocket and considered writing another letter. What would Marianna do if he wrote to tell her he'd be in Indiana in the coming weeks? He shook his head and stood. No, he wouldn't do that to her. She had made a decision and had chosen Aaron. If he felt God telling him to fight for Marianna he would, but he didn't feel that. Instead, he knew he needed to wait and to pray.

He put his shoes back on, rose, and headed back to his rental car. There were millions of people in L.A., but Ben had never felt more alone as he drove back to the hotel. He just had to trust that what he'd written to Jordan was true—that God would heal the brokenhearted. And as far as Ben was concerned, he was at the top of that list.

Ten days later Ben found himself in Cleveland, not that the town looked any different from any other place he'd been. They drove in at night and spent all day at the venue. To him all cities looked the same—a sea of smiling faces, mostly women.

He leaned closer to the microphone. "It's said the best songs are those that stir emotions for the musician. Music is more than chords and tempos. It's more than lyrics. Half of every song is created with my fingertips on the guitar and with my voice. The other half focuses on the heart."

"You can have my heart!" A girl near the front row shouted.

He winked at her then continued without missing a beat. "The singer must believe the words he sings to make it a beautiful song."

A man in the front row cleared his throat and the woman next to him chuckled as if understanding a private joke. A woman in row five rose and hurried out of the room.

"Stick to singing," Roy had told him over and over. *"That's what they pay to see."*

But if he had to be on the road, at least he could do God's work.

Ben's gut tightened and he spoke faster. They'd come to hear a song, but he couldn't let them leave without knowing his faith, his heart. "This song is important to me, because it makes me think of someone I care for. I don't have her in my life. I doubt I ever will, but God has given me the peace to walk away from her. Of course"—he chuckled—"I'd rather have her, but sometimes what we get seems like second best, especially when it has to do with matters of the heart."

A collective "oh" rose from the women in the audience, and Ben imagined numerous women elbowing the guy they'd come with as if saying, "You should be thankful."

And with that he started playing the song that the world loved, but that broke his heart nearly every time he sang it.

"Entered my cabin, all warm from the fire,
Muscles were achin', worn out n' tired
From hard work like granddaddy did—
Ever' day of his life."

Looking out in the crowd Ben saw many beautiful women, but none seemed as beautiful to him as the memory he had of Marianna. He took a breath and continued on.

"Got my cabin deep in the woods
But need somethin' more to call it all good
To fill the aching hole in my life—
Cuz every warm cabin
Needs a good wife

You're nothing alone, you're everything together
Aches all fade when someone helps you weather
the hard times,
Come fill my heart, come fill my life—
Every warm cabin
Needs a good wife

My granddaddy told me, "If you wanna be whole,
Son, find a good woman who fills up your soul.
Whose smile brings sunshine, whose laughter rings true—
'Cuz son, life ain't nothin' 'til you do."

Then came the day I looked in your eyes,
I knew granddad's words were heartfelt and wise.
Your smile, your laughter proved my grandad knew
A thing or two about life.

Your gray eyes a'dreamin', your smile so warm
could melt all the ice from the cold winter's storm,
And by the March thaw, my soul came to life
When I asked gray-eyed girl to be called my wife.

You settled my heart, you warmed up my life
The day you agreed to be called my wife.

You said:
We're nothing alone, We're everything together
Aches all fade when someone helps you weather
The hard times,
I'll enter your heart, I'll enter your life
Every warm cabin,
Needs a good wife

Baby,
We're nothing alone, we're everything together
Aches all fade when someone helps you weather
The hard times,
You entered my heart, you entered my life
Every warm cabin, needs a good wife

Got a warm cabin, got a good life,
Got all I need
Ever' day with my wife."

Ben finished the last chords and opened his eyes. The auditorium was full and all eyes were on him.

Focused on his tears.

CHAPTER TWELVE

uth's hands folded and then unfolded on her lap. She cupped them again as if holding an invisible warmth inside. The Carashes' woodstove heated the room, but that wasn't the warmth she tried to grasp. It was the prayers lifted up. Words of care for each other.

Folks back home would say it's wrong. All of it . . .

Gathering like this. Talking out loud in prayer. Bringing attention to yourself by speaking what's on one's mind to God—as if He needed any guidance figuring stuff out. The problem was . . . something about it felt right to Ruth. Her heart grew warm to hear her and Abe's names on Deborah Shelter's lips. Tears rimmed the edges of her eyes to hear Deborah's daughter praying for Marianna's adjustment back to Indiana and her relationship with Aaron.

"May Marianna and Aaron's marriage be founded in truth and stitched together with faithfulness," Sarah prayed. The tears came because Ruth could think of no more beautiful prayer than that. Yet as the muscles tightened in her neck, threatening to cut off the flow of air, she realized neither truth nor faithfulness had joined her and Abe together—not at first. Over the years feelings for Mark had unraveled, and thick threads of love for Abe had taken their place—not with neat stitches but with jagged lines that came as God carried them through the hard times together.

Ruth found it easy to let her mind wander when those praying spoke of people and problems she did not know, but her senses jerked awake when Abe stirred on the sofa seat beside her. He cleared his throat.

Surely he wasn't going to—

"Dear Lord, I come before Ye a man of feeble words. I did not grow in a home that spoke words of prayer aloud, yet their love fer You was known. Help me in my own family to show them what loving Ye is all about. I'm faltering 'cause this is a new path, a different way. But it feels right. It's a way of love . . ."

Ruth waited to see if he would continue, but after a long pause another voice rose up. The tremble of Abe's arm pressed against hers. With slow moments, she released her clenched hands, allowing the warmth she'd captured there to move up to her heart. She reached out and placed her hands over Abe's folded ones and the trembling stopped.

His words were true. This *did* feel good and right, and that was the problem. Ruth had allowed emotions to overtake her before, and they led to the wrong places—places of pain. Marianna had almost done the same. Ruth had seen the way her daughter had looked at Ben Stone and he at her. She shook her head in slow increments. To let emotions run wild wasn't always the answer. Like wild horses, they pulled and raced down destructive paths.

She let out a low breath, thankful Marianna was in Indiana far away from Ben, and then attempted to refocus her mind on the prayers around them.

And as the others prayed, she silently added in prayers for her children—for Levi and Naomi and the baby to come. For their wedding. For their life together.

She prayed for Marianna and Aaron, but as she thought of them she didn't know what to pray. Aaron seemed like such the perfect young man, but Marianna's letters of late had seemed discontent.

Lord, if he's not the man for her, please show my daughter. Ruth didn't know where that prayer came from, but it was something to consider. She'd been the one to invite Aaron Zook to come visit them . . . but she never thought it to be a matter of prayer. Until now.

In fact most things in life she'd never really considered praying about. They lived their lives devoted to God . . . so why had she never thought to talk to Him much?

Marianna entered the Troyers' home for church service and it seemed like just another day—similar to the ones growing up. The same homes, the same buggies, the same people. Only the children were different. As some grew, they begot others to take their places.

She entered with Levi and Naomi, and she couldn't help but notice eyes upon them, especially her. She was certain if she'd already been baptized that she'd have some confessing to do. Her lack of formal commitment to the church was the only thing that had kept an elder from visiting. Of course she'd have to get baptized before the wedding. She and Aaron had yet to set a date, so she still had time.

She entered through the front door. The members of the community sat in familiar places. They sang the songs she knew and read familiar Scripture verses.

When it was time to kneel, Marianna did so willingly. Her heart warmed in full surrender to God. In the aisle behind her a young mother directed her toddler, showing her how to fold her hands and lower her head. Marianna thought of her own children someday. She had this—this community, these people, this learned reverence to offer, but because of Ben's influence she also had so much more.

Marianna had seen by example how her parents attended church and devoted themselves to others. She'd attended many a barn raising and delivered a meal to a family in need, but until Ben, she hadn't been sure she knew how to follow God. She was thankful now she knew how to listen to Him through His Word and prayer, instead of coming up with her own ideas.

When the time of silent prayer was over, the congregation lifted from their knees and returned to their seats on the benches.

She thought of her friend Jenny in Montana. An ache settled on Marianna at the thought of Jenny's hard growing-up years. What she'd been given had been a gift—a loving family and home filled with care and tenderness, the knowledge of God, a community who'd watched out for her best interest.

She scanned the faces of those in her Amish community. Was it worth trying to share more with them? Maybe what they had was enough. After all, what they did have was a great treasure in each other and their simple faith.

The poems and lessons she'd learned through repetition would be there for life. She told herself she wasn't turning her back on those things, just adding to it what God intended to be added from the beginning, a personal relationship with Him.

After the service was over, Marianna moved to help the other women in the kitchen. Most were kind to her, but some kept their distance. It didn't bother her too much. Mem had gained back their trust, hadn't she? It would take time, but she'd be back in the community again.

Naomi moved around the kitchen with slow steps. More women ignored her—pregnant and not married. That wasn't something one saw every day at an Amish church service.

Naomi tried to brush off the stares as she cut slices of pie. What would happen if they knew that besides Naomi being pregnant, Levi was not the father? As Marianna set out jars of sweet pickles on the tall tables, she scanned the faces of the young men. . . was one of those the father? Could he be part of their community? Could he be in this room?

She looked from face to face—and then her gaze stopped on Aaron.

Marianna shook her head. She would *not* think of that as a possibility. Yes, Aaron and Naomi had gotten close for a time after she left. And yes, he admitted kissing Naomi. Still, he swore he hadn't done more.

As much as Marianna wished he hadn't kissed Naomi, hadn't grown closer to her than he should, she was thankful things had only gone as far as they had. But then, Aaron's character wouldn't allow more. Some young man didn't have values or willpower, but her Aaron did.

Yes, Aaron's character was sound. Marianna shook her head. She should just be thankful for that, and that things between him and Naomi had stopped at a kiss.

And that Aaron and Naomi weren't the ones committing their lives to each other this summer.

CHAPTER THIRTEEN

s the days grew hotter, and the baby's birth grew closer, Marianna decided to move from Aunt Ida's house and stay with Levi instead—to be there for Naomi. Today she'd talked Naomi into getting out for a while. They went to town for groceries, and Marianna told Naomi she'd treat her to lunch.

Growing up, days like this didn't happen often. Working at the West Kootenai Kraft and Grocery, she met people who ate there nearly every day. She hadn't eaten in a restaurant since returning home, but had to admit she looked forward to it. But before they could relax and enjoy lunch, she had to get some shopping done.

Naomi was looking at the fabric next door, and Marianna volunteered to get the groceries. She glanced at her list—oh yes. She needed a bag of beans for tomorrow's supper. With quick steps she walked toward the bins of bulk goods. She heard a man clearing his throat and noticed a tall man walking down the next aisle.

With all that had been happening lately, she hadn't thought much of the Englisch driver—the man her mother had once loved. But there he was. He wore a baseball cap pulled down over his eyes, and she placed a hand on the cream-colored metal shelf, touching a bag of lentils as if considering the price.

He was handsome, she had to admit, but still it seemed strange he'd once held her mother's affections. What was it that had made Mem decide on Dat instead? Was it the simple fact that Dat was Amish? Marianna had no doubt her mother had made the right choice, but how?

Over the months that she'd been back, she'd heard more about this driver—Mark Olsen. One woman said he was divorced. Another said he'd recently gotten out of jail. Many refused to hire him as a driver unless there were no other options.

Still, not every Englisch man is alike. She turned her back to the man and put two bags of beans into her shopping cart. Ben was Englisch, and he was different. She couldn't imagine him not following God, not pursuing what was right.

She finished getting everything she needed on that aisle. Would she be able to move to the next one over without being seen? No luck, she was exiting her aisle the same time Mark exited his. He slowed and glanced her direction. She turned away and moved toward the bin of oats, hoping he wouldn't follow. She let out a sigh of relief when he moved to the checkout counter instead.

Marianna's heart pounded in her chest as she realized that as soon as the baby was born, there'd be a wedding, and if there was a wedding, Dat and Mem would return.

What would happen if Mem happened to run into Mark? Or worse yet, what if he found her . . . making it clear what he'd already told Marianna—that he hadn't forgotten their love.

Marianna picked up a few more things. She watched Mark leave the store and then approached the front counter.

"Beautiful day, isn't it?" She struggled to push thoughts of a meeting between her mother and Mark out of her mind.

"Uh, yeah. I guess so." The blonde woman's eyes widened. "I've always liked spring."

"Me, too. I'm glad to be able to hang my laundry outside, instead of around the woodstove." Marianna smiled. "I love getting dressed and smelling the sun on my garments, don't you?"

The woman nodded. She tilted her head and studied Marianna, a strange look in her eyes. It was then Marianna remembered: she wasn't in Montana! Conversations like these—between the Amish and Englisch—weren't done here.

Marianna paid for her items and then grabbed up her bags, started to leave—then stopped. Done or not, there was no call to be rude. She offered the woman a smile. "Have a nice day. And thank you for all your service. It's much appreciated."

The woman nodded and a responding smile filled her face. "Wow, thanks. I think you just made my day."

Naomi lifted the edge of a bolt of fabric and rubbed it between her fingers.

"It's microfleece." The storekeeper approached. "It's nice and soft but not too heavy. Perfect for a summer baby."

"*Ja.* I think I'll take two yards." Naomi pointed to a light blue fabric. "I've already made three baby blankets, but I'm sure one more won't hurt."

As the woman nodded and pulled the bolt of fabric from the store rack, the jingling of the bell on the store's glass door drew her attention. Naomi turned and her smile faded as Aaron walked in with Mrs. Zook. Instinctively, her hands went to her stomach. As if feeling her eyes upon him, Aaron lifted his head, his eyes meeting hers.

Mrs. Zook continued on to the back of the store, her eyes fixed on the clearance rack. Instead of following her, Aaron moved Naomi's direction. She turned back to the fabric, not knowing what else to do.

"Hi there." Aaron strode up and paused by her side. "Haven't seen you in a while."

"I saw you Sunday. At church." Naomi acted as if she was engrossed in a bright fabric of bunnies and ducks. "I served you pie."

"*Ja*, that's right."

They stood there in silence before Aaron took a step closer. "Did Levi bring you to town?"

Naomi shook her head. "No, Marianna did. You're marrying a good woman."

"I know. And where is Levi?"

"He's at work." Naomi looked around. "Shouldn't you be there too?"

He shrugged. "It's my mem's birthday. She asked I bring her to town and help her pick out fabric for a quilt."

"And she won't think anything of you talking to me?"

"No." He brushed his blond bangs from his forehead. "Why should she?"

The tension in Naomi's chest built, and she again considered running from the store. "So she doesn't know?"

"Know?"

"*Ja*, know that I'm carrying your child." The words slipped from her mouth more easily than she expected they would.

Aaron took two steps back, running into a rack of fabric and making a loud clang.

She turned to him, daring to fix her eyes on his. "Why, Aaron, are you acting surprised?"

He leaned closer and lowered his voice. "And why are you acting as if I should know?"

"How could you not? You were always the expert at math. We were together . . . oh about nine months ago." She cocked one eyebrow. "Or did you forget?"

"Of course not." He turned away. "I just assumed . . ." He swallowed hard, his Adam's apple bobbing. "I assumed because you're marrying Levi that he was the father."

"I had no choice. I found out just days after you left for Montana."

"You should have at least told me." His voice lowered a notch.

Naomi sucked in a breath, holding it. Those moments with Aaron had been so special. He'd been so tender and caring. He'd helped her forget about Levi, and for a time she thought he truly did love her. As she walked around the house she imagined he'd built it for her. She tried to convince herself, as she was consumed by his kisses, that he'd forget Marianna. But that wasn't the case.

Pain stabbed her heart to see him. To look into his blue eyes. It was the same pain she felt the moment he told her he was going to Montana to see Marianna. She'd packed a lunch and had taken it over—any excuse to see him one more time. One more chance for him to choose her . . . but he'd walked away and boarded that train instead.

Naomi wiped her eyes, refusing to let one tear drop. She'd cried enough tears over Aaron. Thankfully, Levi had stepped up—had been the man she knew Aaron could never be.

"And would it have made any difference if I would have told you sooner?" Naomi crossed her arms over her chest. "You built a house for her, Aaron. You went to Montana to get her. You love *her*—" Her voice lowered to a whisper. "How could your child and I ever compete with that?"

Without another word she went to the cash register and paid for her fabric, and then she walked through the door without looking back.

There was no need.

No reason to let him see her tears.

After shopping, Marianna found Naomi waiting outside the grocery store with her bag of fabric. She had a distant look in her eyes . . . Probably because of the pregnancy. Marianna couldn't imagine the fatigue that must set in so close to the baby's due date.

After loading up their things in the buggy, Marianna led the way into the restaurant. Naomi followed, keeping pace right behind her. Marianna was sure if she stopped short Naomi would plow into her back. The young woman had seemed nervous from the moment Marianna had found her. She'd had a small purchase of fabric but told Marianna she would do more shopping at a later time.

Marianna saw a table open and sat down. What had gotten Naomi so bothered? Instead of asking, she told herself that all would be explained at the right time. Marianna didn't need to go poking and prodding for the truth like Aunt Ida learned to do so well.

"What are you doing?" Naomi leaned close to Marianna, but didn't sit in the empty chair.

Marianna peered up into Naomi's wide-eyed gaze. "What do you mean?"

"What are you doing sitting here, out in the open?" Naomi leaned closer. "In the middle of all the Englisch?"

Marianna looked around and for the first time noticed the glances. The prying eyes.

"I . . . I'm sorry." She stood and followed Naomi to a corner booth.

Naomi took the seat with her back to the rest of the restaurant, as if not seeing them would make the Englisch evaporate into thin air.

"You've changed, Mari." Naomi shook her head.

Marianna picked up her menu and flipped to the back page. "I don't know what you mean."

"Times past you'd never wanted to eat in a restaurant. We musta passed this place a hundred times and never'd come in. It's like . . ." Naomi paused placing a finger over her lips as if trying to keep the words tucked inside.

"Like what?" Marianna set down the menu. Her hands felt clammy and her hunger turned to dread.

"It's like you're one of *them*." Naomi cocked one eyebrow. "Levi left to live in the world a time and you'd never know it. He's come back and fits in just the same. But you . . ."

Marianna tilted her head. "Because I sat at a center table you think that?"

"Not so much. It's other things. I've seen you watching folks, studying the Amish like the tourists do. Like it's all new to you instead of how you've lived from the day you were born. Yer words are proper too—Englisch proper—and to hear you talk about God like you do. Talking like you know Him and speak with Him and telling others they should do the same. Well, it's different. We have our ways, Marianna. Faith is private. Only the prideful person would suggest how another should live."

Marianna leaned back, pressing her shoulders against the vinyl seat. She knew what Naomi was talking about—her suggestion to read her Bible and pray. She lowered her gaze and shook her head, whispering a quiet prayer for patience.

Wait.

Marianna knew the words she wanted to say, but also knew they'd bring about no good. Still, they replayed in her mind. *I suggest you spend more time with God and you point a finger at my pride? You're carrying a child conceived outside the marriage bed and you accuse me?*

She took in a deep breath then released it. "I'm sorry you feel that way." She didn't try to explain. Didn't try to defend. She knew that to do either would just help tip their already distant relationship.

Naomi nodded but didn't respond. Instead, she looked down at her growing stomach and placed a hand over it, spreading her fingers. Her eyes widened as if she felt the baby kick, but Marianna didn't ask if it did. As she watched the tender moment, a strange uneasiness washed over her. It was as if invisible hands had gripped her neck. Everything within her wished to push from the booth, to look away, to hurry away.

Why? Why do I feel this way? I should be happy. Levi's returned to the Amish. We'll have another member to our fam—

She couldn't finish the thought. Her mind wouldn't go there. It couldn't go there. This baby—something to be celebrated—

made the hairs on her arms stand on end. But why? Why did this feeling creep over her like hundreds of ants?

"Excuse me." Marianna placed the menu back on the table and slid from her seat. "It feels a little warm in here." She brushed a trembling hand across her forehead. "I think I need to splash some water on my face."

Naomi glanced up and nodded. "I hope you're not coming down with something."

Marianna swallowed down the emotion that was balling up in her throat. "*Ja*, me too."

She looked around and found the bathroom, hurrying toward it. Why had they'd stopped to eat? Suddenly the last thing she could do was enjoy lunch.

Her stomach turned, sickness overcoming her, and she hurried into the farthest stall closing it behind her. The air felt heavy and thick and she struggled for breath. Tears rimmed her eyes.

What's wrong with me?

She lowered the toilet seat and sat. Her knees quivered and she placed her face in her hands. A sob attempted to burst from her lips but she pushed it deeper inside.

The door to the bathroom opened and she heard footsteps. Every muscle froze. Wasn't there anywhere she could be alone with her thoughts?

"Did you see that?" A woman spoke. "Walking in with her chin held up like that. The nerve."

"You'd think she'd consider what she'd done and not act like she was living right."

"Her parents should talk to her."

"*Ja*, I do agree."

They continued on and Marianna held her breath, telling herself not to make the slightest noise. Not to give her presence away. Bad enough these women were talking about Naomi like this. It would be most awkward if they found her there!

The more they talked, the more she recognized their voices. Mrs. Klees and Mrs. John, who were part of their community,. Marianna didn't talk to them much but she saw them at church.

She pulled her feet back, tucking them to the sides of the toilet. *Please, don't let them notice the door to the last stall is closed.* As she listened, the queasy feeling she had a moment before evaporated like dew under the sun. Instead a new feeling rose up in her.

Anger.

How dare *they talk about Naomi that way—as if she were the only Amish girl to find herself in this situation.*

If Marianna were brave, she'd confront them—point out their poisonous tongues. But she was anything but brave.

"I feel so bad for her parents." Mrs. John's tone dripped with self-righteous pity. "The poor Sommer family has already faced so much. Imagine if it were *your* daughter, trouncing around talking about God in such a prideful way. A shame."

Their words hit like a fist to her gut. *Her? They were talking about her?*

Marianna blinked back tears. What was she was doing here? She hadn't tried to be difficult. She was trying to share hope and joy in God—what was so bad about that?

The women left, and she waited another few minutes before she exited. She kept her head lowered as she walked to the table and sunk into the booth.

Naomi sipped on a glass of water, but from the look on her face it was clear she wasn't comfortable either.

Marianna reached out and touched her hand. "Why don't we head home and make our own lunch? The food isn't that good here from what I heard, and we don't need to waste money on that."

Naomi nodded and a relief crossed her face. They hurried out, eyes fixed on the door. Let people say what they want . . . Marianna knew that God saw things differently. He loved Naomi's child, too, even though in the world's eyes it was more of a topic of gossip than a celebration of life.

But right then and there Marianna decided to change that. They could talk about her. They could point fingers at Naomi. But as much as Marianna was able, she would make certain this child felt special and loved.

Aaron woke up in the night and sat up in the bed. A child's cry had woken him, and it wasn't until he'd jumped out of bed that he realized it had been a dream. The cry, that is, not the child.

The child was anything but a dream.

From the first time he heard about Naomi's pregnancy, he'd wondered. Yet when Levi's note to Marianna said he and Naomi were getting married Aaron assumed—was even relieved—the baby wasn't his.

Out of nowhere came a hot fist of anger. Aaron turned and punched his pillow. Why hadn't Naomi told him? Fear plowed through his brain, and he felt as if his whole world had been tipped to his side. *What if Marianna finds out?*

He couldn't let that happen. He replayed the moment she entered the small room he'd built at their cabin. He'd imagined their child there—his and Marianna's. And now?

Should he pretend nothing had changed?

Would it be possible to let another man raise his son or daughter?

What if Naomi is lying? How did she know for sure the child was his instead of Levi's? Most importantly, did Levi think it was his child?

Aaron didn't know what to think or what to do. He lay back in the bed and pulled his covers to his chin.

Hurt replaced the anger. Worried tagged along next. If Marianna hadn't moved, none of this would have happened. He just hoped this wouldn't ruin everything.

He closed his eyes and knew that he would do what he had to do. Nothing would keep him from the woman he couldn't live without. And if holding on to Mari meant ignoring the fact that the baby Naomi carried was his . . .

So be it.

CHAPTER FOURTEEN

*B*en rose and noticed the tour bus wasn't moving. It must have stopped somewhere in the night. Where were they? He didn't have a clue. His head was foggy, and he stumbled toward the front in search of the coffee he smelled.

Greg Jackson, his backup guitarist, held out a cup of Starbucks.

Ben nodded, taking the cup. It was French roast with a bit of cream and sugar, just how he liked it. He took a sip and though it hit the spot, it couldn't compare to coffee back at the West Kootenai Kraft and Grocery. Memories, memories, they stung his heart as he swallowed, then sat on the sofa next to Greg.

The morning light hit the man's face, highlighting dark circles.

Ben took another sip. "You're up awfully early."

Greg chuckled. "Man, are you kidding? Out late."

Ben's eyes widened.

"Yeah, missed the bus but my date gave me a ride. Thankfully we only went seventy miles last night."

Maybe he should talk to the man, tell him it wasn't cool how he messed with women's emotions at every stop, how he took advantage of them and left them emptier than before. It wouldn't matter, though. Ben had given the same lecture a dozen times. He'd even talked to Roy about it. Roy had talked to the guys but it did little good.

Ben picked up his Bible and headed to the back where his bed was. With each step he felt it coming—the thick throat, blurry eyes. The emotions welled up and he sat on his bed and pulled his knees to his chest.

God, what am I doing here? I'm not doing anyone any good. I feel my soul being stripped away.

He opened his Bible to read, but the tears blurred on the page. Then the tears came and with it a heavy sob that was so loud it probably woke up the rest of the guys.

He was alone.

Useless.

He wanted out, but for some reason he felt God telling him to stay.

God . . . I don't want this life any more. Can't You put me somewhere else? Anywhere else?

He laid back in bed, telling himself it wouldn't hurt to be twenty minutes late to rehearsal for once. And then he just lay there and prayed. He prayed for himself and the other band members. He prayed for his friends back in Montana. He prayed for Marianna, that she would continue to seek God wherever she was. That's what really mattered.

He also prayed that if God's plan was for her to be with Aaron, that God would bless that union. Bless them.

That prayer stung the most.

His prayers carried him through the day. The concert was

a joy that night. And he was still smiling when he went out for hamburgers with the guys after the concert.

They went to one of those chain restaurants that was a mix between Denny's and the local bar. He glanced at the wall lined with old junk—a child's tricycle, an old baseball mitt, a watercolor of Elvis. Who was the genius was who turned garage sale finds into decorations? He smiled to himself when he realized God did that—turned the useless into a good find.

The other guys had joined him. Not one had headed off with a pretty girl at his side. That was something to celebrate. They ordered hamburgers and talked about what they were going to buy with all their cash once the gig was up. It was hard to imagine his songs—mostly one song—could support a dozen people on the road.

"Babe alert." Joe Smink poked Ben's rib cage.

Ben turned to see what Joe was talking about, even though deep down he knew he shouldn't.

The woman's long-legged stride, knowing smile and eyes fixed on him, telling Ben she'd been at the concert. He always knew when woman were. They approached with fixed gazes that made him feel as though the price of their admittance also paid for his heart—at least for one night.

Ben squirmed in his seat wishing he'd just gone back to the bus.

The other band members' hungry eyes scanned the woman, from her low-cut top to her pointed heals. Still, her eyes fixed on him.

"Hey, can I join you?" The woman slid in to the vinyl booth before Ben had a chance to respond. "I was at the concert. It was great. I heard you before, Ben Stone, years ago, but I have to say I enjoyed you even more this time."

"Really?" He raised his eyebrows. "I can't believe you paid to see me . . . twice."

The woman laughed and extended her hand. "I'm Tasha."

Ben took her hand, soft, warm. Her long fingernails were painted red. The first thing Ben thought of was that the woman hadn't worked a day in her life—not Amish work anyway. Things like cooking, baking, sweeping, washing. He missed Marianna's trimmed nails and calloused hands.

"Listen. I was wondering if you were up for going for a drive? I don't live far from here."

One of the guys wolf-whistled, and heat rose up Ben's cheeks. The strength he'd gained from this morning was still with him. He could see through her. See that she had a hole the size of Texas in her heart and was hoping for him to fill it. Or at least try.

He smiled at her. "You're a nice girl, but I'm really not interested. If you want to have dinner with us I'll buy you a burger."

Snickers sounded around the table and this time it was the woman's face turning red.

She lifted her nose and narrowed her gaze. "No thanks, Ben Stone." She spit his name. "Sorry I bothered you."

The woman rose, turned, and strode away. The band members' laughter followed her.

Instead of feeling good about what he'd done, Ben felt horrible. The way he acted wasn't kind or godly. He lowered his head, wishing he could rewind and try that again. "Man, that was dumb."

Greg turned to him. "Change your mind?"

"Yeah, that *was* dumb." Joe added in. "You might want to run after that."

Ben slid from the booth and rose. "I know I did the right thing, but I should have treated her better." He could see the woman striding across the parking lot with long strides. Her head was lowered. She paused by the side of a sports car with her hands dangling at her sides. Without looking back at the restaurant she got in the car and drove away.

How many lonely people had been in the audience tonight? How many had walked away with no more hope than they'd walked in with?

He tucked his hands into his jean pockets. "I'm heading back to the bus. I'll catch you guys later."

"What about your hamburger?" Greg pointed to the waitress who carried a full tray their direction.

Ben pulled out a twenty from his wallet and tossed it onto the table. "One of you guys can have it. I'm not hungry anymore."

Dear Marianna,

I've lost track of how many letters I've written. It has to be a dozen at least. I still don't know when I'll be giving these letters to you. Or if I ever will.

Lately I've been thinking about children. It seems silly I know. Your life is occupied with other things—other people. There is no date for our wedding (even though I wish it were so), but I cannot stop from thinking about how you would be as a mother.

My own mother is kind, but distant. She's quicker to point out what I've done wrong than what I do right. My artistic talents—she thinks they are nice but would rather have me work a real job. I know you are not like that. I have seen you with your younger siblings. I've noticed the way you listen when they talk to you and the way you snuggle them on your lap.

Of course the most important thing you have that you can offer your future children is your faith. You are an example of all that is right and good. You don't take your role as an Amish woman lightly. I respect that. In fact, seeing your example has made me consider my own faith more.

Sometimes we do the things we do, and serve the way we serve, because of what we feel is right. And then sometimes we see others and they show us new ways. They remind us of the faith of our forefathers . . . and live in a way that brings to mind why those things should be remembered. Your steadfast faith has been an example to me, even if you didn't know it.

Written with the pen of the man who sees your faith and considers his own in a new light.

CHAPTER FIFTEEN

aomi sat up in bed and gasped for air. A strong, knotting contraction pulled her breath from her lungs. Her eyes spread open and she searched for light. Instead, darkness spread in every direction. The room was dark. The night beyond the window was dark, and she still had two and a half weeks to go before the baby was due.

She opened her mouth to call for her mother—to try and tell her that the contractions had come, but a moan escaped her lips instead. When the pain ebbed, she relaxed back into her pillow to catch her breath. Tears filled her eyes, but she wiped them away.

It was then she knew it wasn't her mother she needed. It was Levi and Marianna. She needed Levi's strength. She wanted Marianna's prayers.

She slipped on her robe and slippers, lit the lantern in her room, and tiptoed outside with the lantern swinging in her hand. The spring air was warm and it smelled of damp soil, fresh grass, and rain. The rain would come, she just hoped it wouldn't come too hard before the midwife was fetched.

She hurried to the dawdi haus, the glow of the light guiding her steps. Rocks bit through the thin bottoms of her slippers, but she ignored the pain. Her heart pounded with the realization that the time had come. The baby would soon be here!

Her lower stomach knotted up again. "Levi!" Her lungs struggled to fill, so intense was the pain.

She placed the lantern on the porch and braced herself against the door. The pain peaked hard and tight. Her fist pounded on the wooden door and a squeak escaped her lips.

She heard fumbling from inside and a minute later the door opened. Golden light bathed Levi's face, and she fell into his arms.

His heartbeat pounded against her cheek, and his arms wrapped around her, holding her up. "Is it time?"

She nodded. "*Ja.*"

He led her into the house, through the living room and to his bed. Before she lay down he stripped the dirty sheets and remade it with clean ones the midwife told them to keep on hand. She sat down on the edge of the bed and wiped the sweat beading on her brow.

Levi studied her with concern in his gaze. She attempted to offer him a slight smile, but she could tell he could see right through it.

"The midwife. I need to go get her."

"Levi!" Naomi's fingers wrapped around his night shirt. "Don't go."

Levi studied her, and then he took her hand. "This is happening faster than I thought it would. I won't go. I promise. I'll send Marianna."

Naomi looked to the window. "But that night's so dark."

"She'll be fine. She doesn't have to go far."

Another contraction hit and Naomi turned to her side, covering her face with her hands, trying to breathe. Levi leaned closer, making soothing circles on her back. A minute later the pain released and Naomi's body relaxed. Without a word Levi rose and hurried to the extra bedroom, pounding on the door.

He returned a few minutes later and stroked a hand over her hard, round stomach. "Marianna's on her way, but if the baby comes too quickly we'll be fine." He winked. "I'm an expert at birthing calves and colts."

"Do not think that makes me feel . . . better." Another contraction began, and she closed her eyes. "Just pray." Her voice was breathy and low. "Pray for me and this baby."

He lowered his head and she trusted he was indeed praying. When the contraction stopped, he rose and hurried to the washbasin. Returning, he wiped her brow with a cool, damp cloth.

She reached for his other hand and gripped it. She could never have done this without him here! How did she ever deserve a man who would stand by her in such a way, with concern for her and not for himself?

She didn't want to know where she'd be if Levi had left, walked away.

Another contraction came, and she was almost grateful, for she didn't want to imagine life without him—not for a moment.

Marianna hitched up the buggy quicker than she ever had before. With a hasty motion she pushed the lap robe to the back and with a flick of their wrists they were on their way.

She knew from experience that most first-time labors took their sweet time, but she questioned if that would be Naomi's case. The pains seemed to be coming close together. She set the horse at a quickened pace.

There was nothing she could do but pray as the buggy carried her forward. Back in Montana they had a phone in their shed. How useful that would have been to just ring up the midwife. Useful, but a "trapping of the world" according to her bishops.

The steady *clip-clopping* of the horse's hooves stilled from the urgency of the moment. There was no such thing as speeding when it came to driving a buggy. One could only go as fast as the horse was prepared to go. As she settled back into the seat, the quietness carried her thoughts to God.

Her first whispered prayer for a safe delivery for Naomi was followed a prayer for Ben. At first she questioned why this name entered her thoughts, but the Lord's ways—she knew—were His own.

Wherever he is, Lord, be with Ben. I'm not sure why you've placed this burden on my heart, but let him know that You are there for him, and let him know there are others who still care. If he questions the place You've put him at this moment, may Ben find the answer in You. If he wonders if You still have a plan, find a way to assure him You do.

The words came as soft whispers, and as she prayed Marianna realized that the things she was praying for Ben were things that burdened her own heart. She too needed to know God was there and others cared. She questioned the place she was at. Did God still have a plan? Was she still in line with it?

Am I just trying to put my problems on Ben? Or is he going through the same things as I am? Does he have the same questions?

Either way she knew that didn't matter. If Ben needed

strength for those things, so be it. If not . . . well, prayers sent up to God never went to waste.

She noted the midwife's house up ahead and her mind was stirred back to the present. She'd be an aunt today. A new life was always something to celebrate no matter what else happened—even if the things she prayed for never resolved as she thought they ought.

Ben sat on the bed in his bus and pulled the guitar out of his suitcase. He strummed for a few minutes. *God . . . why? Why did You bring me here? Why make me a star. Because I know that's from You, Lord . . .*

The image of that woman who'd tried to pick him up at the restaurant drifted into his mind. She'd seen him in concert not once, but twice. Obviously she saw something she liked. The only question was, had she seen any difference in who he was now and who he'd been then?

The first time on tour he'd been just a kid—barely twenty. He lived with his roommates and the only thing they'd had in the fridge was booze. He'd been dating Carrie, Roy's daughter, at the time. But that didn't mean he didn't bring home other girls every now and again. His life had been headed for a train wreck until his buddy Jason drank himself to death on Ben's living room couch. The tour stopped after that and the trial followed. Ben had been acquitted, on one condition. For the rest of his life he had to write one letter a week to an underage drinker who'd been caught drinking or arrested for a DUI. He'd continued writing those letters, even when he was on tour. And hopefully those he wrote to understood his change. The thing was, those in the audience now had no idea he was different from what he used to be.

In the years since Ben's last tour he'd given his life to God. He moved to Montana to have a quieter life, to focus more on God and the people He placed in his life. Sure, between songs he shared a little about Montana, about his faith, and about writing "Every Warm Cabin Needs a Good Wife" with the audience, but what if he shared more . . . shared how God had *really* change his life?

Roy wouldn't like it. In fact, Roy already shot down the idea when Ben mentioned it months ago. But then, the crowds didn't pay to come see Roy. They paid to come see him, and if they really wanted to know him . . .

Well, Ben would let them do just that.

Naomi's eyes fluttered closed as weariness attempted to pull her into its grasp. Each time she drifted off to sleep another contraction jolted her awake. Her eyes popped open. A gush of wetness warmed her legs. "What is it?"

"Just your water," the midwife said as she hurried into the room. Marianna followed. Naomi's shoulders relaxed some to know they were there. Levi looked at the women and for the first time Naomi noticed how pale he was.

Levi gazed down at her, wiping her damp hair from her face. "You are doing gut, Naomi."

"Thank you . . . you can go in the other room and wait. If it's more comfortable for you."

"*Ja,* I can do that." He leaned forward and kissed her forehead and then hurried out of the room.

Another pain gripped her, and Naomi's hands reached for the iron bed frame, pulling against it.

The midwife checked her and then leaned her face in close. "I came just in time. On the next contraction you can push."

Naomi nodded and did as she was told, but it didn't make a difference. The minutes ticked past, and her body grew weak with the effort.

The midwife came to the side of the bed and brought her face close. "Look at me. You're making progress, Naomi. Don't give up. I believe one more push will do it, the baby's head is crowning."

Naomi gasped. She tossed her head from side-to-side. "I am not sure. I don't think I can." She looked to Marianna, and her friend lifted her finger, wiping tears from Naomi's face. Tears she didn't know she'd been crying.

"I'll be right back." Marianna hurried from the room.

A moment later she returned, Levi at her side.

Naomi reached for his hand. "Are you sure? Are you okay being here?"

Levi smiled. "More than anything. I jest thought that was a nice way you were asking me to leave."

"I wan—want you here." She barely got the words out before she looked to the midwife. The woman nodded, and Naomi knew what she had to do. She had to push through the pain.

Levi wiped her brow again. "One more. One more."

With all that was in her Naomi bore down. A cry escaped her lips and at that moment her child entered the world.

"It's a boy!" Marianna's voice, filled with wonder.

Naomi's hands reached for her son.

The infant's shuddering cry filled the room. The midwife cut the umbilical cord and then placed the baby on her chest. His body was pink. His hair light. He looked up at her with squinty eyes.

With a small gasp, the tears came heavy now. Joy over being able to see her baby at last, but worry tinged the edges. What did Levi think now . . . now that he saw the child—the physical evidence of what she'd done?

Levi had stood by her and asked few questions. She told him she'd met someone when she was out with a friend and things got out of hand. She never confessed it was Aaron's baby. Levi had never tried to explain to anyone that he'd been the honorable one.

She'd asked his forgiveness, and he'd offered her grace. She supposed he found it easy to love her because they'd built that foundation over the years, but what about this child? Would Levi be able to love a baby not his own? The truth stood on her chest, pushing the air from her lungs.

"He's beautiful." Levi whispered in a hushed tone. "I can't believe it. We have a son, Naomi. I have a son."

A cry of relief pushed from Naomi's lips, and she lifted her eyes to Levi. Excitement brightened his gaze.

Levi bent down and kissed her forehead. "He's beautiful."

She tried to take in all the baby's features, but tears blurred her eyes. Just as happy as she was to see the small, pink bundle, happiness filled her chest and seeped out of her pores to hear Levi's words.

His son. Levi called this baby his son.

She looked up at Levi, love flooding her. What did she do to deserve a man such as this? "Will you name him, Levi? Will you name the baby?"

"Of course." He smiled at her. "He's a beautiful boy, Naomi. I'd be honored to give our son a name."

The baby squalled, and Marianna stepped forward to get a better look. Her eyes were tired. No one had slept much last night. Still, the small one was worth staying up for. They passed him around and marveled at his perfect nose, his small fingers, his feet that seemed too big for his tiny, wrinkled body.

Naomi had finally drifted off to sleep, and Marianna sat by Levi as he held his son.

When the morning warmed, they moved to the back step. The late morning sun elongated shadows around them. "I think it's pretty amazing Naomi wants you to name the baby. Have you thought of a name yet?"

Levi nodded. "I was thinking Samuel. We can call him Sam for short. He's one of my favorite men in the Bible. I appreciate how his mother dedicated him to God's service and let another raise him. I'm no Eli, and this boy's mother will still be raising him, but I like the idea that our children belong to the Lord." Emotion caught his voice in his throat. "It's an honor in being part of training him in the way he should go."

She could tell her brother's tears bothered him, and she gently slugged his arm to lighten the moment. "You sound so mature. Not like the Levi I know."

"Thanks. I'll take that as a compliment. I also *feel* mature— maybe because I'm a father now."

She smiled. "And it sounds like you've been reading your Bible."

Levi nodded. "Some. I have been trying to make time in my day."

"That's gut. I think you should. It makes all the difference. You need to make it a priority."

Levi shifted in his seat, and she could tell their conversation was entering dangerous territory.

"But enough about that." She pushed off from the porch step and stood. "You don't need me telling you."

His gaze softened and she was thankful he hadn't reacted like some of the women. In her own quiet time, she brought each of them up in her prayer. She also prayed that God would show her how to be gentle. The Lord Jesus desired change in others, but His way wasn't always hers.

"Do you need anything from me? I can make you a sandwich or watch the baby if you wish to rest."

He shook his head. "I am fine. I have a few things I need to tell Sam—about our life. About our family."

She pressed her lips together and she crossed her arms over her chest. She felt warm inside as if spring had birthed in her heart too. "All right, I'm going to lay down myself and leave you two boys to your little talk."

Ben got back from his morning jog, and noticed an envelope from Annie from the West Kootenai Kraft and Grocery waiting for him on his bed. Just seeing the store's name on the return address label caused his heart to jump into his throat. Ben was already sweaty, but a rush of heat traveled over him as a image flashed in his mind. It was of Marianna sitting across the table from him at the store. Her eyes were bright as laughter poured from her lips. He bit his lip and tried to swallow down the emotion. It didn't matter how much wishing he did, praying they did, that was a place they'd never be together again. His gut ached realizing that.

He tore open the envelope, wishing Annie had somehow managed to smash down some baked goods and include them inside. No luck. Instead there was a small stack of mail and a note from Annie written on blue and white stationery.

Dear Ben,

> *We sure miss you around these parts. Every time Jenny goes down to Eureka she comes back with those tabloid magazines that show pictures of you standing in the line at Starbucks or climbing off your tour bus. Sarah told me to tell you that she doesn't understand why you'd pay five dollars for a cup of coffee when it's only one dollar here at the store. Millie says to tell you that she bought your CD for everyone on her Christmas list. (All of us in these parts can attest to that.) Edgar says you need a hair cut.*

> *Edgar also kept bugging me because your mail was stacking up. I threw out all the junk mail and here are the bills and such. I hope you make it up to these parts soon. If you do let me know, we can have a concert here at the store. I reckon it wouldn't be near as fancy as those places you're playing in these days, but you'll never have a crowd with bigger smiles and more love pouring from their hearts as all of us.*

> *Love you lots!*

> *Annie*

Ben looked through the mail. Annie was right. Most were just bills and those were already being taken care of through automatic payments. But something caught his eye.

A handwritten letter. From James Folk. He'd prayed for that name before—many times. It was one of the kids he wrote to.

Seeing the letter from him was almost as exciting as receiving a Christmas card from Marianna. He tore it open.

Dear Mr. Stone,

> *I'm sorry it's taken me so long to write you back. It's been almost a year since you wrote after I got caught for drinking and driving. I read your letter back then—well, at least most of it. I wasn't very interested at the time. Your talk of God was something a guy who was enjoying doing his own thing didn't want to hear at the time.*
>
> *Then, when my mom was helping me pack up my things for college, we found your letter again. She recognized your name. We wondered if you were the singer who my mom likes. We checked online and found out you were. I took that letter to college with me because, well, because I never had a letter from someone famous before.*
>
> *At college I found out my roommate Mick was a Christian. This bummed me out at first, but the more I watched him, the more I wanted to be more like him. He seems content nearly all the time and not caught up*

with all the drama of college. Remembering you were a
Christian, too, I pulled out the letter again.

I've read it at least once a day for the last month.
And the more I read it, the more sense it made. The
weird thing was that my roommate was telling me some
of the same things you wrote in your letter. I thought that
must be God talking to me, because things like that just
don't happen.

So what I wanted to write and tell you is that last
night I prayed the prayer you included in the letter. I'm
going to tell my friend tomorrow. I know he'll be excited,
but I wanted to have a day to just let it sink in. I feel a
difference already. I'm more excited about my future.
Mostly I have hope. I just wanted to write and tell you
that. Just think—I'm never gonna be alone again. I know
God will be with me wherever I go.

I know you're busy with concerts and stuff so don't
feel you have to write me back, but if you do I included
the address to my dorm. Thanks again for writing. It
means a lot. And I'm gonna have to tell my mom she was
wrong. You're not cool because of your music. You're cool
because you took the time to write to a guy like me.

Thanks again,
James

Ben wiped away the tears he hadn't realized he'd been crying
and sank down onto his knees, next to his travel bed.

"Thank You, God." He not only thanked God for this kid's
salvation—which was something to rejoice about—but also for
letting him know he was making a difference.

He pulled out his notebook and looked over a list of kids' names he'd written letters to since he'd been on the road. He knew now that his job was to just keep sending the letters. It was up to God to impact the people He chose, wherever and whenever He chose.

"God be with them. Be with Roni, and Claire, and Dean, David, Eric, Kennisha. Let them know You love them. Let them know that when they turn to You that You'll have good plans for them, even when it feels like they're on a bus headed to who knows where . . ."

CHAPTER SIXTEEN

*E*ven with the bright lights on him Ben saw the older man. He looked familiar, like someone Ben used to know. He nodded at Ben and waved. It wasn't the wild wave of a fan but a soft wave of familiarity. *Do I know this guy?*

Ben tried to keep his mind on his music, but at the same time he wracked his brain trying to remember where he'd met the man. Maybe a former teacher or coach from school?

No, he would have remembered that.

As the concert started to wind down, the energy in the room grew. The letter from James had renewed him, his passion. Reminded him that sharing God's truth changed lives. He looked past the bright lights and scanned the crowd. God had given him a platform, a message, for a purpose.

The cheers from the crowd increased. Everyone waited for the song he was most well-known for. But before he sang about the warm cabin and the man who needed a wife, Ben set down his guitar and approached the mic.

"You know behind every song there's a story. When I first started this tour I would talk about the young woman I fell in love with in the mountains of Montana. I shared how my house seemed emptier after I met her because she wasn't in it, and everyone like that story." He wiped at the smile on his face. "It was a good tearjerker. Seems people love to cry." Laughter carried across the audience.

"But that was just part of the story. See, there's a reason I ended up in Montana." Then Ben told about how he'd been caught up in the wrong kinds of things and how good people he cared about were hurt.

And killed.

"I was a broken man after that. My stupidity had caused another's death. When I went up to Montana I found peace there, but I didn't know why. It was during that time I started reading my Bible. I started getting to know some of the good folks that called West Kootenai home, and they invited me to church.

"Sittin' on that pew I heard about a Dude who knew everything I'd ever done—everything—and loved me anyway. Not only that, He didn't want me to carry the pain of those mistakes any longer. In fact, He gave His life so I wouldn't have to."

"Preach it, brother!" someone called from the back.

Ben smiled. "I prayed a simple prayer that first Sunday. I told Jesus He could have my life if He'd take my sin with it. The amazing thing was He gave me more back—peace, joy, love, Himself."

Claps erupted around the auditorium.

"And that, my friends, is the backdrop for this song. I'm still praying for a good wife, but until then I have peace knowing God is by my side. With each mile my tour bus drives I find myself surrendering more and more to Him—to God's will and God's way." As the claps grew louder, Ben picked up his guitar and started playing the song that everyone had been waiting for.

"Every warm cabin needs a good wife," he sang.

After the show, Ben wasn't surprised to see the older guy from the audience standing outside his dressing room as he exited.

"Hey, Ben." The guy patted Ben's back.

Who *was* this man? "Hey yourself."

"So I see that Roy sucked you in again. Put you on the road." The man chuckled.

Ben stood straighter. Now he knew they'd met before, but where?

The man extended his hand.

Ben took it, shook, and then released it. "I'm sorry. I know that I know you but . . ."

The man laughed and ran his hand through his graying hair. "I'm sorry. I think we only met once, years ago. The first time you were on tour. I'm Denny Fairweather."

"Denny." Ben slapped his leg. "Of course. The songwriter. I should have known. I think I used two or three of your songs on my first CD. And I have two of your songs on this new one. No wonder you were smiling so big as I sang them. Wow." Ben studied the man's eyes and saw something there. It wasn't just the finding of a long lost friend. He saw a peace that he recognized. "It's so good to see you!"

Denny nodded. "Yeah, I feel the same. It was a great crowd, lots of energy. And they seemed to like my songs, which is a plus."

Ben studied the man. He looked like an average guy you'd find standing in front of you at the grocery store line. Well, except for the fact that his talent for writing music was legendary—at least to Ben.

Ben squeezed the older guy's shoulder. "Want to head out and get some coffee? I'd love to catch up."

Denny's face brightened. "Sure. I'd consider it an honor."

Ben chuckled. "Well, that makes two of us then. And since you're more familiar with the area, I'll let you lead the way."

They went to a little diner not far from the civic center where the concert had been held. It was the kind of diner that had been around fifty years and nothing had changed. The booth had red vinyl seats and chrome accents. There were a few people scattered around the booths, and from the way they all chatted back and forth, it appeared they were regulars. As Ben looked at the menu offerings: meatloaf, Reuben sandwiches, BLTs, he guessed they hadn't changed the menu in fifty years either.

It felt strange to be here with the man whose songs he sang as his own. The guys from the band had gone out with a group of women—true groupies. Ben's heart grew sad at the thought.

"So, have you been on the road long?" Denny took a sip of coffee.

Ben nodded. "I think this is my twenty-fifth show and I have, uh, about two dozen more."

"So, it's the midpoint."

"Yeah."

"And after that, are you going back to record more songs?"

"That's the plan. I'm supposed to be writing them as we go along, but too often I'm distracted. I like looking outside the bus window and seeing parts of the world I've never seen before." He didn't tell Denny that as he looked out the window he often thought of Indiana. They were only a few states away. He was closer to Marianna than he'd been in a long time. He took another bite of his pie. "Of course, my hope is that you'll come up with some new stuff and save my skin."

Denny chuckled. "Oh, I have a few more songs up my sleeve. I was hoping Roy would request some more. In fact that's the reason I came. It always helps me write better when I get to know the singer I'm writing for. So tell me, Ben, about that song. The one about the cabin. Were you writing about someone special? You never really said anything about her tonight."

"Yeah. I thought she was someone pretty special. I don't know what she thought about me. I hoped for a while that she liked me, but it never went anywhere."

"Do you think it will someday?"

"No, no it won't. We're too different. She moved away from where we both used to live, and I don't even know if I'll see her again." Pain pierced Ben's heart as he said those words.

He paused for a moment and tried to figure out what else to say—how to explain Marianna without mentioning that she was Amish. Marianna wasn't beautiful in comparison to supermodels or movie stars. She didn't wear fitted and stylish clothes. Her hair didn't fall in soft waves around her shoulders. But there was something about her he couldn't forget. Her gentle spirit, her inner beauty, her heart for God . . .

And her smile.

"She's just a simple woman—simple on the outside, but inside anything but," he finally said. "She has a sense of humor and loves to help people. She's an amazing cook . . ." He let his voice trail off.

Denny cocked an eyebrow. "So I have to ask. Why are you here talking with me instead of in that cabin of yours with her?"

Ben took a bite of his pie. "Well, mostly because she chose a different path. A different man. She left . . . and well, I didn't like sitting around there waiting and hoping that she'll come back."

Denny tapped his fork against the table, as if bothered by Ben's words. "And you didn't go after her?"

"No." Ben shook his head. "I've been praying about it . . . and well, I'm waiting for God to let me know when—if—the time is ever right."

"Maybe that's why I'm here." Denny grinned. "To prod you on."

"Are you saying that God sent you to tell me that?"

Denny shrugged. "Well, I haven't heard a loud voice from heaven, but I did feel a nudging to come and meet you. I liked what you shared tonight about what God did with your life. I have a similar story. In fact, I used to tour too. I played in that civic center many a times."

Ben studied the man's face. He wasn't sure why, exactly, but he knew he needed to pay attention. "So why aren't you still on the road? Your music is good. Really good. And your voice is too. I've heard the demos."

"God gave me a talent. I'll confess that. The thing is that just because I'm a singer doesn't mean I need a stage. He's shown me a different way."

Ben's throat tightened. Could that be possible for him? To find a place to settle? To not have to struggle with the traveling, the band, the women? Could he have a family and a home and still write and sing for God...and let God show him how to use his songs from there?

Goose bumps rose on his arms. *God, is this message from You? If it is, I want it . . . I want what You have for me. I'm ready for it. Ready to surrender all.*

"I want to hear more." Ben finished off his pie and then motioned to the waitress to bring him another piece. "I wanted to hear how God led you to songwriting, Denny. I gotta hear how you do it . . . how your songs make a difference without you being on stage."

"Sure. Of course."

Ben folded his hands and placed them on the table, wishing he could calm his pounding heart. "I also want to talk to you more about Marianna . . . you're the only one I've told her name to. I want to know if you think I should go to her . . . because suddenly something inside tells me it's time. Now's the time."

Ben's heartbeat quickened as his cab approached the civic center. Denny's house was in the opposite direction and he still had a long drive tonight. Ben told Denny he didn't mind catching his own ride. Ben smiled and his head bobbed along to the jazz music the taxi driver played on the radio. In fact from the way he felt inside—the new hope he had—he almost could have walked on air back to the bus.

Yet Ben's euphoric feeling sank as the taxi drove closer. He gripped the door handle, afraid to open it.

A police car was parked in front of the bus and a policeman stood outside the door, talking to their bus driver.

"What did the guys do this time?" He paid the taxi driver and then strode up the bus.

"Hey, officer, is there a problem?"

"You Ben Stone?"

"Yeah?" A cold sensation traveled down his body. "Oh man, no one's hurt are they? I told those guys to watch themselves."

The officer shook his head. "It's nothing like that. I'm here because there's a warrant out for your arrest."

"My *arrest*?" Ben took a step backward. "I'm sorry, there must be a mistake."

The officer shook his head and pulled a print out from his pocket. "It says right here that five years ago you were acquitted for the death of Jason Robinson. The deal was you didn't have to spend any time in jail as long as you continued to write letters to teens."

"Yeah, that's right. I've been done that. I've done it every week since I walked out of jail."

"I don't think so, son. Your parole officer's the one who put out the warrant. Seems the letters have been stopped for over a month."

Ben turned to the bus driver. "Frank, can you tell them? I've written the letters. In fact I gave them to you to mail. You can vouch for me—"

Frank lowered his head, and Ben's stomach sank to his knees.

"Man, I'm sorry." Frank turned and took two steps to the dash. He opened a compartment and pulled out a small stack of mail. Returning, he handed it to Ben. "I've been meaning to find a post office, but you know how Roy is about sticking to a schedule."

Ben stared at the letters in Frank's hands, then he took them and turned to the officer. "You can see what the misunderstanding is, officer. I'm really sorry about this. I'll make sure they make it into the mail tomorrow."

The officer shook his head. "That's not going to work, Mr. Stone. I'm not the judge and jury here. I'll take those letters for evidence, but I'm afraid I'll have to take you in. It'll be up to the judge in L.A. to decide."

"So . . . I'm under arrest?" Ben swallowed hard. Roy's fury filled his mind. It had been a simple mistake . . .

"I'm so sorry. I can testify." Frank looked from Ben to the officer and back to Ben again. "I'm so sorry."

The officer lifted a hand. "I'd be happy to take your statement, but right now I need to ask Mr. Stone to follow me to my car."

Ben sat in the small interview room of the Los Angeles jail staring at a two-way mirror. Did anyone watch from the other side?

When he'd first been driven away in the police car panic overtook him. What about the tour? All the fans who'd already purchase tickets? The media?

Sure enough, when he exited the L.A. airport in handcuffs, the media was waiting. Cameras flashed, questions shouted.

Ben scrunched down in his chair and lowered his face into his hands. "What have I done?" He'd set out to lead a quiet life in Montana, and he ended up on the road. He'd wanted to be part of a community, to build friendships and become a friend. Instead he stood on stage and spoke to crowds. His deepest conversation lately had been with Denny. And then—just when he'd decided to reach out to Marianna—this happened.

How could he go to her now?

"God, are You there?" he whispered into the still air of the room.

Ben didn't know when he'd get out. Didn't know where he'd go and what he'd do when he did. He studied his hands. They weren't the hardworking hands that he'd had in Montana. He didn't recognize them anymore. He didn't recognize himself either as he looked in the mirror. Maybe God didn't recognize him either, with his long hair and trendy clothes. What would Marianna think if she saw him like this—looking like a rock star and sitting in a jail cell? She wouldn't believe it. *He* couldn't believe it.

The door opened. Ben glanced up just in time to see Roy stride in. It wasn't hard to spot the disapproval on his face. He tossed an *L.A. Times* newspaper onto the table in front of Ben.

"Have you read today's headline?"

Ben shook his head. "This isn't the Holiday Inn. It's not like they serve me coffee and a paper in the morning."

He dared to glance down at the paper. It was opened to the Entertainment section and an image of his face filled most of the page. *"Every warm jail cell needs a good wife?"* the headline read.

"Ha ha, very funny." Ben folded his arms in front of him.

Roy sat across from him. "What were you thinking, Ben?" He drummed his fingers on the tabletop. "How hard is it to find a post office and drop the letters into a slot?" Ben saw more questions flint through Roy's eyes. Questions he didn't ask. Had word got back to Roy about other things—how he "testified" on the stage? Roy studied him as if trying to figure out who this stranger was.

"I messed up."

With the declaration, Roy's squared shoulders softened and the hard jut of Roy's chin lowered a notch. He ran a hand through his graying hair. "It's not the end of the world, I suppose."

Ben sighed. "So tell me the damage."

"Well, your tour's cancelled, but we expected that to happen. They got one of the old Backstreet Boys who's trying to resurrect his career to take your place. You know, Ben, you screwed up, but the law chose to make an example of you. They ran with it. If you would have been in Montana and missed some letters you might have gotten a phone call. They blew it out of the water because of your newfound fame." Roy cleared his throat. "So we're going to help them."

"Excuse me?"

"I've talked to the judge and we're setting up a press conference." Roy glanced in his watch. "Someone should be here in ten minutes to take you to the shower and give you a clean jail cell uniform." Roy pursed his lips and nodded. "Prison-cell orange is a good color on you."

Ben raised his hands. "Wait, wait, you want me to talk to the media about this? Won't it hurt my good-guy image you've worked so hard to build?"

"Actually no. I want you to tell the truth. I want you to tell everyone how you messed up and how you've changed. I've heard that you shared a little about it at yesterday's concert. You can do it again."

For the first time since he saw that cop car, the burden on Ben's shoulders lightened. "Really? You know I'm going to mention God."

Roy smiled. "Well, I heard lots of people last night give Him the thumbs up, so that might not be too bad."

CHAPTER SEVENTEEN

evi walked from the field to the house, wiping his brow with his handkerchief. The scent of soil clung to him but he didn't mind. It felt good to work hard and know that he was providing for his family.

He and Naomi's father, Mose Studer, had been putting seed in the ground. They'd been out since sunrise, and now it was nearly dark. Their only breaks the whole day had been dinner and supper, which Naomi's younger sister Charity had brought out to them in metal pails.

Levi walked into the house expecting to find Naomi in her room asleep. Instead she was sitting in the rocking chair. She rocked ever so softly with Samuel asleep against her chest. Her dress was damp near her collarbone, beneath the baby's open mouth. Naomi's long red hair was down as if she'd been brushing it out and hadn't had the chance yet to put it up in her sleeping kerchief. Naomi looked up and smiled at Levi as he entered.

He stopped short and sucked in a slow breath.

"What?" Her eyes widened. "Is something wrong?"

He neared her and pulled a simple dining room chair closer so they sat knee to knee. "No, nothing's wrong at all. I—I just don't think I've ever seen you look so beautiful."

Pink tinged her cheeks, causing her freckles to disappear. "I don't think—"

"Shhh . . . Levi lifted a finger and placed it to her lips. "Don't argue with me. I know yet what I'm talking about."

She nodded, smiled, and adjusted the baby so she was cradling him in her arms.

Levi reached out a finger to stroke his son's smooth skin, then realized his hands were still dirty. Soil clung to him. He should go get washed up, but he wasn't ready to leave them—not just yet. "Has Sam been good today?"

"*Ja*. Nothing to deserve a talkin' to yet."

They sat there in quiet comfortableness, content to marvel over the baby.

After having Samuel, Naomi had moved to the dawdi haus, too. She had taken his old room, Marianna had the guest room, and Levi slept on the couch. When he was able to sleep, that is. When he wasn't wide-awake and overwhelmed at being a father and, soon, a husband.

He stood. "Be right back."

After washing up and changing his clothes, Levi returned and reached toward Samuel. "May I?"

Naomi nodded. "*Ja*, that would be nice. I never realized such a tiny little guy could get so heavy."

With slow movements and tender hands, he took the slumbering baby. Samuel's breathing quickened but his eyes remained closed.

Levi settled his son in his arms. "So, I was talking to your dat today."

"*Ja*, what did he say?" Naomi moved the laundry basket and found her sleeping kerchief. With precise movements she pinned it on her head.

"He said that we can get married now. If it's all right with my parents, we can go ahead and set a date."

"Really?" She turned and pink again flushed her freckled cheeks. Then she bit her lower lip with her perfect, white teeth. "Your parents, they won't have a problem with it, will they?"

"No. They wondered why we were waiting. Of course they don't know—" Levi halted his words, but he could tell from Naomi's face that she knew what he was going to say: *"They don't know that Samuel is not my son."*

The thing was, Levi felt like this boy *was* his. He knew he'd protect him with his life. He was ready to commit to Naomi. Ready to commit to Samuel too. As far as he was concerned, the boy would never know any father but him.

He'd see to that.

Ben followed the officer to the mini-stage they'd created in the police precinct and sat in a gray metal chair. Two dozen reporters fanned around them, their cameras set. He looked to Roy and then back to the crowd. They told him he could start when he was ready.

Ben began by telling of his first tour. He told of how hard fame had been on a young man. "I didn't quite go off the deep end, but it was close." He saw one of the female reporters in the front row smile. "Soon I found myself caught up with women and booze . . . and I partook plenty of both."

He shared about the party at his place and how when he went to bed Jason had been passed out on the couch. "When I went in the next morning his face was blue. When I ran to him he was cold. I tried to find his pulse. My buddy and I called 911, but it was too late. He was gone.

"For the last five years I've been writing letters to teens who've abused alcohol, telling them my story and asking them to reconsider their paths before they lost a friend or even their own lives. Some have written back.

"I regret to say that in the last month I've been on the road and I failed to get those letters sent. I just want my fans to know that I'm accepting my error and will pay the consequences, whatever they may be." His voice caught in his throat and tears moistened his eyes. All noise around the room stilled. A few of the male reporters looked away.

His foot tapped as he saw the cameras focused on his face. "I want to take this time to talk to those out there who might have a problem like I had. If you're an underage drinker and think you're cool, know there is nothing cool about burying a friend. Jason missed out on getting married, having kids, buying a hot rod . . ."

He lifted his lips in the slightest smile. "Or maybe you're like me and you have a void inside and you're just trying to fill it. I felt like I was missing out on something. I thought the next can of beer or the next pretty girl would make everything better. They never did. They only made things worse. The only thing that can fill that void in your life is a relationship with Jesus Christ. He knows you better than anyone. He gave His life to take away your sin and—"

A reporter in the front row cleared his throat and then signaled to his cameraman to cut off the recording. The man turned off his camera and a few others did the same. Still, some stayed on him, so Ben continued, his voice rising in fervor.

"I messed up and if I were to ask around in this jail I bet a lot of others have messed up too."

Laughter sounded from some of the reporters.

"But I know one thing to be true. When I asked Jesus to fill me with His life, the only way He could do that was to remove all the old stuff that remained. I'm a different man than I was back then. Sure I mess up still, but at least I know where to go when I need it—to God."

He nodded, signaling that the interview was done. Ben looked to the officer next to him and started to stand, but the guard motioned for him to remain where he was.

"Mr. Stone, Mr. Stone!" Each reporter tried to call louder than the others.

He pointed to one in a rumpled brown suit. The man stood. "First, I have to say I'm thankful for you telling the truth and standing up for what you've done. You don't know how rare this is for someone too fess up to their mistakes. Second, I have to ask what the woman thinks of this?"

Ben cocked an eyebrow. "The woman?"

"You know, the one from the song," another reporter called out to him.

A small burst of laughter split Ben's lips. "Truthfully? I haven't communicated with her in a while, but I doubt she even knows."

Another reporter, a short woman with frizzy red hair raised her hand. Ben signaled to her.

"Mr. Stone. I've been to Montana, to the area where you used to live, and since you're being honest I have to ask a question. Is the reason this woman isn't aware of your present circumstances because she's Amish?"

All eyes turned his way, and the cameramen who'd started to put away their cameras pulled them out again. He sat a little straighter. How should he answer that question? He wasn't ashamed of the truth, but he didn't want any reporters to start snooping around West Kootenai.

He rose, signaling to the officer that he was done. "No comment."

"Thank you, Mr. Stone!" the woman called over the noise of the other reporters. "I believe you just answered my question."

The police car drove Ben to the airport, and Ben noticed Roy standing next to the private jet. When the car stopped the officer opened the back door and let Ben out.

"Mr. Stone, you're free to go."

"Thanks." He stretched out his hand and shook the officer's hand. Then Ben turned and strode to the plane.

The officer cleared his throat. "Uh, excuse me?"

Ben paused and turned.

The officer reached into his car and pulled out a CD and a pen. "Would you mind signing this for my daughter? Her name is Moriah."

Ben reached for it. "This is a first."

Roy was quiet, thoughtful until the plane took off. Then he leaned forward and a smile lit his face.

"You hit it out of the park. The media is going nuts. We have a lineup of interviews planned. I thought we could set them up in Montana. They can get a view of the mountains—"

"No. Roy, no." Ben held up his hands. "That's not going to work. I can't do that to my friends. That's the whole point. It's a quiet place."

"Okay, well. We'll give you a week or so to relax, to settle down, maybe write a few songs and we can fly you—"

"You're not getting it. I'm done. At least for a while." He pressed a hand to his forehead. "I need time to figure things out. I thought I needed to make a way to support a wife, but this . . . this isn't me."

"You." Roy gritted his teeth and growled out the word. "I should have known. You messed things up last time. Why did I think things would be any different?"

Ben didn't know what to say. He felt ten again, getting reprimanded for not getting good enough grades.

"You have no idea what you're throwing away. You're at the top. You've got the attention of a nation . . . do you think you can just walk away? What do you think you're going to do now?"

"I don't know. Maybe write a few songs. I haven't really thought about it."

Roy threw up his hands. "Yeah, well have you thought about what this does to me—to my reputation? How am I going to explain?"

"I don't know what to say. I'm sorry."

Roy set his lips in a grim line. He grabbed a plastic water bottle and threw the cap across the cabin. Ben knew that if they were anyplace other than on an airplane Roy would have stalked off. But there was no place to go. It was still a four-hour flight to Glacier International Airport. So instead Roy just sat there, glaring at Ben—who'd never truly understood the cliché "If looks could kill" until this moment.

CHAPTER EIGHTEEN

The spring air smelled of pine trees and sunshine, and Ben took a deep breath as he strode up the wooden-planked sidewalk to the West Kootenai store. Beyond the store a red barn sat in a green meadow. Beyond that, rolling hills covered with pines, and beyond that, jagged mountain peaks rose into the clear sky.

"Home," he said to himself as he entered the store.

"Ben!" Sarah waved from where she was stocking store shelves. He'd been back a few days and each time he entered the store he was greeted with a wave and smile. He liked that. His friends had asked little of his concert tour and had hardly mentioned his arrest and press conference. He liked that even better. To them he was Ben, their friend, not Ben the recording artist. And that's why he'd come home.

If only . . .

He shook his head, pushing thoughts of Marianna out of his mind.

Ever since he'd gotten off the plane he'd been second-guessing his decision. Maybe because the messages on his phone and the e-mails hadn't stopped. Some for media interviews, others for private concerts. All offered to pay well, and as he'd looked around his small cabin, he dreamed of putting away more money for a nicer house. Besides, he didn't like the fact that Roy was hurting from his decision. He'd picked up the phone a few times to call and apologize—and maybe to work out a deal that would help them both—but each time there was a stirring inside that told him to wait.

Lord, give me an answer. Show me the right way.

He grabbed a handheld shopping cart and pulled his shopping list from his jean's pocket.

The door opened behind him, the small bell jingled, and he turned. A stranger walked in—or was it a stranger? There was something familiar about him. Ben had seen the man before. A memory stirred.

Yes. He knew him. The last time Ben had seen him was in L.A., when Ben was still in high school. Tyler Parison. He'd climbed Mt. Everest at age thirteen. The youngest person ever to do so. He'd written one best-selling book, and then another. By eighteen there were talks of a TV series. Then . . .

Parison just disappeared. There'd been rumors that he'd moved to the northwest, but no one knew for sure where he was.

Ben looked again. It was Parison all right. He was tall, but stoop-shouldered. His black hair touched his shoulders.

A woman entered behind him, a baby on her hip. Another boy, who looked to be four or five, trailed them, carrying a stick.

Ben smiled their direction as he pulled two cans of baked beans off the shelf and placed them in his shopping basket. The family made their way to the restaurant and settled around a booth. Their heads leaned over the menu as the small boy discussed an upcoming Easter egg hunt and the baby pulled napkins from the dispenser. They seemed like a regular family, nothing the media found interesting. Something stirred inside Ben—

Envy.

Not for all the guy had been, but that he'd had the guts to walk away.

Is that Your answer, Lord?

Annie approached. "Do you want to see something?" She patted Ben's shoulder. "I got a package in the mail."

He nodded and set the basket on the counter. Then he followed her to the office, pausing just inside the doorway. A quilt lay on Annie's desk, draping over it, a covering of beauty. Blue, brown, gray, and green . . . the pattern was obvious. The layers of fabric displayed lakes and hills and mountain peaks. Beautiful.

"It's Montana." She smiled.

"That it is. Marianna?" His heart ached as he said her name.

"Yes, she'd been promising to make me a quilt ever since . . ." Annie tucked a strand of blonde hair behind her ear. She didn't finish. She didn't need to.

Ever since she gave the first quilt to me.

He took another step forward and fingered the edge, appreciating her neat stitching. "She did an amazing job."

"She always was a great worker. I miss her around here. She wasn't here for even a year, but Montana seems emptier without her." Annie walked to her desk chair and sat. She folded her hands and placed her elbows on the quilt, leaning forward.

"You know, I need to apologize to you, Ben. I'm glad you're back. Saying what I said to you when you left, it wasn't right. It's been bugging me."

Ben's eyebrows furrowed. "I'm sorry. I don't know what you mean."

"You're being kind." She offered a sad smile. "I put my foot in my mouth when I told you to stay away from Marianna. I told you that pursing your interest in her would only hurt her, hurt her family. I thought that her being Amish and you . . . well, not Amish . . . that it would never work out."

Ben nodded. Annie had been firm, speaking with conviction. He had taken her words to heart. "You were right."

"Was I?" She shook her head. "I thought I was, but I was speaking outta turn." She rose and moved to the window, crossing her arms over her chest and looking out to the potholed gravel parking area. "I had to be so firm with my words because I was afraid . . ."

"For Marianna?"

A long sigh escaped her lips. "Afraid for myself. My heart. The questions I was asking myself and didn't want to answer."

"I'm sorry. You must be talking female or something. I don't understand."

"I'm talking in circles, I know." The older woman turned back and looked at him. "I'm talking about my feelings for Ike. You don't get to be my age and single without doing a good job of pushing people out of your life. Oh, I'm all nice and dandy until I find myself attracted to someone. It scares me. I long for love but my fear of rejection and a broken heart is far stronger."

"Okay, I get that. But what does it have to do with me? With Marianna?"

"Don't you see, Ben? If you could fall in love with an Amish person and have everything turn out okay . . ." She swallow hard. "If you and Marianna worked things out. If you could figure out your relationship and live in harmony with the community—and with the blessing of God—then I wouldn't have any excuse. I'd have to open my heart to Ike. I had no right to tell you to walk away and let her be. That was my own fears talking. I hate to think that because of my words you could have missed out on the love of your life."

"You think a little highly of yourself, don't you?" Ben chuckled and cocked an eyebrow. "The truth is you weren't just the only one who was telling me to slow down, to back away. God spoke the same to my heart and . . . well, as much as I respect you, Annie, He has a little more pull."

She opened her arms and wrapped him up in a quick hug. "I was so worried I'd ruined everything. I tried to call your cell phone a few times when you were on the road, but I didn't want to bother you with the concerts and everything. But well, Ben, after hearing the song on the radio and realizing it was yours . . . and that you were talking about Marianna, I've felt just awful."

"It wasn't just you, Annie, really it wasn't. God was getting His point across. He still is."

"Is He still saying to stay away? To let her go?"

"No." He sighed. "I feel Him telling me to be ready."

"Ready to go to her?"

Ben shrugged. "I'm not sure. I just figure that if God could create everything we see, then if He wants me to make a move—when He wants me to make a move—He's clever enough to figure out how to let me know."

CHAPTER NINETEEN

*R*uth sat at the kitchen table. The children were in bed and a gas lamp hung over her, casting light around the room. Abe stared down at the letter from Levi, and a smile touched his lips. He must be reading about their new grandson—his chubby cheeks and light hair. Abe was looking forward to seeing the baby with his own eyes—almost as much as she was.

It was only the second time she'd wished the Amish were allowed to take photographs. She would like to see Samuel's features, to see how similar he looked liked Levi when he was a babe. The other time she'd wished she'd had a photo had been after their daughters' deaths. If only she had one photo—just one to remember them by. Her memory was the only thing that held their captured smiles, and she hoped it never got to the place when those memories faded. The more the years passed, the more their faces had slipped away. And now there would be more changes.

Ruth spread her hand over the table. They wouldn't be in Montana for much longer. After the news of Samuel's birth last month she'd been waiting to hear when Levi and Naomi would have their wedding. Their oldest son had written her to say they'd like to marry in two weeks, and was that too short of notice for them to come? The returning to Shipshewana wasn't the problem. The questions came with what to do with the house there—keep it or sell it?

An even deeper problem . . . was Mark.

Her stomach churned. She could try to avoid him, but the area wasn't that large. If they were there for any length of time she was sure they'd run in to each other. Could her heart handle it? She'd had a hard enough time over the years keeping the emotions at bay. What would she do when she stared into his face? Looked into his eyes?

Ruth let out a sigh. "It seems that we should pack up as much as we can and bring it with us. I can't imagine us having Indiana as our home any more yet, don't you think?"

"Is this what you want, Ruth, to return? To pack our things and come back to Montana for good?"

Ruth picked up David's shirt from the table. He'd caught the sleeve on a tree branch. She pulled out thread and a needle to patch the hole.

"Sometimes I miss the house." The softness of her voice surprised her. "There are memories there. The girls sitting at the kitchen table, sharing stories of silly things back and forth. Looking out the kitchen winda to see their trees growing and stretching into the sky."

Abe nodded, and she could see a battle within his gaze. He had memories too. There were people in Indiana he cared for. He'd built that home, tilled the land. Yet his battle seemed to be for their family now. To plant them in a better place and show them a new way—a way Ruth still struggled to understand.

"We came because of Levi choosing the way of the world . . ."
Abe turned to the window and eyed the snow. "That's not the case
any longer."

"It would be good to be near Levi now. And Marianna." She
bit her lip. "To see the grandbaby would be nice, but the boys
seemed to be settled here. They have good friends and love the
trees and mountains." But in truth, as she thought about returning, it wasn't the boys that worried her. They'd transition back
soon enough. Instead . . .

Ruth's head started to ache. There were so many voices in
Indiana, each stating their opinions. There were so many eyes,
watching her, watching Abe, watching her kids. Accountability
was good, no doubt, but thinking of going back was like picking up a sack full of rocks she hadn't realized she'd been lugging
around until she got to this mountainous place. Then one day,
as she walked through the pines, she realized she was no longer
carrying that burden.

Abe nodded. "Ike said the owners will let us rent here as long
as needed, and I would like to experience West Kootenai as summer nears."

"Another year wouldn't bother me so, but if we think we'll be
here at least that long, I would like my things. My fabric and pat-
terns are back there. All my dishes and gardening supplies. I miss
my own bed and some of my books. If we could afford it I would
like to pack up and bring all of it."

A smile slid onto Abe's face, and she realized they had their
answer.

He rose, took his jacket off the hook and slid it on, then put on
his hat without a moment's hesitation. "I'll go call to Ike and see
what he suggests. He talked before about finding a driver."

She didn't say anything about Abe using a telephone. She just nodded and smiled.

"*Gut.*" Ruth rose and smoothed her skirt with her hands. And at this moment it felt as if her sturdy shoes walked on a floor of clouds.

The truck pulled up and Ruth eyed the trailer on the back. It was bigger than she expected and she figured it was large enough to carry her things. What she didn't bring she could, of course, give to Marianna to start her own house.

The door to the large brown truck opened and a sinking feeling settled in the pit of her gut to see Ben Stone climb from the driver's seat. Without calling out her typical welcome, she turned and stomped back into the house.

"Abe!" Ruth hurried past Ellie, whose eyes were still filled with tears. Joy and the older boys were going with them, but the younger kids were staying with the Shelter family. It would be too much to care for the little ones while packing up the house too. "Abe!"

She gripped the oak handrail and then hurried up the stairs, her heart pounding. She found him in their small closet, zipping up the suitcase with their things.

"I'm here, Ruth. Don't know what you're all worked up about. It's a long drive yet and leaving on time isn't a problem when one's going to be riding for thirty hours."

"I'm not going. We're not going." The words shot from her mouth.

"Why's that?" He turned, his eyebrows *v*-ing. Though he asked a question, his words were more like a statement.

"I cannot believe you did this. He cannot go. Ben Stone cannot go to Indiana."

"Of course he can. He's been touring with his music, but he's back now—you knew that. Says he's always wanted to see Indiana, best part is he's not charging us. He even got a friend to loan him the truck and trailer for free."

She clenched her teeth, attempting to hold back angry words, but they refused to be dammed. "I don't care if we have to pay twice the money. Ben cannot drive us."

Abe took a step toward her. "And why is that?"

"You know why."

"Are you worried about our daughter, Ruth?"

"Of course I am. This . . . seeing him . . . Ben being there can change things."

"If Marianna loves Aaron and wants to marry him as she claims, we should have no worries. Besides, Ben's good company to talk to. More than once we've gotten together to discuss the Bible. He's been patient with all my questions."

The angry feeling that had been rumbling inside Ruth calmed, but just slightly. "Abe Sommer, in all my years I'd not remembered once when you went to the bishop, asking questions about the Bible." She perched a hand on her hip.

Abe rose, carrying the suitcase down the stairs. "That should tell you something, shouldn't it? Sometimes ya don't know how hungry you are till you see a man with a big ole' steak, mashed potatoes, and a generous piece of strawberry pie."

Marianna tucked Samuel's blanket around him as they walked into Davis's Mercantile in Shipshewana. Levi and Naomi had some shopping to do in town and she'd asked to come along. With her Montana quilt finished and shipped to Annie, she needed to get fabric to start another. Naomi was buying groceries, and Marianna thought it would be easier for her to hold the baby while looking at fabric squares than for Naomi while loading up a grocery cart.

Samuel's mouth was slightly open as he slept, and Marianna was sure she'd never seen such a precious face. She headed to her favorite store, A Stitch in Time, when she noticed Mrs. Zook exiting. The woman paused as she saw Marianna approached, and she tipped her lips up in a smile.

"Look at you, Marianna. It's been so long." She stretched out her hand and gripped Marianna's shoulder. "You shouldn't keep yourself a stranger. We are going to be family soon and all."

"*Ja.*"

The woman didn't even cast a glance at the baby.

"I've jest been helping out my brother and Naomi. Little Samuel here has been most *gut*, but he's had colic some. It's amazing how someone so little takes up so much time. But I'll talk to Aaron when I see him. Should be coming over tonight." She rocked the baby as she talked. "It's been since Christmas from when I've been over and I agree that's far too long."

"*Ja, gut.*" Mrs. Zook looked down at the baby. "Tell your brother I offer congratulations?"

"I will—" Music flowing through the store caught Marianna's attention. Her stomach fell and her knees softened. She straightened her shoulders, trying not to give away the lightness flooding her.

It was Ben's voice! She was certain it was his. She'd know it anywhere. "It was *gut* seeing you. I need to pick up some things." Without waiting for Mrs. Zook to respond, Marianna hurried to the back of the store and cocked her head to listen.

Your gray eyes a'dreamin', your smile so warm
could melt all the ice from the cold winter's storm,
And by the March thaw, my soul came to life
When I asked gray-eyed girl to be called my wife.

You settled my heart, you warmed up my life
The day you agreed to be called my wife.

You said:
We're nothing alone, We're everything together
Aches all fade when someone helps you weather
The hard times,
I'll enter your heart, I'll enter your life
Every warm cabin,
Needs a good wife

Her heart did a double-beat. First to hear his voice—to hear Ben's voice all the way in Shipshewana, Indiana—and then to hear him sing about a gray-eyed girl . . . was it possible? Could he be singing about her?

"So you like this song too?" The sale clerk neared, pointing to the speaker from where the music flowed.

Marianna readjusted the baby in her arms. "*Ja*, uh, it's nice. It's the first time I've heard it." She patted her kapp. "I don't take to listening to much music, you know."

"No, of course," the woman clucked her tongue. "Oh, it's been popular for months. He was supposed to do a concert in South Bend next month but it was cancelled."

"He?"

"The singer, Ben Stone."

Hearing his name, heat rose to her cheeks, and she hoped the woman didn't notice. What would the woman think if she were to tell her that she knew Ben—knew him well. In fact, she believed the song was written about her. She shook her head. The woman wouldn't believe her at all. That someone like him could have ever cared for someone like her.

"So, is he going to reschedule?" Marianna tried to keep her voice nonchalant.

"Doubt it." The woman puckered her lips. "He was in jail last I heard. Something to do with killing a friend." The woman shrugged. "I don't keep up with all those entertainers, but a story like that is hard to miss."

CHAPTER TWENTY

*W*ith wide strokes of the broom Marianna swept Aunt Ida's barn. She'd already done the evening chores and was taking her time waiting for Aaron to show up. Aunt Ida had invited them both over for dessert—the first time since the baby was born. Her aunt was sure to have an opinion on all that was happening with Levi and Naomi and their upcoming wedding. Marianna just wanted to make sure she had Aaron by her side when she talked to her aunt. She needed his stability. His presence.

The barn door opened and Aaron stepped through. His eyes fell on hers and in four long strides he was there, sweeping her up in an embrace, pulling her close.

Since hearing Ben's song in the radio she'd been wound up like Aunt Ida's alarm clock, but at the warmth of Aaron's arms, Marianna melted into his embrace.

She wrapped her arms around his neck, her fingertips finding the soft skin between his hair and his shirt collar. She spread open her hands and her palms stroked his shoulder blades and down his arms' tense muscles. His strength overwhelmed her. She needed Aaron's strength right now.

What had the woman meant when she said Ben had been arrested for killing a friend? Surely the woman had been mistaken. Surely it was another singer . . .

Aaron held her as she clung to him, and then he pulled his head back, trying to look at her face. "You doing all right, Mari?"

"Shhh . . ." She snuggled her head into his neck.

"Marianna?"

"I'm all right. I jest missed you that's all."

He held her and she pressed her cheek against his chest. She closed her eyes and told herself to remember this—to hold fast to the feeling of being in Aaron's arms without the questions and concerns of the world pressing in on her.

He pulled back. "So did your parents get off all right?"

She nodded and took a step back. "My uncle Ike called one of Levi's Englisch friends and told him to give us the message. They're coming with a driver to pack up all their things."

"Are you okay with that?" Concern filled Aaron's gaze.

"*Ja*, I believe I am. It's the right decision for the family, although I wish Dat would let Levi and Naomi have our home here. It would be *gut* for their growing family."

Aaron's hands released from around her waist. "*Ja*, too bad." He lowered his head and looked away. "Maybe Levi will have to work hard to build her a home like I built yours. I didna have my father give me a home."

She pulled back and studied his face. There was something behind that statement she couldn't understand. Pride in his own efforts? Disapproval over her brother's decisions?

"Well"—he smiled—"we better get inside, don't you think?"

She nodded, but inwardly cringed. For the first time, Aaron reminded her of his mother. Not so much his words, but the accusation behind them. And as she thought about that, she knew she'd heard such a tone from him before. Not so blatant, but there all the same.

Marianna shuddered and couldn't help wondering . . .

How long would it be until such words were aimed at her?

Marianna had only heard Ben's song once, but she had a hard time shaking the words—his voice—from her mind. The next morning, after helping Naomi with her chores, Marianna headed over to visit her friend Rebecca. Though Rebecca still lived with her parents, she was still set on leaving the Amish. If anyone would understand Marianna's torn emotions, Rebecca would. They packed a small picnic and walked to the creek they'd often visited as children.

They sat underneath a shady tree and new life sprouted up in every direction. Above, two birds chattered and sang and Marianna couldn't help but smile at the gift of bird song.

Yet even though the day was beautiful, Rebecca looked thin, pale. She shivered and scooted so she could have more of the sun's warmth upon her. The slight tremble reminded Marianna of snow upon tree branches in Montana, quivering on a windy day.

Marianna pulled a sandwich wrapped in wax paper out of their brown paper sack and glanced at her friend. "Can I tell you a secret?"

Rebecca's head tipped up and a slight smile lifted her lips. "*Ja*, especially if it's about a certain boy."

"Well . . ." Heat rose to Marianna's cheeks. "*Ja*. It is. I heard something yesterday . . ."

Rebecca gave her her full attention. "Jest looking at your face, Mari, I can tell you're in love. It's what you always hoped, isn't it . . . those feeling all stirred up inside? The knowing of your care for him."

"Yes, well, I didn't know what to expect. And it's not appreciated. I mean, I shouldn't let my feelings be running away like this."

"Not appreciated? You have what you always wanted, who you always wanted. You focused on getting the best, Marianna, and Aaron's that."

Aaron. Marianna nodded. Then, like a knife piercing her between the shoulder blades, she knew she couldn't tell Rebecca that she'd been thinking about Ben.

That had to remain her secret.

Marianna nodded. "He is, isn't he? Everyone in this community respects Aaron."

"So . . . Rebecca scooted nearer. Her eyes sparkled as if a warm candle burned in her gaze. "The secret?"

"The secret." Marianna clasped her hands together. "Um . . . Her mind moved from the memory of holding Ben's guitar to the kind way Aaron had cared for her siblings. Aaron was a good man. "I was just going to say I having a feeling my brothers are going to be more excited about seeing Aaron than me. They got along well when Aaron was in Montana." She blew out a soft breath.

"I doubt that." Rebecca scowled. It was clear she'd been hoping for juicier news. "*Ja*, well, your parents should be coming back soon, right? Then you'll all be together again."

Marianna nodded, but deep down she had a feeling that wasn't going to be the case. How could she explain that things wouldn't be easy here in Indiana? Yes, she'd see them again, but how would Mem would deal with Mark being so close? How would both her parents face leaving their home?

"*Ja*, they should be here tomorrow, jest in time to rest before getting up for church service on Sunday."

"Wait, tomorrow's Saturday?" Rebecca sat up. "That means today's Friday?"

Marianna nodded.

"I thought it was Thursday. I have to work today." Rebecca rose and brushed dirt off her skirt. "I'm sorry, Marianna." She called back over her shoulder as she hurried to her house. "We'll have to do this again, soon!"

"We will!" Marianna called after her. And as she settled back into the grass she realized she was alone. She could use this time to think, to pray. To seek God on things that mattered most to her heart.

Marianna sat near the creek for hours. What a gift. One she hadn't expected. For most of her life she wouldn't have imagined spending a day like this. "Idleness is the devil's worship," Mem had said nearly every day of her life. Her father often joined in, declaring from the very first book of the Bible God told them to work by the sweat of the brow to produce food. She knew her neighbors mistrusted a soft and leisurely life and wanted to keep their children from being lazy, but wasn't there a balance? The Bible talked about Jesus going away to pray and David writing hymns on the hillside. As she sat there, a hymn she knew from childhood rose in her heart.

"*Wo ist Jesus, mein Verlangen, mein geliebter Herr und Freund?*" Where is Jesus whom I long for, my beloved Lord and friend?

Here, her heart told her.

She didn't have her Bible with her, but she played over in mind the special verses she had memorized. She prayed for Aaron, for Ben, for her parents, especially Mem. She prayed that God would break the bonds that remained where they shouldn't be, and strengthen the relationships that should be strengthened.

As she prepared to leave, she thought about what Aaron would say if he knew she'd spent most of the day idle. She considered what Ben would think too—and that brought a smile.

He'd be proud of her. He knew well that idleness with God performed more in one's soul than a week's worth of busy work.

Golden sunlight stretched over the Indiana cornfield as she walked back. Well, at least it would be a cornfield soon. Now it was only dark rich soil. She picked up a clump of dirt and it crumbled in her fingers. Within days a team of horses would be in the fields, breaking up the soil. It amazed her how, if one added too much water, they'd get mud, but with the right amount of light and water and seed, life would burst forth—nourishment. How was it possible one small seed could produce a plant that stretched its arms to the sky?

She wished she'd thought of the power of the seed before she spent time with Ben in Montana. The seed of attraction for him had been planted the moment he helped Ellie get her coloring book out of the puddle with such care.

A laugh slipped through her lips. Ben had talked so sweetly to Ellie not understanding she only understood Pennsylvania Dutch. Was that only a year ago? It seemed like much longer. In fact, it was hard to realize that Ben hadn't always been a part of her life. Her care for him was tucked away in a special part of her heart.

But should it be? Maybe she would have to find a spade to dig it out. Doing so would hurt . . . and that realization helped her to understand her mother even more. And as she walked back to Levi's place, she prayed that God would do some digging in her mother's heart as well as hers.

The trip took longer than expected. A flat tire in Fargo and a touch of food poisoning for Abe through Minnesota slowed them down. They arrived in Shipshewana just as church was being let out. It was being held this week at the Studers' place, which was right next door to the Sommer house.

Ben parked the large truck and trailer out front, and the older boys jumped out and headed to the creek, memories propelling their every step. Ben eyed the large white farmhouse. A porch wrapped around the front. The wooden steps were worn and slightly sagged. The green paint on the porch was worn off on the path to the front door, and he tried to picture the many feet that had journeyed over the spot through the years. Marianna's home.

Mr. and Mrs. Sommer—with baby Joy on her hip—didn't waste a moment heading down the road to see their friends. Ben stood by the truck. Should he follow?

Just as he decided to wait it out, Mr. Sommer turned and motioned to him. "You're welcome to join us. They always have sandwiches after service if you're hungry."

His stomach rumbled, and he walked after them with cautious steps. He'd never been invited to an Amish service back in Montana and he guessed having an Englischer show up for their lunch wasn't common here, either.

As he approached the yard, Ben looked at the people gathered—a sea of women wearing dark dresses, perfectly pressed.

The men wore cotton shirts, suspenders, and straw hats with wide brims. These people seemed more proper, for lack of a better word, than the Montana Amish, like they'd all spiffed up for a funeral. Their eyes studied him and there were only a few smiles. Funny how he felt comfortable singing in front of tens of thousands of people, but his nerves got to him in front of a hundred plain folks.

Ben ran a finger under the collar of his shirt, wishing the ground would open up and swallow him whole. He stepped a little closer to Mrs. Sommer, as if she were his shield of protection from the prying eyes.

An older woman approached Ruth, a smile spreading on her face. "It's *wunderbaar gut* to have you back, but I wished it were for good."

"I know, Ida, but just cause we're going now doesn't mean we'll never be back." Mrs. Sommer looked over the woman's shoulder, scanning the faces. "I do appreciate you caring for Marianna. Did she come today?"

Marianna. At the mention of her name Ben's heart jump-started as if it had been beating at half pace all these months.

"*Ne*, I'm sorry." Ida shook her head. "Poor little Samuel had a fever last night and she stayed to help Naomi with his care."

Ben hung around a while until Mrs. Sommer approached. "You can head back to the house if you'd like. The renters are out and the house is unlocked."

He nodded and walked back up the gravel road. Had Mrs. Sommer sent him back because of his discomfort—or that of her friends and neighbors?

He walked up the steps, the weight of his thoughts slowing his movements. He'd been to the Sommers' house in Montana many times, and it felt strange to realize this had been their home for so many years.

Inside, the whitewashed walls were bare. The door opened into a large common room with the kitchen on one side and the living room on the other. A simple table, with benches running down each side, spanned the two rooms. Ben pressed his lips together as he imagined Marianna sitting there, serving her brothers and sisters. A gas lantern hung over the kitchen sink, and two more were placed around the living room. The couch looked as if it had seen better years, but a brown recliner near the front window appeared almost new. Ben guessed it belonged to the newly married couple who was renting the place.

"It's a beautiful home, a perfect place to raise children."

Ben turned at Mrs. Sommer's voice. She'd followed him in when he was unaware. Mr. Sommer stood there too.

"It seems strange being back. So many memories. Of rocking my babies by the woodstove during cold winter nights." She spoke to Abe more than Ben, and a knowing look passed between husband and wife.

"It was God's will, Ruth." Abe placed a hand on his wife's shoulder, and Ben understood they were talking about the two daughters they'd lost. Ben stepped back, feeling as if he was interrupting a private moment.

He turned back to the front door. "I'll go open up the trailer and you can let me know what needs to be loaded in. There's a few hours of sunlight still and we can get some big stuff loaded up." Without a response he took two long steps to the door and then stopped short. A slim Amish woman stood in the doorway, the sun streaming in behind her made her kapp glow on her head. He didn't recognize her at first—until she spoke.

"Ben?" Marianna's voice was no more than a whisper. "Is that you?"

His heart hammered to the ceiling and back as her voice danced like music to his ears. A thousand words filled his mind—things he wanted to ask her. Things he wanted to tell her. He balled his fists and urged his feet to stay planted. He wanted to hurry toward her. He wanted to pull her into his arms and tell her not a day passed that he didn't think of her.

But instead, he just brushed his hair back from his forehead and smiled. "Yes, Marianna, it's me. It's really me."

Tears sprang to Marianna's eyes, and she didn't know why. She bit her lip and held the tears back, staring at the man she'd been wondering about for so long.

Ben's hair was longer than when she'd last seen him, but he was so much more handsome than she remembered. Her stomach danced, and her chest grew warm, as if all the sunlight streaming through the doorway behind her pooled right inside her heart.

Their eyes locked, and she wanted to tell him she'd heard the song. His soft smile told her that he'd indeed written it for her. There was a depth of love in his gaze she was glad to still see, but she felt guilty for relishing in it so.

Looking past Ben, Marianna's eyes focused on Mem and Dat. Mem's eyebrows were folding down, but was that a smile she saw on Dat's face?

She hurried across the room and her father opened his arms. She ran into his embrace. Her fingers grasped his shirt like they had when she was a child.

"It's so good to see you both. I'm so glad you're back." She turned and placed a soft kiss on her mother's cheek. "And I bet you can't wait to see Samuel. He's so adorable and Levi is a doting dat."

She noted excitement on their faces, but what would they say if they knew the truth? That Levi hadn't fathered a child? To her it proved his love even more. He treated the babe no different than if it had been his own flesh and blood.

She turned back to Ben and cleared her throat. "I am surprised to see you here. I had no idea. In fact . . ." She pointed a finger in the air. "Some woman at the fabric store told me you were in jail." Marianna laughed. "You of all people."

Ben swallowed and the color dropped from his face. Dat's hand squeezed her shoulder. The look, the touch, told her it was true.

Marianna's hand covered her mouth. "No, I'm so sorry . . . you don't have to explain." She mumbled between her fingers.

He shrugged. "Nothing you shouldn't know." He tucked his hands into his jean pockets. "You know about the letters I wrote as part of my parole for my part in my friend's death years ago. The letters didn't get mailed while I was on tour. It's as simple as that . . . it wasn't my fault but it took me off the tour."

Marianna took two steps two him. "I'm so sorry."

"I'm not." He glanced from Marianna to her folks. "I'd rather be here . . . with friends."

She nodded and could tell his words were sincere. Maybe she'd talk to him about the music and his tour later. Maybe if they ever got time alone, but now? Now she just soaked in the fact that he was here—which worried her as much as it pleased her.

And on the heels of that realization came another, more sobering thought.

What will Aaron think to know Ben is in town?

Marianna stood in the hall, looking into her bedroom. It seemed smaller than she remembered, with the simple bed and the chest of drawers. She saw the hooks on the window on which she used to hang a blanket to darken the room at night. It seemed like another girl who'd slept there.

Footsteps sounded from behind her, and without turning she knew it was Ben. He paused behind her and his presence sent shivers coursing through her.

"Anything need to get moved out of this room? We can fit that dresser—"

"No." The word pushed from between her lips. She grasped the doorframe with her hand. "These things aren't going to Montana."

"So this is your room?" Ben squeezed by her and entered, looking around. "This is where you grew up?" He sat on a bed, running his hand over the bedspread. "It's nice."

"Thank you."

Ben stood and walked to the window, taking in the view. "It's beautiful." Then he pointed to the two trees. "I heard your mom saying something about those."

"The trees, yes, they were planted right after the death of my sisters. To remember them . . . although I'm sure my parents will never forget." She stepped into the room. No need to feel uneasy.

This was Ben. He cared about her as a friend and was curious about her life.

She swept her arm. "This room was my sisters', before they died. They slept together on that bed."

Ben bit his lower lip. "That must have been hard, growing up. Being here without them."

Marianna fingered the top hem of her apron. "Actually, it was. I've never told anyone, but I used to hang a blanket over the window at night. I didn't want them looking down from heaven seeing me sleeping in their bed and wearing their dresses."

"I can't imagine, Marianna. I'm so sorry."

She turned to him and smiled. Within a matter of minutes all awkwardness had left. It was just Ben—the one who was so easy to talk to. In fact, more than anything she wished she could sit beside him and share more of her childhood stories. She had a feeling he'd enjoy hearing about her Indiana life.

Voices carried up from downstairs—Mem and Dat talking about what to take and what to leave.

"It was kind for the renters to let my family stay in the house—make a mess of everything," she said. "I appreciate you coming, helping my parents with that."

He shrugged. "That's what friends do."

Marianna stood. "Well, I'm glad you're a *tall* friend." She smiled. "I have some things I can't reach on the top shelf of the closet. Was wondering if you could get them down." Her gaze dropped, as she turned her back to him.

Whistling came from Charlie, walking down the hall with a box of his things. Marianna heard the screen door slam as yet another box of their things was taken to the large trailer outside.

She heard Ben pull the boxes out of the top of her closet and turned toward him. She wasn't sure what was inside, perhaps childhood toys. She hadn't touched those boxes for years—if ever—and the layer of dust on top of them proved it.

As she took the boxes from his hand she noticed a cut on the back of his thumb. It was red and swollen.

"What happened?" She lifted her eyes to meet his gaze.

"Just banged up. Nothing bad."

"I can get some bandages. We have some under the sink downstairs . . . or at least that's where we used to have them." She couldn't remember if those were some of the things Mem had packed up to take to Montana the first time.

"Aw, no, there's no need. I'm just tender from lack of hard work. Too much time plucking guitar strings and not enough on manual labor."

"I heard the song, Ben." She lifted her eyes to him. The way he studied her made her feel beautiful. She touched her kapp and tucked a strand of dark hair back into place. She never felt as beautiful as she did when Ben looked at her.

He nodded and then lifted a hand to her cheek. "Everyone's asked who the girl with gray eyes is . . . it's been my secret. And I can't believe—" Emotion caught in his throat. "I can't believe I'm sitting next to her."

"Don't get all sentimental on me." She rose and opened the box. Old dolls, shoes, and handmade greeting cards inside were nestled inside. "Maybe if you write another song it should be more clear." She grinned. "Might as well just sing my name."

Ben picked up one of her old dolls and eyed it for a moment, then looked back at her. "I would have if I'd known it would be okay with you." His gaze grew intense. "I only attempt to hide my true feelings because of my concern for *you*. I'm not worried about what people think about me . . . about us . . . my concern is for you. So the question is, How would you feel, Mari, if I did sing your name?"

She bit her lip. At first a rush of warmth came to her chest. Her name sung over the radio, playing in stores like the fabric store. Not just here but all around the country. Everyone knowing . . .

Everyone knowing. It would bring as much angst as joy. Not because she didn't think Ben was wonderful. She did. She always would. But letting others know that would mean one thing: that she'd walked away from what her people believed. For she could not stay Amish if she gave her heart to an Englischman.

She met Ben's questioning gaze. "It would mean a lot to me. It would honestly mean a lot." She put an old journal into the box. "And that's the problem."

Ben didn't say anything. He didn't have to.

They both knew how impossible all this was.

Abe and Ruth didn't do much packing since it was Sunday—just prepared everything for the real work that was to happen tomorrow.

Abe was sad he wouldn't be able to see Levi, Naomi, and the baby until tomorrow, due to the baby's fever. More than anything he wanted to embrace his son—to welcome him back into the fold.

"Have the wildflowers bloomed? Has Trapper been good? Oh, you'll have to say hello to Annie and the others for me when you remember." Marianna crossed her arms as if trying to hold in her emotion.

Abe cocked his hat and smiled back at his daughter. She seemed more grown up. He should face the fact his little girl wasn't so little and would be a married woman soon.

Abe sighed. "It sounds like you're missing Montana."

"I am, Dat, and I can see from your eyes you find it funny. You like being right. Don't you?"

"I can't confess that. No good Amish man would. It's prideful you know." He moved to Marianna's side and placed a soft hand on her back. "The good news is that you'll come back and visit us often—once a year at least."

A quick movement of her fingertips wiped away a tear she didn't want him to see.

A conflict waged within Abe. He knew if he asked Marianna to return with them, she would. Not because she'd feel obligated to obey, but because she cared for that place and its people.

Yet he couldn't take her away from all she ever wanted—to have her own home and family and to be married to Aaron. Abe also couldn't help but compare Aaron with himself—a good Amish man. Aaron cared for his daughter. He was a hard worker. He'd done everything right to win Marianna's heart.

Pain tinged Abe's heart. He'd spent so many months all those years ago questioning if Ruth would choose him—choose to remain Amish and become his wife. He'd had no greater joy than when she'd come to him and confessed he was her choice. There had been rough days and hard spots after that, but she'd chosen him. Abe had seen the same joy on Aaron's face when Marianna agreed to be his wife. And while Aaron's love for Marianna was clear, was that enough? Did she want more?

And, even beyond that . . . did God want more for his daughter?

CHAPTER TWENTY-ONE

The rooster outside had roused Ruth early, and she made her way downstairs to the kitchen. It was strange being here again, everything so familiar, yet so foreign. Each inch of this house had a memory attached to it, or so it seemed. But it wasn't home. There were no whispering pines outside the windows or neighbors down the road that knelt with her in prayer, speaking words aloud to God's heart.

On the table Abe had left his Bible open. Ruth sat down and read the section he had underlined.

"The Lord your God is with you, the Mighty Warrior who saves. He will take great delight in you; in his love he will no longer rebuke you, but will rejoice over you with singing."

"Imagine that." She whispered the words aloud although no one was in the room. Imagine the God of the universe cared about her enough to sing over her with a song.

She looked out the window to the trees that had been planted in memory of her daughters. She read the Scripture again and tears filled her eyes and rolled down her cheeks.

He delights in me.
He no longer rebukes me.
He saves.

When she returned all those years ago—full-hearted to Abe—she'd asked God's forgiveness too. She'd walked away from a relationship with Mark but the realization of what she'd done—where her emotions had led her—had hurt so many. She'd broken God's heart. She'd sent ripples of shock through the community.

After time, the pain faded from Abe's eyes, and those in the community seemed to forget her shameful actions, but her own guilt had trailed behind her like untied apron strings. And then, after her daughters' deaths, those strings tightened, cutting off her ability to breathe.

It's punishment for how you acted, a voice in her mind told her. *You hurt those you love and now you'll know what hurt—real hurt—is.*

She hadn't told Abe she felt that way. He carried his own guilt, having been the one who fell asleep while driving the buggy. She'd told him over and over again that it wasn't his fault.

Mostly because it was hers.

But what if . . .

What if the accident happened just because they lived in a world where bad things struck everyone, good or bad? What if the accident had nothing to do with her?

Peace fluttered in her heart like a dozen butterflies. God loved her. God forgave her.

Ruth rose and washed her hands in the sink, and then started washing some of the strawberries that one of their neighbors had dropped off last night. She knew that sometime during the week she'd see Mark, and before that she'd have more time to pray. To listen to the song her heart told her God was singing over her.

Going to Montana for good, they'd leave behind many things. She wanted her feelings for Mark to be one of those things. If she kept turning to God and reading His Word—remembering His love for her—maybe that would be possible.

Over the years she'd heard rumors about Mark. He'd been married two times, maybe three. He had children from a few different women. A foul taste rose in her mouth to think she could have been caught up in that. Ruth wrinkled her nose and then took a bite of a strawberry hoping to wash the taste away.

What had been so appealing? It wasna Mark himself. Maybe it was the emotions. The pounding of her heartbeat, the flush of her cheeks. The forbidden fruit. She bit her lip. Those feelings had held her prisoner for so long.

Looking around at what needed to be packed up, she noticed Abe and Ben had carried down her hope chest from upstairs. That was yet another thing that needed to be sorted through.

Since the children still slept, she decided no time was as good as the present for getting started. She opened the trunk to find crocheted dish clothes and beautiful table clothes that she'd been given for wedding gifts. There was an old, tin teapot that used to belong to her grandmother, and nestled under it there was something wrapped in brown paper.

She lifted it in her hands and turned it over. Could it be . . . ? Ruth unwrapped the paper and a smile filled her face.

Her cup. Her precious china cup. The one she'd cherished as a girl. But . . .

Ruth frowned as she turned the cup over in her hands. How could this be? It wasn't at all as she remembered. She fingered the flowers, the edges of the cup, and that's when it happened.

Like a blast of light in a dark and dreary room, she understood.

She saw the cup as it was. Even more, saw herself as she was. And with that understanding, came a rush of laughter.

She'd been so foolish. So blind.

"Lord, I see." She closed her hands around her treasured cup. "I finally see. And I thank You." She lifted her face to heaven.

"Thank You with all my heart."

Ruth heard whistling outside. She returned the cup to her chest and hurried to the window. Abe approached from the barn, his eyes fixed on the fields he'd tended for so long. He was a simple man. A good man. Abe was the right man—not because he was Amish, but because he had a good heart and was dedicated to her and to their family.

And because she loved him. She knew because it was flooding her, right now. And thankfulness too. She'd made the right decision then, and they were making a right one together now.

Abe must have sensed her eyes on him because he glanced up.

She waved to him as he headed out to the fields, and he waved back, a broad smile on his face. *He* was her life, not this community. Not this home. He and their family.

She could go anywhere if she was with him.

She heard the sound of footsteps upstairs and from their heaviness knew it was Ben getting ready for the day. David and Charlie still slept, and Joy did too.

Last night, Marianna had headed back to Levi's place, saying she'd return this morn with Levi, Naomi, and baby Samuel.

What would Levi think of his sister's Englisch friend? Ruth had a feeling he'd like Ben—maybe even more than he cared for Aaron. Ben was likeable in that way.

At that thought, Ruth placed a hand over her heart. What if God had chosen Abe for her not because he was Amish, but because of the man he was? Could it be . . . could God choose someone for her daughter not because he was Amish, or Englisch, but because he was the right man for her—for her future and her faith?

Ruth swallowed hard, shaking her head. She couldn't let her mind think of that. Marianna had her mind set on who she was set to marry. Ruth just had to trust that her daughter was being diligent on seeking God's heart on the matter.

The sound of voices carried down the road. Ruth wiped her hands on a dishtowel and hurried outside. Sure enough Levi, Naomi, and Marianna strolled toward her. In her son's arms was the newest addition to their family. Ruth couldn't help it. She hoisted her skirt and hurried toward them.

Reaching them, she offered Naomi a quick hug and then stretched out her arms to the baby.

Levi smiled. "Mem, meet your grandson." He handed her the small bundle.

Ruth sucked in a breath as she noticed the baby's fair skin, light fuzzy blond hair, and light blue eyes. She studied him, but couldn't see much of Levi in his features. Of course, with babies it was so hard to tell.

She smiled as she kissed her grandson's cheek. "Joanna was light like this. That's who Samuel must take after."

Levi nodded, and Ruth noticed he and Naomi exchange glances.

"Oh and yer family too." Ruth chuckled. "He's only part Sommer after all."

She held him up to her, breathing in his baby scent. It made her realize Joy had grown so much.

"He's beautiful." Ruth looked into her son's eyes. "A gift from God no matter the circumstances."

The visit with her son and soon-to-be daughter-in-law was pleasant, but far too short. After breakfast the young couple headed back to Naomi's parents' house to work on plans for the wedding. She and Abe had errands of their own, and they headed to town to settle up accounts at the grocery and bank. They'd left Ben and Marianna to pack up the rest of the house with the help of the older boys. Marianna also insisted in keeping Joy, stating it would be too soon her baby sister would be traveling back to Montana.

"Why don't I head to the bank, while you talk to Dee at the grocery store?" Abe suggested.

For as long as Ruth remembered she'd had an account at the store that had gotten them through lean winters. Dee was always good at providing them with credit until they could pay in the spring. Yet as she entered the store it wasn't Dee she saw first. But there . . . standing near the shopping carts . . .

Mark.

She paused in her steps, touching her kapp to make sure it was still in place. She looked over her shoulder before remembering Abe wasn't there to back her up.

"Hello, Ruth." He smiled. "I heard you were in town."

She nodded and crossed her arms over her chest. A buzzing

filled her insides as if she'd just swallowed a beehive. "*Ja*, jest back for our son's wedding . . ." Ruth's quivering moved to her knees.

"You look the same, Ruth, as young and beautiful as your daughter Marianna."

She placed a hand on a shopping cart to steady herself. "I do not know how to answer that."

"You can say thank you."

Mark's eyes bore into her, and she did not like it one bit. He studied her as if he had a right to this—a right to her time, attention, heart. "It's foolishness, that's what it is. You have no right."

"So because you're a married woman I cannot tell you how beautiful you look? How I feel?"

An Englisch woman entered the store and hurried by, not giving them a fleeting glance.

Ruth turned her head, unable to look into the intensity of his gaze. His desire was clear. Mark had always been intense and clear about his feelings.

Her emotions swelled, but then the Scripture verses she'd read just this morning replayed in her mind. God loved her. His love was true. Abe loved her . . .

And then another verse came to her, one she'd read a while back. Seeing Mark her heart told her what it wanted, but what had that verse said? "*The heart is deceitfully wicked.*" The thumped mass inside her chest was that, all right. It wanted to smile at Mark, to offer him a hug of greeting.

Dear Lord, help.

As soon she let loose the prayer, a response filled her mind. She motioned to a quiet corner just inside the store, and Mark followed her there, seemingly pleased she hadn't turned him away.

Ruth pressed her fingers to her temples and looked up into his face. "I need to tell you something. It's something you need to hear, Mark." His name was soft on her lips.

She blew out a slow breath and began. "One year my grandparents took me to the flea market in Shipshewana all by myself. I was so excited. Before we arrived they told me I could pick one special item jest for me. They believed I would choose a special treat, but my eyes focused on a beautiful china cup. I had to have it. They considered it an usual request, but they agreed. Looking back now, perhaps a part of me was tired of being plain. Even though I'm Amish I've always been drawn to beautiful things." She looked back at him. "And forbidden things."

Mark smiled at her words and took a step closer.

She held up her hand. "I'm not finished. I drank from my cup a few times, and once my sisters knocked it off the table. It dropped to the floor and a corner of it chipped. After that I was so fearful of it shattering, that I put it away. In my hope chest. And when I married Abe it was one of the things I moved into our new home.

"A few times over the years I considered pulling out my china cup, but I was afraid the kinder would break it."

Mark lifted one eyebrow, and Ruth could tell he wondered where this story was going. She set her chin, determined to finish her story in her own good time. "I came across that china cup today, when I was packing up my things. Nearly dropped it when I was sorting through my hope chest." She wrinkled her nose. "Funny thing, though, wouldn't have mattered none. You see, it weren't china at all but hard plastic. And the intricate flowers I admired so was a sticker decal."

She lifted her chin, and met his gaze without flinching. She kept her tone firm, but kind. Even hard words could be spoke with kindness. "That's what my feelings for you were, Mark. I thought for so long they were something to cherish, but this whole time they've been fake. Worthless."

Mark shifted side to side. She saw his neck turning red. This wasn't what he expected, wanted.

"Yer story doesn't make sense, Ruth, I saw something different in your eyes. When you looked at me, I saw you still cared."

"Of course. I will always care. You are a part of my youth, my past, but not my present. There are emotions there, ain't no denying that. They're emotions I tried to tuck away and protect like that china cup, but when I heard you were back, and I studied those feelings, I realized they're nothing but a fraud. My feelings of care fer you was mixed with my longing to leave behind my Amish ways. The motives were wrong for sure. I wanted to be loved, but what you offered was not love. It was unhealthy desire."

Even as she spoke, she felt the certainty within. This was truth. "I've found true love in my husband, Abe."

He flashed a scowl. "So that's it?"

"Well, *ja.*"

He reached out a hand, touching her arm. She took a step back.

"Will you at least pray for me, Ruth? Pray I'll find a love like you have?"

"I wish I could, but that'll jest tie my heart to yours. Instead, when thoughts of you come up, I'll thank God. For the gift He has given me in my husband."

Mark ran a hand through his hair. "I'm uh, glad for you. For the life you have. I'm sorry to have bothered you." With that he turned and strode away.

Seeing him go, Ruth's stomach tingled as if she'd leapt off the top of the barn. She watched the back of Mark's head as he stalked off. Gray dulled his shiny black curls.

Footsteps approached from behind and she turned. Abe stood there.

He paused before her, looking down. "When I started for the bank something gave me pause. I felt drawn to turn around and head this way."

"I wasn't surprised to see Mark. He's one of the reasons I didn't want to come back here for long." Her voice trembled.

Abe stepped closer. Ruth tried to swallow but her throat was tight—as if a cob of corn was stuck in her windpipe.

"I know."

She stared at her husband. "You do?"

"I heard you, Ruth. All you said to him. I followed you inside—standing just over there—and heard every word." He stepped forward and placed a hand on her shoulder. From the look in his eyes he wanted to do more—to pull her into his embrace—but he resisted. She knew it was because they were in public.

"Remember that love letter you wrote to me on our first anniversary? The one that told me all the things you loved about me. The one that I still keep with my socks?"

She nodded. She'd done that after overhearing someone in church say how she'd written one for her husband. Heat rose to her cheeks.

"This"—he pointed to the doorway where Mark had just had exited—"this means even more than that. Telling him you loved me and had no interest in hurting our marriage meant more to me than any love letter."

She nodded. The deep love in Abe's gaze brought tears to her eyes. "It's true," she whispered.

"I know. I know something else too. We're not going to Montana to run away, Ruth. We're going to find what we've just had a glimpse of. A new relationship with God. A fresh start at our love. I can't wait for the next twenty-five years."

Abe covered Ruth's hand with a rough palm. It was the hand of a hardworking man—a man who gave everything for their family.

A man she loved with all her heart.

CHAPTER TWENTY-TWO

Instead of having her things taken to Aaron's house, Marianna had them delivered to Levi and Naomi's place. It seemed silly to move things into the house Aaron built when the date for their wedding hadn't yet been set. They both agreed it would be better to wait for Levi and Naomi's big day. Then they would talk. Then they would plan . . .

In the other room Naomi sang to little Samuel as she gave him a bath. Marianna looked over the boxes of things she'd stacked around her small room. She looked again to the dusty box she had Ben pull from the top shelf. Were there any things inside that Mem could take back for Ellie and Joy? How special that would be to have her younger sisters playing with the same dolls she had as a child.

Marianna lifted out the dolls and noticed some worn journals underneath. Opening them up, she noticed her mother's handwriting. Marianna dropped down onto the bed, still staring at the words. A knot in her gut tightened. Should she read them?

Before she second-guessed herself, she skimmed over the page:

I had to get a new journal. Marilyn had scribbled on the old one and I couldn't write a word inside. I just broke out into tears crying every time I tried.

Abe went out and spent the evening in the barn again. It never used to take him two hours to muck the stalls. He came in smelling of the Lexol leather conditioner and Neatsfoot oil he used to care for the horses' harnesses. It's so lonesome here inside the house with the younger ones sleeping. I try to think of warm memories, but my mind soon wanders. I thought I'd caused Abe enough pain as it was, but now . . . the pain of losing the girls is unlike anything I've known. The worst part is we deal with it alone, each hiding away in our own thoughts.

There Mem had stopped. On the next page was a recipe for granola. And the page after that was a list of seeds Mem had wanted to buy for her spring garden. Marianna flipped through the rest of the pages and she noticed none of the rest were Mem's personal thoughts. There were cute things she and Levi said. There were more recipes and even a sketch of a quilt design.

What had made Mem stop?

Marianna thought about her own journals she left in Montana. Heat rose to her cheeks at the thought of anyone reading her words. She was thankful now Mem's journal hadn't shared more. Still, how had Mem and Dat made it through those hard times?

Taking a smaller box, Marianna pulled out the things for Ellie and Joy and carried them to the living room. Naomi sat there nursing Samuel. Levi was nowhere to be found.

"He's out in the barn," Naomi said, as if anticipating her

question. Marianna nodded and headed out the front door. He'd been staying out there a lot.

As she entered, he tilted his chin to her as a welcome. Sitting on a milich bench, Levi turned the harness over in his hands studying the stitching, especially the stitches near the hardware. He took it apart next, undoing all the buckles, giving each piece a stress test, twisting it and turning it to see if it would break.

"Like father, like son." She sighed.

"What?"

She thought of her mother's journals but didn't want to tell Levi she'd read more than she should have. "Oh, I jest know Dat does that when he's tired or stressed. He gives all his harnesses the once-over. Stays out later in the barn than needs be."

His gaze narrowed. "Better to have a broken harness in your hands than one on your horse."

"*Ja*, of course, but I don't think it's your harness that's worrying you so."

She turned away from him. From the corner of her eye she watched him approach. He crooked his arm and caught Marianna with a soft elbow around her neck, pulling her into a gentle hug.

"Hey now." She tugged against his arm, pulling out of his embrace.

"How do you do that? I can't hide anything from you, can I?"

"I've learned to study you. Since I was small I could tell if you were the one who stole my cookies from my lunch pail." They stepped apart. "Something's bothering you. You want to talk about it?"

Levi put down his harness and let out a slow breath. "It seems natural a man should be doing a lot of thinking the week of his wedding. Especially . . ."

"Especially with the birth of Samuel and wonderings about . . . his father?"

Levi nodded. "I'm his father, but I know what you mean." He buckled the harness back up and then hung it on the correct hook. "I—I just consider marriage a big step. I just want to make sure she's the right one."

"Is she?"

A smile split Levi's face. "*Ja*, yes she is."

Bubbles bounced in Marianna's stomach and even though they were talking about him and Naomi she couldn't help but think of her and Aaron. "And how do you know this?"

"I know because I can't imagine her not being there when I have good news. I know because I look forward to seeing her smile. I know because the thought of her being with another man tears me in two. *I* want to be the one she wakes up to every day."

As he spoke those words, the barn around her faded to gray. Marianna knew . . . she knew deep down . . .

She'd made the wrong decision.

Marianna moved to the bench he'd been sitting on and sat, placing her hands on her knees.

Dear Lord, I haven't been truthful with myself, have I?

The problem was, truth—the truth hiding deep in her heart—would ruin everything.

Marianna walked from the barn to the house and noticed a car parked on the road close to the dawdi haus. Dusk had faded the world around her into muted colors. Yet it was light enough to see a young woman in Englisch dress waving at her. Marianna's mind was still foggy from her conversation with Levi and it took her a minute to realize it was Rebecca approaching.

Rebecca ran up wearing jeans and a pink T-shirt. She paused before Marianna. "Do you have plans today?" She smacked her bubble gum as she spoke.

"No, I don't think—"

"Good, then we're going somewhere." Rebecca tugged on her arm, leading her to the car.

"What are you talking about?"

"I know you and Ben haven't had a chance to talk much since he's been here. It seems that he was in town today, running an errand for your parents, and my boss, who is Ben's biggest fan, nearly fainted. She couldn't believe he was in Shipshewana or that he was friends with you. She demanded he come back tonight for a concert."

"A concert?" Marianna paused in her tracks, touching her kapp.

Rebecca blew out a sigh, held Marianna's arm firmer, and continued to the car.

"When are you going to remember you haven't been baptized yet? You can listen to music tonight. I insist. It's *your* Ben. I refuse to have you miss this."

Ben was already singing when they arrived. He wore a light blue T-shirt and sat in a chair in the center of the room. The tables had been pushed to the side and more chairs had been set up. People circled him in rings, like swirls around a cupcake. Someone had brought in a small sound system and he leaned forward into the mic. Her heart leapt as she listened to him. Heat rose up her neck and it was as though his voice embraced her. The music swelled and the emotion in her heart did too.

She hadn't realized how much she missed his voice until this moment. Tears flowed.

She tried to stay hidden in the back, but as Ben started to sing the song "Every Warm Cabin," she couldn't resist any longer. She had to leave. She couldn't sit and listen to this. She'd been a fool for trying to keep him at bay—for refusing the love he offered her, but there was nothing she could do about it. Her mother had been strong. She'd turned her back on the Englisch man she'd loved. Marianna told herself she could do the same. She *had* to do the same.

She rose and moved toward the restaurant door, when the guitar stopped.

"Marianna!"

Gasps carried across the room and whispers filled the space where his music had been a moment before.

"Is that her? The girl from the song?"

"How do they know each other?"

"Surely he isn't singing about an *Amish* woman."

She heard the scrape of a chair leg on the floor. He was rising, following her. She quickened her pace. Why had she come at all? She should have known hearing Ben's music—his voice—would stir her feelings.

Her hands pushed against the glass door. It opened and she hurried out to the sound of crickets meeting her ears.

"Marianna!"

She knew he wouldn't give up until he talked to her. Taking a deep breath, she allowed her steps to pause and turned around, staring into Ben's handsome face. She balled her hands into fists and all her love for God turned to anger.

How could You let this happen to me? Why did You have to bring him into my life?

"Thank you." The whispered word slipped from Ben's lips.

Her chin quivered from his closeness. "For wh-what?"

Ben smiled. "You've been running from me all week. Thank you for stopping."

From over his shoulder she could see that all those who'd been listening to the concert had turned and were now watching them through the window.

"We have an audience," she whispered, pointing.

"I'm used to it."

"They're all going to know—"

"Know what? That you're the girl in the song?"

She nodded.

"I don't see a problem with that. Do you?"

Marianna crossed her arms over her chest and tapped her right foot on the sidewalk, trying to release some of her nervousness. "Well, I am promised to be married to an Amishman."

Ben shrugged. "That's not my fault. In fact if you'd like to we can go find Aaron." He pulled a set of keys from his pocket. "I have a rig. We can remedy that tonight."

He smiled again and seeing that smile was like a punch to the gut. Her toe tapping stopped and instead she stomped her foot, blowing out her frustration in a quick breath. "Do you think this is a joke? Do you not realize this is my life? This is my town, Ben, and you've made a spectacle of me. Do you not think it will get back to my parents—and the church—how you ran out after me? Aaron's going to find out and his family too. That's the family

I'm supposed to be a part of soon. They're going to hear. They're going to know . . ." She lowered her head and placed her hands over her face.

"I'm sorry. I—"

"You're sorry that you weren't thinking? Is that what you were going to say?" She turned her back on the fans staring out the window. Turning her back on him.

"Why did you come here, Ben? Why do you have to make things so hard?"

"Things wouldn't be hard if you didn't have feelings for me. You do have feelings for me, don't you, Marianna?" He placed a soft hand on her shoulder.

She jerked her shoulder away, refusing to answer. Refusing to even consider . . .

Ben cleared his throat. "I know this isn't the place or the time, so I'll let you keep walking, but I want you to know that I've waited . . . and I'll keep waiting. Until you make a vow to another I'm not going to give up hope."

Her hands started to quiver like aspen leaves in the wind. She didn't know how to answer that, so she replied with the only words that came to her mind. "You better get back in there, Ben, they're waiting to hear the rest of your song."

CHAPTER TWENTY-THREE

*T*he wedding wagon pulled up, and Marianna wanted to take a look inside. So many Amish weddings were held outdoors, a cooking wagon made it easier to prepare the two wedding meals. More than satisfying her curiosity, though, Marianna needed a distraction. After talking with Ben the other night, she hadn't been able to sleep much. His words continued to play through her mind.

"I'll keep waiting. Until you make a vow to another I'm not going to give up hope."

Marianna followed Aunt Ida inside, noting the five gas stoves, cookware, and the large coffeemaker. The wedding was tomorrow, but friends and family had already gathered to help prepare.

While the women buzzed around inside the wedding wagon, hard at work, the men gathered in the side yard. She knew Levi was with them. Custom required that the bridegroom cut off the heads of the fowl that would be cooked up for the wedding feast.

Men walked through the coops that sat alongside Naomi's parents' barn, picking out the best chickens, ducks, and turkeys. In the wedding wagon, women prepared dressing, stuffed the foul, washed dishes, and peeled potatoes. Pies covered every free bit of counter space, and some of the older children had been put to work cracking nuts. Marianna's Uncle Abe and Uncle Levin, Aunt Betsy's husband, supplied hot water from large kettles. Other menfolk emptied garbage cans and constructed tables from wide pine boards and trestles. She knew before the men journeyed home for the night all the fowl would be placed in a large outdoor baking oven.

Marianna set to work peeling potatoes in the deep metal sink, but her mind wasn't fixed on the task at hand. Instead she imagined standing in front of all her friends and family, reciting her vows before Aaron, before God. Even now her tongue felt thick as she thought about saying those words. Yet how could she not go through with it? He'd built a home for her. It was what everyone expected—

But could she do it?

Could she vow her love for one man when her heart had already given it to another?

Naomi's aunts had been cooking since yesterday, and by the time Marianna had walked across the lawn to Naomi's parents' place at 7:00 a.m., they were already there, continuing where they left off. Inside the house six tables were set up on three sides of the living room and in the kitchen. Chairs filled the rest of the space.

It had just turned 8:00 a.m. and crowds had already gathered, everyone in their places for the wedding. For as long as she could remember, Marianna had always looked forward to weddings. It was not only a great occasion for the bride and bridegroom, but for the guests—especially the young people who got to see friends and cousins they hadn't seen for a while.

This time, though, dread weighed on Marianna, as if she walked with concrete shoes. Did those attending wonder about her and Aaron's plans? How would she respond? She needed to talk to him, that she knew, but not today.

Today she needed to celebrate a love confessed and vowed.

Marianna made her way to the front row with the others in the bridal party. By nine o'clock the house was full. As those gathered sang, Levi and Naomi were led into the other room by the ministers. She looked beautiful in her light blue dress with a white apron. It looked similar to the dresses they wore every day but the lighter color of the dress made it special.

Marianna knew this was a time they were given instructions concerning the duties of marriage. What did the ministers tell them? Did they discuss the importance of faithfulness and speaking the truth? If so, how did Levi and Naomi respond? How would she respond?

After three songs were sung, Levi and Naomi returned holding hands. Marianna rose with the rest of the bridal party and moved with Levi and Naomi to the row of benches called the minister's row. Marianna kept her eyes on the preacher, refusing to look at Aaron who sat across from her.

The bishop's vigorous voice rose as he shared stories from God's Holy Word. He relayed the story of Adam and Eve and how God had created a special woman perfectly designed for Adam. He also shared the uprightness done by Noah's sons who did not intermarry with unbelievers. Marianna had heard it all, but for some reason each sentence of his stories pierced her heart.

At noon the sermon ended, and the bishop asked Levi and Naomi to come forward. After they answered a series of questions, Marianna held her breath as the bishop placed his hands over the clasped hands of Levi and Naomi.

"You have now heard the ordinance of Christian wedlock presented. Levi, are you now willing to enter wedlock together as God in the beginning ordained and commanded?"

Levi looked to his red-headed bride, and Marianna couldn't miss the intense love in her brother's eyes. Marianna couldn't see Naomi's face but she imagined the same look in her gaze.

Levi nodded. "Yes."

"Are you confident that this, our sister, is ordained of God to be your wedded wife?"

"Yes."

Then he turned to Naomi. "Are you confident that this, our *bruder*, is ordained of God to be your wedded husband?"

"Yes."

He looked to Levi. "Do you also promise your wedded wife, before the Lord and His church, that you will never more depart from her, but will care for her and cherish her. And if bodily sickness comes over her, or in any circumstance which a Christian husband is responsible to care for, you will do your duty as her husband until the dear God will again separate you from each other?"

"Yes."

The minister's eyes looked to Naomi. "Do you also promise your wedded husband, before the Lord and His church that you will never depart from him?"

"Yes."

The couple then clasped their right hands together and the bishop continued. "So then I may say the God of Abraham, the God of Isaac, and the God of Jacob be with you and help you together and fulfill His blessing abundantly upon you, through Jesus Christ. Amen. You are husband and wife."

A smile radiated from Levi's face. Tears of joy filled Naomi's eyes.

With the wedding complete, the events of the day were just starting. Marianna worked alongside the others as they trans-formed the room for serving lunch. And then they fed the crowd family-style in three shifts.

She smiled and chatted with the others as the dishes were cleared, washed, and reset. Then as the high summer sun dipped lower on the horizon she joined the others as they sang their traditional wedding hymns and songs. As they sang, snacks were passed around. There was still the Amish wedding dinner to go, followed by the songs of the *vorsingers*.

And when the time finally came, Marianna listened to the words more closely than she ever had before.

We alone, a little flock,
The few who still remain,
Are exiles wandering through the land
In sorrow and in pain . . .
We wander in the forests dark,
With dogs upon our track;
And like the captive, silent lamb
Men bring us, prisoners, back . . .

Marianna understood this pain far too well.

When they continued the next song, she couldn't help the tears that filled her eyes. She wiped them away and raised her voice above the others—as if that would make everything better.

Listen to me, all peoples of the earth.
Listen to me, young and old, great and small.

If you want to be saved, you need to leave sin,
follow Christ the Lord, and live according to His will.
Christ Jesus came to the earth to teach men the right way
    to go,
to teach them to turn from sin and to follow Him.
He said: "I am the way the truth and the life,
no one comes to the father except through me."
He who longs for Gemeinschaft with Christ
and who wants to take part in His kingdom,
needs to do what Christ did while he was on the earth.
He who wants to reign with Christ must first be willing
    to suffer for His name.

And in singing those words, she knew. That was where the problem lay. She was willing to suffer for Christ—to turn her back on all Englisch ways—if that was what He asked. The problem was . . .

She didn't know.

Was that what God was asking of her? As much as she wanted to answer yes, she couldn't. Because deep down, she had a feeling . . .

She should not dismiss Ben—not just yet.

CHAPTER TWENTY-FOUR

en sat in the room that used to be Marianna's and from his perch in her window took in the long line of buggies parked on the road. He'd been invited to the wedding, but he knew they'd only done so to be kind. Abe and Ruth seemed relieved when he said he'd rather just stay home.

He wanted to be there for Levi—to get to know him better—but Ben knew with an Englischer there most of the Amish would be more focused on him than the ceremony. Besides, he didn't know how his heart would take hearing two people reciting vows to each other when the woman he loved was on the arm of another.

"What am I doing here?" he whispered into the empty room. "God, why can't You just release me? Why can't You take away this love that I have for her? I'd rather be empty of love than heartbroken. There has to be another way . . ."

Footsteps sounded behind him, and Ben turned. A young woman stood there wearing Amish dress. She looked to be Marianna's age, but she had a hardness about her. There was a knowing in her eyes, too, that told him she was all too familiar with the ways of the world.

"Sorry to interrupt." She attempted a smile but it paused halfway up. "I know you don't know me, but I've been a friend of Marianna's for a long time—for as long as I can remember. I'm Rebecca, and there are some things I need to talk to you about."

He stood and faced her. Whatever this girl had to say he wasn't going to take it sitting down.

"She's talked about you a little, not much, but things like this don't need words."

"Things like what?"

"Love." She remained in the doorway, expression somber.

A chuckle burst from Ben's lips. "I'm sorry . . . I think you have the wrong person. Marianna's engaged to someone else."

"*Ja*, that's true." The young woman removed her kapp and shook out her hair. She then bent down and pulled a pair of jeans and a t-shirt out of her satchel. "Can you hang on a minute, I need to go change out of these clothes."

Ben's mouth dropped, and he studied her face. "Did you say you're Marianna's *Amish* friend?"

"*Ja*, I was raised Amish, but I'm still in my *rumspringa*." She untied her apron and pulled it off. "I know it's silly but this is a busy tourist season at the cafe and I make better tips when I wear my Amish clothes. So can you hold on just a minute?"

He was in Marianna's house, which is the only place he was welcome around these parts. It's not like he had anywhere to go. "Uh, sure."

He walked outside and sat in one of the wicker chairs on the front porch. The sun was bright and a variety of flowers bloomed around the property, but even they couldn't lift his mood. He considered leaving before Marianna's friend came out. Maybe he should head down to the creek to toss rocks in the water. He didn't need Rebecca to tell him that Marianna loved him. He saw it the moment their eyes met. Her face had been full of joy, when she first saw him in Indiana. And if her parents hadn't been there he was sure she would have rushed into his arms.

But what did that matter? Marianna had made her choice. She was here, wasn't she? She was still engaged to Aaron. He didn't need to go to her and try to win her heart. He could do nothing as long as she ran from the truth—the truth of his love, the truth of God's freedom.

Three minutes later Rebecca exited the door. She pointed to the chair next to him. "Can I sit there? I promise I won't bite."

He rubbed his hands down the front of his jeans. "Uh, sure."

Rebecca picked a pansy from one of the window boxes and twirled it in her fingers. "It's silly, you know, you being here, loading up furniture like your muscles are your greatest asset. No offense or anything, but I heard that you were supposed to be in Los Angles right now, recording."

"Yes, well, I just thought I'd do a friend a favor."

"And . . ."

"And, what?"

"And to see Marianna."

"Yes . . ." He smiled. "It's true."

"Well, there's only one way to win her heart."

"And what is that?"

"You have to express how you feel."

He shook his head. "I tried to talk to her the other night."

"That's your problem, Ben. You tried using words. You need to express yourself the way you know best. Through song."

Ben cocked his eyebrow. "You want me to write a song that Marianna's Amish tradition doesn't even allow her to listen to?"

"She'll listen. You should have seen the joy on her face when she heard your Good Wife song. You're talented. I have a feeling this is just the beginning for you."

He looked away and shook his head. "Well, that beginning is going to end before it starts. I've decided I don't want that type of lifestyle—one on the road. I can't live that way."

"Who says you have to travel and sing? One of my customers a while back said that he was a songwriter. He wrote songs for others to record."

Ben glanced back over at this woman who seemed just as uncomfortable in her jeans and T-shirt as she did in her Amish clothes. She didn't seem to fit in either world. Yet as she spoke, something stirred inside. Something that told him to stop and listen to the words of this unlikely advisor.

He crossed his arms over his chest. The idea of still using his music without having to travel both excited him and scared him. What would Roy say? Would people be interested in his songs? Would he be able to write from Montana—to stay there and build a home there for . . .

"Still, not traveling doesn't solve everything. Even if I wrote the perfect song, Marianna still might choose him."

"Sure, she might, but don't you want to try? No dream comes true until you wake up and go to work. Besides, you have some time. It's not public knowledge, but Marianna and Aaron are talking about not getting married until November, which is typical for Amish weddings. That's a long time away, and if anything, the waiting makes things more favorable on your side."

"What do you mean by that?"

She shrugged. "I can't tell for sure, but there's something strange going on with Aaron. My mother used to tell me that what's whispered in the dark will be shouted from the rooftops—I think that's in the Bible somewhere. I just have a feeling that the more time Marianna spends with Aaron, the more she'll discover he's not the man for her."

"So how do you know I am?"

Rebecca tilted her head up to him. "I may be wayward according to my people's beliefs, but I can tell when someone truly loves God. There's something special about you, Ben, and Marianna will be foolish if she doesn't realize that. I'd never tell her to leave the Amish, but I can tell her to seek God's will. And I hope when she does, it will lead her into your arms."

"You can hope all you want but it doesn't matter. I'm leaving in the morning. Don't think I can do much songwriting, romancing, before then. Not that I agree with you. Not that I think I should. Marianna needs to take the next step. Only then will I know I have a glimmer of a chance."

If the wedding lunch had been simple, the wedding dinner was anything but. It was a time for additional friends and neighbors to show up.

Before everyone arrived, Marianna asked Aaron if they could slip away for a short walk. She hadn't seen much of him lately, and she missed the time they had together in Montana. Here Aaron worked. He cared for the house. He helped his father. He didn't have time to talk with her or to sit and dream.

She held his hand as they walked through a small meadow. A dozen cows chewed their cud near the creek, glancing up as they passed.

"Aaron, I was thinking, maybe we could spend some time together tomorrow. I've been reading my Bible and—"

His smile faded and his eyebrows lowered. "The English Bible?"

"Of course. You know I don't read German any better than you do. There's some passages I've been reading. Some stories I think you'd like, and . . ."

Aaron looped his thumbs through his suspenders. "There's no need. You know what I think of the English Bible."

She could tell he was trying to keep his voice calm, but anger tinged his words.

"*Ja*, but I thought if you read it, maybe you'd see—"

He whispered something under his breath she couldn't understand. "It's jest as my father said. You think a woman accepts you for who you are, but as soon as you take her into the marriage bed she's already crafting ways to change you." He cleared his throat. "Seems you're not even waitin' that long."

Heat rose to her cheeks, and she wished there was shade nearby. Marianna fanned her face. "Is that what you think, that I'm trying to change you? It's our faith, Aaron. The faith of our Anabaptist ancestors was built on God's Word."

"I thought I was *gut* enough for you." His words seemed more sad now than angry. "Thought all I provided was *gut* enough."

A sigh escaped her lips. "I don't mean to sound ungrateful. I wish I could help you understand."

"I know yer having second thoughts . . ." Aaron lowered his eyes. "You can't hide that from me. But why?"

As he asked the question, she pictured her nephew. Samuel had grown and changed. His hair was blonder than ever, and his eyes were the bluest eyes she'd ever seen. She only knew one other person with eyes like that. She looked up and focused on those eyes.

"I'm not sure how I look at you, Aaron. It's just that I have this feeling deep inside that something's not as it should be. I can't explain it." She let out a heavy sigh. "I'm tired of trying to figure it out. And the truth is I feel you've changed too."

"Maybe because you don't look at me like you used to, Mari, not with the same respect. It's as if you knew . . ." He turned and moved toward the back door.

She shot to her feet and followed him. "What, Aaron? Knew what?"

He glanced over his shoulder at her. "The truth, Mari. It's as if you knew the truth of Naomi's baby."

Was that relief she saw on his face as he uttered those words?

Marianna paused her steps and for a moment she thought she would tumble. Her knees grew weak, and the fear that had nestled deep inside her exploded to her mind and heart. Looking at Aaron's face . . . she knew.

"It makes sense." The whisper escaped her lips.

She glanced at Aaron again. "He looks just like you." Her stomach lurched and a quivering hand covered her mouth. She wanted to turn and run. She wanted to grab his shirt and ask him how he could do that—not only be intimate with Naomi, but also lie.

Levi. Her brother had no idea, and she was glad. He considered Aaron a friend. It would be a double slap to his face.

Aaron let out a slow breath. "I don't know what to say."

"You can tell me the truth. I want to hear it out of your own mouth. Is that baby yours?"

"*Ja.*"

Even though she expected the answer, it came as a fist to her gut.

"I'm sorry, Marianna. I lied to you." He punched his left fist into his right hand. "I was so stupid . . . so lonely." His eyes glittered with the beginning of tears. His cheeks blazed. A strand of sweaty blond hair clung to his forehead and the innocence of it made her think of the boy she once knew, but nothing about Aaron was innocent.

"I love you, Marianna," he uttered through strident breaths. "I'm so angry at myself for letting this happen. It wasn't anything I planned."

"But you told me . . . you told me it was only a kiss." She struggled to breathe. The air refused to fill her lungs.

"Didn't you jest hear me? I lied. I was afraid to tell you the truth. You're so . . . so pure."

A scoff escaped her throat.

"As soon as you got the letter from Levi, telling you about Naomi, I hoped the babe wasn't mine. Before that . . . well, I tried to forget. Tried to pretend it didn't happen." Aaron paused.

Then his words came forth like a flood, as if he was searching for a way to make it right. "I don't know what to tell you. Levi had abandoned her. You were gone. We found comfort in each other . . ." He stepped closer and put a hand around her shoulders, pulling her to him. Strength had escaped from her body and she fell into his embrace.

He held her and rocked. His voice choking out more words. "I didn't plan on it. Naomi didn't either. It just happened."

Rocking in his arms she stared into the blue sky, her gaze fixing on a distant cloud. She wished it would come and offer up rain—to cry for her the tears that refused to come.

"After the first time we knew that's not what we wanted. I was s . . . so afraid to tell you. So afraid of what you'd think of me."

"Wait, the *first* time . . . there was more than one time?"

He ran a finger under his collar. "Do we have to talk about this?"

"Aaron, in a few months' time I'm supposed to commit my life to you. And now—now you can't even tell me the truth? You can't even talk about something that's going to affect the rest of our lives?"

"It was more than one time, but not many. We were just lonely."

"And from that you created a child. You have a *son*, Aaron. A son that my bruder is raising as his own. I—I never thought it was you. Levi told me months ago he never slept with Naomi in the family way before they were married." Her voice softened with each word. "I just assumed it was some guy she met . . . anyone but you. You've always been so noble, so good, so kind. I thought you loved me."

"I do, Marianna. Just because I made a mistake doesn't mean things have to be different."

Mustering the strength, she pulled away. "*Ja*, it does." The moistness of the grass wet the hem of her skirt, but she didn't care. "You say you love me, but you would have had me believe the lie that this was not yer child? What will happen when the child grows, Aaron? He's part of the community and his looks make it clear he's your son. As he grows he'll just look like you more. Don't you think folks will start asking questions? Don't you believe the child will want to know who is father is?"

"I suppose I didna think much about that. Levi and Naomi love each other."

"And you'll just let my bruder raise your child? Do you not think you have responsibility? Financially and in care? I don't know, Aaron. The way you've done this—you're not the person I thought you to be. The person I thought you were would step up and do something. Would take responsibility. Maybe that's what hurts the most."

He didn't say anything, just looked away.

She brushed off a piece of meadow grass that clung to her arm. She didn't know what to do or where to go.

"What does this mean, Marianna? Now that you know the truth—is the wedding still on?"

"I don't think so, Aaron." She waited for the sorrow, the grief of the loss to cut into her, but instead, a heaviness she'd hadn't realized she'd been carrying lifted.

It was as though she was suddenly free.

"I'm not mad at you, Aaron. I'm just sad. Sad that all this happened. Sad our dream didn't come true. I'm sad you believed you had to lie to me. I'm sad you didna open yourself up to me. I'm sad you have a son and won't have a relationship with him as you should. But I'd be more heartbroken if I loved you like I wanted to. I can't make myself love you as a woman should love the man she's planning to marry. I thought I did, for a time."

She sighed. "I always looked forward to seeing you when we were children, and spending time with you. I imagined our life together and I thought that was love. But if it were truly love I'd be heartbroken right now. I'd just be crushed that you'd given yourself to Naomi in that way. All our lives we're told to follow God and do what's right. And I thought I was doing that by loving you—loving the life we could have had together. I don't know. Maybe God has a different plan for both of us. I thought I wanted to live in Indiana, and I can't express how much the house you built means to me—that you thought of me. But more than that, I think I was to you something I'm not. You thought of me as a good Amish woman, and though I've always strived to be that . . . I don't think I am anymore."

And it was then the tears came. She looked up at him through a bleary haze.

Pain filled in his gaze too. "You're not perfect either. It's not like you kept your heart wholly for me. I heard about you and Ben."

She pulled back from him. "You know?"

"Don't you think people talk, especially when they see an Amish woman in the arms of an Englisher?"

"It wasn't like that."

"*Ja*, it might not have been, but I have a feeling. Even if we married you never would have gotten over him, would you?" His voice was thick and she heard vestiges of the hurt she caused, but still that didn't change what he'd done.

"No." She lowered her head staring at her black shoes. "I imagine I never would."

She knew from where the sun sat in the sky she should get going back. They had a wedding to celebrate . . . but deep down all Marianna wanted to do was escape. What should she do now that the perfect man had violated her trust?

What should she do now that she realized her love for the wrong man would never leave her heart?

CHAPTER TWENTY-FIVE

With Levi and Naomi man and wife, Marianna had moved back to Aunt Ida's but she decided to stay at her parents' house with them—the last night within her childhood home. The previous night she'd braved her way through the rest of the wedding, her thoughts far from celebration.

Now that morning's light dawned, Marianna took her time dressing, yielding her will to the dress as she'd always done, in the way that expressed self-surrender. As she did, a strange heat filled her chest—anger. Her parents would be here soon, Ben too.

To say good-bye.

A longing for the mountains, the store, and her Montana friends caused her throat to tighten. Her hands balled into fists and her teeth clenched. Why had Dat insisted she go to Montana in the first place? If she'd never gone, she'd never know now what she was missing.

Her chest seemed to fold in on itself as she tried to clear her mind of angry thoughts, but it was no use. For the rest of her life she'd have these memories. Here in Indiana she'd walk among the fields and dream of mountains. She'd pick wildflowers and remember the sway and scent of the pines.

Unless . . .

Her eyes widened. What was keeping her here now? Nothing . . . but some*one* was keeping her away.

Marianna sank onto the floor, kneeling. Tears filled her eyes and she shook her head. No, she couldn't think of what that life could be like. Couldn't think of Ben.

Yet her mind refused to obey. She covered her face with her hands and rocked back and forth. Her mother had chosen the right way and she still struggled with unwanted affection for Mark. Mem was happy with her choice, happy with her life, and yet, by her own confession, longing still caught her by surprise at times.

How would *she* ever face it?

Marianna wasn't certain. She had longings for what she was turning her back on, and doubts of what she was walking into. How could she stay without her parents? How could she ever return to Montana when Ben was there?

Uffgevva, lay it down. The word stirred in her mind. Her community—and the way they lived—made it clear that turning her back on the Englisch was the only path to choose. She had to lay down her desires for someone not from her community. To live as she knew she should.

"Dear Jesus," she whispered into the still of the morning.

Uffgevva. Lay it down. The phrase filled her mind again, but the voice was gentle. It wasn't an accusation from community members. Instead a sweet, gentle peace flooded her.

Lay it down—your worries and fears. Jesus' peace stirred within. *Give it all to Me.*

She thought about it for a while. Thought about what her community demanded. She also thought about what she'd been reading in the Bible. Over and over again Jesus said to surrender, not to the wills and rules of man . . . but to Him.

A breath escaped her lips, and she dabbed her tears with her thumbs.

Maybe the greatest sacrifice wasn't laying down her will to the good of the community. Maybe it was giving everything—heart, mind, soul, spirit—to Jesus.

Months ago she'd prayed and asked Him to take away her sins. She'd prayed for eternal salvation. She thought she'd given herself to Him, but had she given enough?

Is that what Jesus meant when He said follow Him meant leaving father, mother, brother, sister? Not to physically turn your back on them, but to allow their influence over you to take a distant second place to what God desired?

Was it possible? Could she live a life where she thought of Jesus first—with her love, her attention, and her future? A lightness pushed in where heaviness had been before, and hope stirred. Marianna closed her eyes. It was as if these last six months had been walking through a dark valley and beams of welcoming light crested over the ridge ahead.

Everything she'd learned growing up in this community modeled and expressed a love for Jesus, but wasn't enough. It seemed almost too simple—to trust Jesus most. To love Him best.

Jesus. Her heart lightened as she said His name.

"Jesus." She whispered His name and the corners of her lips lifted in a smile.

He is enough.

And knowing that, she was free—free to love the man who loved Jesus most too. Free to grow closer to Jesus together, as their love for each other grew.

Marianna found her parents sitting by the woodstove, just as she'd seen them almost every day of her life in Indiana. Joy slept in a small cradle by Mem's side.

Marianna moved to the armchair and sat. It seemed odd for her dat to sit there without his newspaper in hand. Mem's hands didn't hold mending or a seed catalog with plans of next spring's garden. It was one of the few times she'd seen Mem so still.

Marianna understood. This moment would never come again. As much as they looked forward to settling in Montana, a piece of their hearts would remain in this house. Memories of laughter around the dining room table. Christmas gifts wrapped in brown paper on the bench by the window. Thoughts of exiting this home one night with three happy children—and returning with one. Marilyn's and Joanna's memory trees standing tall on the property . . .

Such things couldn't just be picked up and moved. Memories couldn't be boxed up with paper wrapping to protect them. Although they would be carried within, those remembrances would fade with every mile they journeyed over to their new home.

She folded her hands on her lap. What she had to tell them would add another load to what they'd already be carrying away.

Might as well just come out with it. "Aaron and I spoke today. We've decided not to get married."

Mem sucked in a breath. "Is there a reason? Surely that decision didn't just come out of nowhere."

"There are many reasons—some I can't explain. But one reason, mostly. I want to follow God's way. For so long, marrying Aaron is what *I* wanted. I've come to realize that marriage to him is not what God wants for me. Aaron is a good man. I pray that he'll read his Bible and be open to following God as diligently as he follows the Amish ways. I jest know that God has a different plan for me. I hope you understand."

She looked from Mem to Dat. Although there was surprise in their expressions they didn't try to convince her otherwise. They took the news in and nodded.

It was clear God had been working on their hearts too. Suddenly things weren't just about how they'd be viewed in their community. It was beginning to matter more about what God thought, and as Marianna looked deeper into her parents' eyes she noticed a peace she hadn't expected.

It was as if they knew deep down that God had a different plan for her too.

Her heart swelled. So this was how it was when you followed God rather than your own leanings or man's teachings. She smiled. All things working together for good.

Marianna was only slightly surprised to find Mem, Dat, Levi, and Naomi—with baby Samuel in her arms—standing in the front yard as she headed downstairs. Last night, when only a few guests had remained at the reception, Mem and Dat had approached Levi with a special gift. The house wouldn't be sold after all. The farm was their heritage—one Dat wanted to pass down to his son. Marianna paused at the window and smiled. It seemed that Levi would be tending the soil this year after all. He and Naomi would be moving in in a couple of weeks, which worked out for the renters too, since they were moving to Charm, Ohio, to be closer to her family.

Something stirred in Marianna's heart as she thought about that. What would her Dat think of her returning to Montana? Of being closer to Ben?

As Mem let Naomi and Levi toward the two trees behind the barn, Dat approached the house. He smiled when he saw Marianna and motioned to the porch swing. She joined him, sitting by his side.

"Mem and I talked last night. We've seen how both you and Ben have struggled—have tried to do the right thing." Dat raised her hand and squeezed. "We've struggled with the thought that if you allowed yourself to love Ben, you'd be walking away from everything, but we know you. We know you can honor our family and love God . . . even if that means you don't follow the way of the Amish in every part."

Marianna tilted her head. "What are you telling me to do?"

Dat smiled. "I'm not telling you . . . I'm allowing you. God has been speaking to me in His Word. If He has chosen a path for you, who am I to stand in your way? Mem and I aren't ready to leave the Amish. We know so many benefits. We love the community in Montana. But we know Ben's love for God, too, and we can't think of a young man we'd rather have you choose. Besides"—Dat winked—"I'm sure you heard him playing that guitar late into the night. You better go find him and hear what he's been working on. I don't want us to have any more sleepless nights while we're on the road."

Her lips parted and her heart seemed to jump into her throat. "We?"

Dat nodded. "We. The four of us adults and Charlie, David, and the baby of course. That's what you want, *ja*, to come back with us? Before the sun hits its peak today we're all going home."

She found Ben sitting near the creek with his guitar. He eyed her and then laid the guitar down.

"I was looking forward to seeing you today." He reached out toward her.

She glanced down at his hand and then extended hers. He wrapped his hand around it and stroked her fingers.

The beating of her heart increased. "And as I was longing to see you." Her hand grew warm where Ben stroked it. He stepped toward her, his wide eyes fixed on hers until their noses nearly touched.

"Ben." His name came out on a whispered sigh, and she turned her head, the feelings overwhelming her. The intensity of his gaze made it hard to breathe.

"Yes, Marianna?" His breath warmed her cheek. His hand tightened until his grip became almost painful.

Then, before she could say anything, he spoke. "I want to ask you something. Will you come back to Montana with us?"

Her heart sank. *Was that all he wanted to say? After all this time?* She shuffled slightly and looked down at her feet. She was such a fool. "Is that really what you wanted to ask?" She looked up at him again, then glanced to his guitar.

He tipped his head. "Do you think there's something more?"

She shrugged. "Well . . . Dat did mention a song."

Laughter spilt from Ben's lips. "Oh, Marianna, there *is* a song. There's also more that I want to ask too. But I've been thinking about this, and as beautiful as Indiana is, we need to get back to Montana. We need to seek God there . . . together."

She saw a twinkle in his eyes. He wasn't rejecting her. Not at all. He wanted her to wait. His smile told her he had wonderful things in store for her . . . for them.

Marianna placed a hand on her hip. "Well, now, I suppose there is only one thing I have to do, then. Tell me Driver Ben . . . do you have room in the back of that trailer for a few more things?"

Though her eyelids weighed heavy from long days of travel, Marianna didn't want to blink lest she miss one inch of the view. Their truck and trailer wound its way up the dirt road that led to West Kootenai, Montana. Late spring draped a soft green blanket over the high mountain pastures. They drove past creeks carrying sparkling, white water down the hillsides toward Lake Koocanusa.

Looking up, the snow still rimmed mountain peaks. Snow that would soon make its way down the mountains. A knot swelled in her throat at the thought of parking in front of their log cabin and seeing Josiah and Ellie bounding out the front door. She pictured Trapper's excited bark and dance, and her smile could not be contained.

Marianna leaned forward. "You can drive a bit faster."

Her parents' laughter joined with Ben's, and she caught his gaze in the rearview mirror.

The truck and trailer crossed the bridge over Lake Koocanusa and wound its way up the mountain road. Twenty minutes later they pulled up and parked, and before she could get her side door open, Marianna saw Trapper, leaping through the open door . . . racing to her side.

She stepped out of the back seat of the large truck. Trapper danced at her feet.

She was home.

Morning dawned in West Kootenai. As soon as the sun's rays brightened the morning, Marianna had been up and dressed. Now she walked down the wooded pines behind their home, her eyes on Trapper. The dog trotted beside her . . . and then, as he neared the still pond, he paused.

Her heart doubled within her, and she crossed her arms and pulled them tight. With a single bark the dog lunged over the hill.

"It could be a rabbit or a squirrel." She patted her kapp, but something inside told her it that wasn't it. Hope filled her over where the next few steps could lead her. And *whom*.

Within a quickened pace she followed Trapper. Her footsteps crunched on the dry pine needles. The scent of new leaves and mountain streams filled her nostrils. Laughter spilled out as she crested the hill, but the log was empty. Her heart fell. *How foolish.* She'd let her romantic thoughts carry her away.

Then . . . movement. Trapper ran along the water's edge and a figure crouched down and opened his arms to the dog.

Ben.

He looked as if he'd been expecting her. Maybe *hoping* was a better word. He'd hoped she'd come, and his face glowed like the reflection of the sun across the water.

Ben laughed as Trapper jumped into his arms. Then with a pat on the wiggling creature's back, he set down the dog and stood. He walked toward Marianna, and she'd never been more happy.

To be here. To see the mountains towering above them. To witness pure affection in Ben's gaze. To feel God's presence beside the still waters . . .

This . . . was joy.

"I was hoping you'd come."

His low voice, his nearness, cloaked her in the purest contentment. Even so, she couldn't help but think of the community and what this would mean.

Always the community. Even with her parents' permission it was hard turning her back on all she'd been raised to believe.

Ben paused before her. He stroked her jaw with his fingers and caressed her neck. "I don't want to let you go again. I learned that the hard way. I was a coward, but now I've been thinking about things."

"What things?"

"Of us doing this every day. Walking through these woods. Praying by this pond. Spending life together. Looking into each other's eyes. Do you feel the same way?"

"I think so. I believe so."

She leaned forward and their lips met. The kiss was hesitant, hopeful. Everything within her grew warm. She'd wanted this for so long. Wanted him for so long.

Ben.

He pulled back from the kiss and wrapped his arms around her, pulling her into an embrace and whispered in her ear. "I want us to be together. To have a life together."

She pulled her hand from his and gripped his forearms. She pulled back farther, looking into his face. "I want that too. And the strange thing is, I believe that's God's plan for me . . . for us."

He kissed her once more, and she could feel his smile on her lips. Then he cupped her face and looked into her eyes. His adoration was palpable. Why had it taken her so long to embrace the truth?

"I love you so much, but I know what that means. By coming to me, I know all you have to leave behind." His blue eyes widened, and he glanced from her eyes to her kapp. He turned, looking away. "It's asking too much . . ."

Lightness, peace, flooded her chest. "I don't want to be stuck in the ways of the past, Ben. I'll always be grateful for all I've learned—the Amish community's love, respect, and care for each other—but I want to step forward into the future. The future God has planned for my life, for our lives. Now that I know about God and His love...I can't stay here anymore, with the things of the past. And now that I know your heart. Ben, I never want to let go."

Marianna's mind echoed his name—*Ben, Ben.*

At last he turned toward her and their eyes met. Joy radiated from his eyes.

She raised an eyebrow at him. "Oh, and about your new song." She grinned. "I hope it's time for me to hear it."

He chuckled and glanced to his guitar, leaning against a tree. "I'm still working on it. The title is *'Marianna'*. And my favorite line goes something like this: 'Marianna . . . the name written with the pen of the man who dreams of a future by your side.'"

She placed a hand to her cheek. "I love it."

"I hope so, because the song was inspired by some letters I've been writing. I've been learning a lot about the Amish. Learning there are some things we can *all* learn from their ways." He pulled an envelope from his back pocket. "Here's the first letter. I thought you'd want to read it."

She pulled lined paper from the envelope. She was about to read when he took it from her hands.

"Actually, let me read it to you." He cleared his throat and began.

Dear Marianna,

The long journey has me weary. The miles have taken their toll, but even in its heaviness my mind can't stop thinking of you. It's strange how often I find myself turning to letters to express my feelings. I suppose it's become my means of communicating. Strange how I now filter my thoughts through the written word. Putting pen to paper seems to calm me somehow.

There's an Amish proverb I've been thinking about. You know it, too, no doubt. The gem cannot be polished without friction, nor the man perfected without trials. It's an easy one to quote when the warm spring breeze is

upon you and the air smells of fields and trees, but the
truth is I'd rather have the friction gone for now. The
trials aren't from outside. If anything I should be happy
that the dream I've held for so long is finally coming true.
Tomorrow is a big day.

Instead, the trials are within. In a perfect world I'd
be able to share this letter with you. No, let me say that
differently. In a perfect world I'd be able to share what's
really going on with my words—by looking into your face
and speaking my heart.

I picture you at this moment, sleeping under a
handmade quilt and dreaming of me. I hope that's the
case. Tomorrow I'll put on a smile and no one will be the
wiser, but tonight I'll still think about you—think about
the truth of what I hold inside that more than anything
I wish I could confess.

Written by the man who dreams of your smile.

He looked up at her and smiled. "I wrote this just days after you left Montana."

"All this time?" Her breath released with her words.

"Yes, Marianna." He kissed the tip of her nose. "I've been loving you all this time."

"I can't wait until you read the other letters you wrote to me. I'm eager to hear the song too. I want to be the first to hear it when you're done. I also want to know what I've missed in your life. I have a feeling you have a few stories to tell."

"That I do." He winked. "So what you're saying is that you're not going anywhere?"

She shook her head and then glanced at the pond, drawing strength from it. Knowing this—knowing Ben—was God's gift to her.

She looked back to him, focusing on his eyes. "I'm not going anywhere. I'm choosing you, Ben. I'm choosing you." She touched her kapp.

"Are you sure?" He took a step back and focused on where her hand rested.

Marianna nodded and lifted the kapp off her hair. A few wayward strands curled against her cheeks, and she smiled.

Ben brushed those strands back from her face and tears filled his eyes.

She touched her fingers to his hand, pressing it against her cheek. "*Ja*, Ben. I am sure. This is the love I've been hoping for. Praying for. You are God's gift to me. One I will cherish always."

She released a pin from her hair, allowing it to fall over her shoulders, and knew she, like her hair, was finally unbound. Free to live as God called. Free to be neither Amish nor Englisch, but only His daughter.

Free to marry the man He had chosen for her.

And as Ben opened his arms to her, she lifted her heart in praise—and stepped forward into a future blessed by her Creator. As his embrace closed around her, she nestled her cheek against his strong chest, listened to the solid beat of his heart.

"Yes, Ben. Oh yes. I am sure."

Layered Dinner

Martha Artyomenko

1 pound ground beef, cooked
1/2 pound bacon, cooked and diced (save grease)
carrots, sliced
cabbage, sliced
potatoes, sliced
canned green beans (if you want)
salt
1/4 cup flour
2 cups milk

Layer beef, bacon, carrots, cabbage, potatoes, and green beans in a roaster pan. Salt each layer lightly. Add flour to the bacon grease and stir until smooth. Add milk slowly, bring to a boil and cook 1 minute or until thick and smooth. Salt and pepper to taste; pour over top of casserole. Bake at 350 degrees for about one hour or an hour-and-a-half, until potatoes are tender.

NOTES:
You can basically use any vegetable you want. I have done it without the bacon, but I like the flavor the bacon gives. You can also do it with cream of mushroom soup if you would like to instead of the bacon/white sauce.

Cherry Crumb Pie

Martha Artyomenko

PIE CRUST:
2 2/3 cups flour
1 cup shortening
8 tablespoons water
pinch salt

2 jars home-canned cherry pie filling or 2 cans cherry pie filling
1 teaspoon almond flavoring, divided

TOPPING:
2 cups flour
2 cups brown sugar
1 cup butter

In large bowl place flour and salt. Cut in shortening until very fine crumbs, using a fork, until your shortening is completely absorbed and you do not see white flour anymore. Add water carefully. Do not overhandle. Add a little less or little more, depending on your altitude and weather conditions. Form two balls and roll out on a floured board to fit a pie pan. Finish the edges in the fashion desired and set aside.

In the bowl you made the pie crust in, put the ingredients for the topping. Cut the butter into the dry ingredients until crumbs form. Fill pie shells with cherry pie filling. Add 1/2 teaspoon almond flavoring to each pie. Top with crumbs.

Bake at 400 degrees for 35 to 40 minutes or until crust is lightly browned and bubbly. Pie shell should shake loose from the tin, if you are not sure if it is done.

Leah's Grapenuts

Martha Artyomenko

This is a very typical Amish, homemade cereal you would eat in the mornings. Especially if you owned a cow.

3 pounds brown sugar
2-1/2 quarts sour milk (fresh raw milk that has gone sour is best, but store milk that is on the edge works fine)
3/4 pounds melted margarine or oil
8 pounds whole wheat flour
1-1/4 teaspoon salt
1/2 teaspoon maple flavoring
2 tablespoons baking soda
2 tablespoons vanilla

Dissolve baking soda in milk before adding to dry ingredients. Add butter and flavorings. This will be a thick batter. If too thick or too thin, add less flour or more milk. Spread in three greased cookie trays (if you want it thicker, use two cookie trays). For think cake—bake at 350 degrees for 30 to 40 minutes or until cake tastes done. For three trays—back for 30 minutes and then text if it comes out clean, if not, bake until knife comes out clean. Break into chunks and you can either rub on a screen to get small chunks or process for a few seconds in a food processor. You do not want them very small as it will be like eating bread crumbs! Spread on cookie trays again and toast in slow oven (175 degrees) until browned lightly and very dry.

Granola

Martha Artyomenko

1/2 cup oil
1/2 pound margarine
2 tablespoons molasses
1 tablespoon vanilla
1 cup brown sugar
1 cup honey
1/2 teaspoon salt
7-1/2 cups oats
1/2 cup sesame seeds
3 cups grape nuts (I use homemade or any cereal is good. I have used a mixture of all sorts.)
1 cup wheat germ
1 pound coconut
(If I am out of anything I just add more oats or grape nuts.)

Melt together oil, margarine, molasses, vanilla, brown sugar, honey, and salt. In a large bowl, mix oats, sesame seeds, grape nuts, wheat germ, and coconut. Pour liquid over top and stir well. Bake for 8 hours at 200 degrees, stirring every couple hours, until browned and crunchy. When you pull it out, if you like large chunks, do not stir until completely cooled. This will give you the large crunchy chunks. If desired, stir in dried fruit after baking, but before cooling.

AUTHOR'S NOTE

Dear Reader,

From the first scene on *Beside Still Waters* I've been eagerly anticipating the last scene of *Beyond Hope's Valley*. A love story is just that—a *love* story. Marianna has gone through many ups and downs on her journey, but from the beginning I knew the happily-ever-after I wanted for her at the end. I'm talking about her chosen man, of course, but I'm also speaking of her growing romance with her Creator. Marianna's heart is different at the end of this book than it was when she first arrived in Montana. She's different.

As I've mentioned in previous author's notes, the plot behind this series was inspired by my friends Ora Jay and Irene Eash. The spiritual journey of this series was inspired by them, too. I have never met two people who are so joyful and eager to share about their relationship with Jesus Christ. Often during the writing of the Big Sky Series I've called Ora Jay and Irene to ask questions about the Amish lifestyle, and we'd usually stay on the phone for over an hour as they shared about what God was teaching them in His Word. They also always asked me what He's been speaking to my heart, too. That's what true Christian fellowship is all about! I'm so thankful for friends like that.

My hope is that as you read *Beyond Hope's Valley* you'll be inspired to seek God about every detail of your life—and share your journey with good friends—just as Marianna did. There are many times we think we know God's will for our lives, but sometimes we are surprised. In my own personal relationship with Jesus Christ I've discovered that His way is always best . . . and He has greater plans for me than I ever imagined!

If you'd like to hear more about what God is doing in my life, please be sure to check out my website and blog at www. triciagoyer.com. I'm also on Facebook and Twitter, and I love to connect with my readers! Make sure we connect there, and they YOU can tell me about how God is speaking to you, too!

With a heart full of thankful to Jesus!
Tricia Goyer

Other Amazing Titles from